WELCOME DEATH

No death could have been more welcome than Evan Morgan's, or more fitting for the Welcome Home celebrations in the village of Llanddewi. For Morgan had spent the war making money and enemies down in the Vale of Glamorgan with about equal facility. In fact, on the night, it seemed as if a whole posse of murderers had beaten a path to the door of the Manor House. It is left to the ingenuity of Sir Richard Cherrington, an eminent but slightly eccentric archaeologist with a penchant for amateur detection on a visit from Cambridge, to solve this intricate puzzle of motives and alibis.

WELCOME DEATH

WELCOME DEATH

by

Glyn Daniel

Magna Large Print Books
Long Preston, North Yorkshire,
BD23 4ND, England.

British Library Cataloguing in Publication Data.

Daniel, Glyn
    Welcome death.

    A catalogue record of this book is
    available from the British Library

    ISBN   978-0-7505-4170-1

First published in Great Britain in 1954
First Ostara Publishing edition 2014

Copyright © The Estate of Glyn Daniel

Cover illustration © Elena Helfrecht by arrangement with
Arcangel Images

The moral right of the author has been asserted

Published in Large Print 2016 by arrangement with
Ostara Publishing

Magna Large Print is an imprint of Library Magna Books Ltd.

Printed and bound in Great Britain by
T.J. (International) Ltd., Cornwall, PL28 8RW

CONTENTS

CHAPTER 1

THE WELCOME IS PLANNED

'Order, order. I call the meeting to order.' The Vicar rapped on the table and the hub-bub of conversation died down. 'Ladies and gentlemen–' He hesitated. 'Or should I say lady and gentlemen?' Hugh Morris beamed through his spectacles and bowed slightly to Miss Mary Cherrington, sitting on his right. She inclined her head and hastily put her hand to her head to hold firm her hat which, uncertainly perched on her piled-up hair, had tilted forward dangerously, its decoration of cherries trying to shake itself free from the other brightly coloured fruits.

The Reverend Hugh Morris was a kindly man – many would say too kindly, too Christian in his charity for this modern world; but for all that village committee meetings seemed to bring out the worst in him. Not that it had always been so. Thirty years ago, when he had come straight from Lampeter as a young curate to this south Glamorgan village of Llanddewi, he had been kindly and polite at the village meetings. And they had dragged on interminably and got little done. That was before he met Dorothy – Dorothy Vaughan. Dorothy was the daughter of old General Vaughan, who lived at St David's Castle, between Llanddewi and Barry. She had married the young curate of Llanddewi, to the delight of Hugh Morris, her own considerable surprise, and the displeasure of General Vaughan, who was planning to send his daughter to winter in India in the hope that she might pick up an eligible soldier or civil servant in one of the better Punjab cantonments. Dorothy Vaughan had been accustomed to organize her father and St David's Castle: Dorothy Morris soon organized her husband, and, when he became Vicar of Llanddewi, through him and the Mothers' Union the whole village, and when he became Rural Dean, the whole rural deanery of the Vale of Glamorgan. Under her firm influence, Hugh became less outwardly kind and – more firm in his dealings with the many committees over which he had to preside – from committees to provide underwear for the starving children of Europe to protest meetings to prevent the Glamorgan County Council from constructing a coast road from Barry to Porthcawl. He was not dictatorial nor discourteous, but firm and businesslike. From Bridgend and Porthcawl in the west to Cardiff and Llandaff in the east his reputation grew. 'An efficient, sensible man,' they said of him, the prosperous farmers and landed gentry and businessmen of the Vale of Glamorgan who gathered in the Bear or the Duke of Wellington or in the private bar of the Bell Inn at Llanddewi, 'A good committee man who can be trusted.' But it was Dorothy in the background all the while who was firm, who was sensible, who could be trusted. There were rumours of translations and preferments, and there is little telling what successful future Hugh Morris might have carved out for himself in the Church of Wales – if Dorothy had always been there.

She died in the influenza epidemic of 1919, leaving behind her a baby son, David, less than a year old. And now, a quarter of a century later, it must be admitted that she was no more than a memory, though a very fragrant one, to the grey-haired, stoutish man who was still Vicar of Llanddewi and Rural Dean of the Vale of Glamorgan. And David, born at the end of the First World War, was, at the end of the Second, a Captain in the Glamorganshire Regiment, on his way home from Singapore to be demobilized. His father sat presiding over the Llanddewi Welcome Home Committee. That was one of the things he had almost forgotten from Dorothy's time: how to run a committee.

The Vicar cleared his throat and smiled. 'I

wonder,' he said gently, 'if we are not getting away a little from the business in hand. We are here charged with the details of our Welcome Home festivities. It was – er – decided long ago at the general village meeting over which I was happy to preside that we should have a Welcome Home Fund at Llanddewi. And due to the very diligent collections organized by Miss Cherrington and Mr Anderson, and I need hardly say again how grateful we all are to them.' He turned and smiled at Miss Cherrington on his right and at the Postmaster on his left. The fruit on Miss Cherrington's hat shook dangerously again; Ben Anderson, a shy but resolute man who was nervous of speaking or of being spoken of in public, blushed and looked down at the table. 'Due to these vigorous collections,' went on the Vicar, 'and to the generosity of the village, we now have sufficient money to achieve our original purpose, which was to give to each man returning from the war a small present of money, and to hold a social gathering in the Village Hall. We have agreed, I remind you, on the present and the social gathering; our job tonight is merely to work out the details. There is perhaps no very useful purpose served, as I see it, in discussing whether it would not be better to have some sport instead of the social evening, or whether it would be wise to take the whole village on a charabanc outing to central Wales, to the Birmingham Corporation Waterworks, or whether the money should be spent, as Mr Evan Morgan has suggested, in putting up a pavilion on the village cricket green.' He glanced down the table to the other end where Evan Morgan sat; a square man, with no neck, with a square red face, in which two very blue eyes were set deep and rather close together. He looked what he was: handsome in an animal way, as you might say an ox was handsome, powerful, ruthless. He had started his working life as an errand-boy in the village shop; his mother had been the school caretaker. Now he owned not only the village shop, but shops in Bridgend, Cowbridge, and Barry, and farms through-out the Vale. He had bought the Manor House in the centre of the village, when old Mrs Fitzhammon-Jones, whose family had lived there ever since the name Fitzhammon had been heard in South Wales, had gone to church in her reading spectacles, tripped over the gateway from Church Street, and fallen down the long flight of stone steps that led to the sunken churchyard, expiring appropriately though inconveniently among the seiried ranks of tombstones, and not far from the Fitzhammon-Jones family vault. The purchase of the Manor House had been a symbolic gesture of defiance on Evan Morgan's part – the more real for not being

13

consciously realized. Evan had given twenty-five pounds to the Welcome Home fund – indeed, was the top subscriber – and Hugh Morris did not wish to offend him. He was in any case only awaiting a suitable opportunity to beg a similar sum from him towards the repair of the chantry roof.

'All these suggestions have been most valuable,' the vicar lied easily, 'but their consideration is – er – not within the terms of reference of this Committee.'

'I am of the opinion,' said Miss Cherrington, who was a little deaf and had not heard, or wickedly pretended not to have heard, what the Vicar had been saying. Her voice was thin and precise. 'I am of the opinion,' she repeated, 'that the charabanc outing should go somewhere else. The Elan Valley is all very well, but we live here in the midst of natural beauty. Was it not Carlyle who said that the Vale of Glamorgan was the "Garden of Wales"?' It was her favourite quotation, and the Mothers' Union heard it frequently, and believed it was not Carlyle but Mary Cherrington who had originated the phrase. 'Let us therefore go,' she went on, 'to some place that will give us some man-made beauties. What about Gloucester, Oxford and Stratford-on-Avon? That would make a delightful excursion.'

'Should have thought the Elan Valley lakes were man-made if anything was,' said Henry

14

Thomas crisply. Henry was the landlord of the Bell, a shortish, bluff man.

'But culture, culture–' began Miss Cherrington.

'Anyway,' butted in Joseph Stanley Thomas, 'I hope the new pavilion will be equipped with a good scoring board. The present one is hopeless. The little boys who score have got to stand on tiptoe to hang up the numbers.' Joseph was Henry Thomas's brother and farmed Sealands, the large farm on the sea coast between the village beach and the golf-course.

The Vicar sighed and glanced hopefully at John Davies, the only member of the Committee who had not hitherto spoken. John was the village schoolmaster, and had been so for longer than the Vicar could remember. If it had not been for the war, he would have retired. He had been kept on through shortages of staff but at last, the war over, he was retiring. This was his final term. John could always be relied on to support the Vicar in bringing a meeting back on to the rails. But tonight he too failed. He took the pipe out of his mouth and said, 'I've been thinking since we had our meeting in the Village Hall. We ought to do something more permanent – like a library and reading-room. And we should certainly add some inscription to our old War Memorial – I mean for record purposes.'

'But no one was killed from the village,' said Evan Morgan. 'Fortunately,' he added ungraciously after a slight pause.

A voice cut in, ice cold, sharp: 'Except my son.' Joseph Stanley Thomas could have kicked himself the moment the words left his lips. He swore at himself under his breath. The others looked away, pointedly – all except Evan Morgan. He stared at Joseph Thomas. 'I'm sorry,' he said, but there was no trace of apology in voice or mien. 'Of course, I meant killed in action.' Joseph bit his lip savagely; he knew only too well what Evan Morgan meant. He choked back with difficulty the words that came tumbling hotly to his lips, the thoughts that chased themselves through his mind. 'You know – heat of battle; shots in anger; all that sort of thing,' went on Evan Morgan.

That was it, Joseph said to himself. That was it. Not killed in action. They would always say that. Sometimes he half wished his son Nigel had been killed in action – shot down in flames over some German town – that is, if he had to die. Nigel was his only child, conceived, if not born, when he and Bella were still in love, during those two short years after their marriage when life was sweet – and love was eternal, and before Bella had begun chasing away after every eligible man in sight, from the cowherd on Sealand Farm to, well, so they said, old

General Vaughan himself. Thwarted of her love and her understanding companionship, he had thrown his energies into his farm and into the upbringing of Nigel. Indeed, Nigel had been his life, and as he grew up Joseph had relived his own life, reshaped into a pattern he had himself never been able to achieve. Nigel had gone to Llandovery and then on to Jesus College, Oxford. He had narrowly missed his cricket blue, had flown with the Air Squadron. When war broke out he had been called to the R.A.F. at once. His father had not known how to live through those first few months of anxiety when Nigel had been engaged in apparently suicidal raids and reconnaissances in Blenheims. But somehow Nigel had survived and his father began to believe that he led a charmed life. He transferred to heavy bombers and did a tour of duty in Wellingtons, and was awarded a bar to his D.F.C. He converted to four-engined aircraft and flew Lancasters through some of the heaviest bombing raids on Hamburg and Berlin, returning unscathed. It was about three months after his D.S.O. had been gazetted that he had been killed; a jeep had been driven back to the mess late at night, overturning and crushing Nigel against a tree. It was said that the driver was drunk, but the details were hushed up and the citation read:

'Wing Commander Nigel Thomas, D.S.O., D.F.C., killed in an accident while on active service.'

Joseph Stanley Thomas clenched his teeth. Not in action. What the hell did Evan Morgan know about action? He who had spent the war fooling around with the Home Guard?

'As I was saying,' went on the Vicar, 'all these points are interesting and must be gone into – some other time. Our concern tonight is the presentation and the social evening. First, the date of the gathering. Most of our warriors have already returned home, including your son – Roger, Mr Henry Thomas. In fact, there are only two whom we now await: Mr Davies, your son Bryn, and my own son David. Both Bryn Davies and my son are at the present moment on their way home by air from Singapore. I had a cable this morning to say that they had arrived in Calcutta yesterday evening. They should be in England tomorrow or the day after, and if the formalities of demobilization do not take very long we should see them early next week. Let me see: tonight is Friday evening. I would suggest that our social evening be a week tonight – that it be next Friday.' He paused. 'Anyone with any serious objections to this idea?'

'Isn't it rather soon?' said Ben Anderson, colouring as he spoke. He liked to have as long as possible for preparing for everything he did. A fortnight seemed more suitable to him.

'Oh, I don't know,' said the schoolmaster. 'After all, it is a welcome home that we are planning, is it not? And it should be soon. Some of our chaps have already been demobbed nearly three months and the war has been over some while.'

Hugh Morris smiled. Things were going better. Together with John Davies, he would manage the meeting yet. 'I don't want to hurry you, of course,' he said. 'I don't want to hurry anyone. Let everyone say his say while he may.'

This was always his formula – Dorothy's formula – when he wanted to hurry them and no one to have any further say. It usually worked. He glanced around the table and went on quickly: 'Those in favour of next Friday for the social gathering and Welcome Home?' He paused. 'Those against? Splendid. We are all agreed. Then next Friday it is, and seven o'clock for seven-thirty. That is the usual time for such functions, isn't it? In the Village Hall. And the form of our entertainment?'

'Usual thing, I suppose,' said Henry Thomas. 'Cold buffet supper' (he pronounced buffet as though it were a blow). 'Drinks. Dancing. That sort of thing.'

'And we may count on your wife to arrange the catering as usual?' Mrs Henry

Thomas had been counted on to arrange the catering at every gathering in the Village Hall since anyone could remember.

'And your son Roger will fix the lights, and a gramophone for the dancing?' Roger Thomas had always done these things before the war, and four years in the R.E.M.E. should have made him at least no less able to do them.

'He'd be delighted, I should think,' said his father. 'Of course, he's one of the chaps whom we are welcoming back, but that doesn't matter. In fact, he's been counting on being asked to do this as usual, and plans to festoon the words *Welcome Home* in fairy lights under the trees at the entrance to the Hall.'

'Excellent,' murmured the Vicar; 'excellent. Nothing could be better. And now the speeches. Who is going to make the speech of the evening and present the prizes – er, our little gifts – to the men?'

'There's one obvious person, isn't there?' It was John Davies who spoke. 'I mean your brother in-law.' There was a murmur of approval and the Vicar nodded his head. He supposed so. Dorothy's brother had made most of the village speeches for the last ten years since he had retired from the Indian Army with the rank of Colonel and come to live again at Llanddewi. Bryn Vaughan had entered into full possession of St David's

Castle on the death of his father, the General, and had thrown himself fully into the activities normally associated with and, in the mid-thirties, still pursued by country gentlemen. He hunted, he fished, he bred horses, he shot, he played golf, tennis, and squash. Two things his fellows among the landed gentry of the Vale of Glamorgan found odd: the first was that he was unmarried, and remained obviously unmoved by the appearance and attentions of all the eligible women who thought of him as an agreeable husband or second husband, and the grounds of St David's Castle as a most desirable residence; the second was his passion for field archaeology. He had made it his aim to visit every antiquity in South Wales, and with tireless enthusiasm he drove around the countryside in a shooting brake equipped with camera, surveying instruments, field-glasses, six-inch maps, and air photographs, tracking down every earthwork, every barrow, every vestige of a prehistoric field-wall or village, resolutely exploring every clue in field or place name which might conceal the presence of an antiquity. Queer chap, the hunting-fishing fraternity said when they discussed him in the lounge of the Country Club in Cardiff. A good chap, of course – but strange. And they put it down to the Indian sun. They pretended they were quite prepared for it when the news was published that Bryn Vaughan had been made Chief Constable of South Glamorgan.

Yes, Colonel Vaughan was obviously the right man to make the proper speech of welcome. 'If that is the feeling of the meeting,' said the Vicar, 'I will get into touch with my brother-in-law.' That was the feeling of the meeting. They might have widely differing views on village policy, but none of them fancied himself or herself in the role of making a speech of that kind. It was much better, as well as more convenient, to wish the speech on to someone who was not there.

'And now the next details?'

'I suggest, Mr Chairman, that we leave the details of the organization next Friday to yourself and Henry Thomas and Mrs Thomas.' John Davies was being helpful as usual. Indeed, it was all going according to Dorothy's maxims. If you want a committee to do something efficiently, break it up into a sub-committee, she used to say, and if that is too large, have a smaller sub-committee, until in the end the work is delegated to one person and then done.

'Is that agreed?' It too was readily agreed. All was well. Everyone had had a chance to express his viewpoint; nobody wanted any more of the detailed work of organization than he could reasonably avoid. The Vicar looked round hopefully. Could he now bring the meeting to an end? He glanced at his watch. They had been discussing things for only an hour. It seemed too good to be true. Evan Morgan glanced at his watch; good, he thought. The Bell is still open.

'Is there any other business before the Committee?'

But it was too good to be true. Evan Morgan spoke up, importantly. 'We seem to have forgotten the share-out,' he said.

'I don't think so,' said Hugh Morris. 'I was going to suggest some such arrangement as this. We will divide what we have collected in half. Half shall be spent on our entertainment next Friday and the other half to be divided among our returned warriors, if we may call them that for the moment.'

'That's just the point,' said Evan Morgan quickly. 'But just how is it going to be divided up?'

'How?' The Vicar was puzzled.

'I think he means,' said Miss Cherrington precisely, and with a shake of cherries, 'in what proportions and amongst whom?'

Henry Thomas groaned. 'I see,' he said. 'More money for officers and less for other ranks, I suppose.' Roger Thomas had been a sergeant in the R.E.M.E. Corps. Henry's brother took no interest in the discussion. If he had lived, he thought to himself, I wonder what rank Nigel would have been when he was demobbed. A Group Captain, or perhaps an Air Commodore? His fancy saw the boy higher in rank than Colonel Vaughan. If he had lived, he said to himself. If he had lived; and the words burnt into his mind.

'Gratuities were given on that basis,' said Evan Morgan aggressively. 'They varied according to rank.'

The Vicar decided to try and dispose of this issue if he could. 'I am sure there were special reasons for varying these gratuity payments,' he said suavely and tolerantly. 'But here our problem is surely a very different one. We are dealing with the return of some dozen or so men to our village. All of them are very well known to us; we do not distinguish between them, or the service they have given us. They all served us well during the war. Now we welcome them back. Our gifts should be divided equally between them all.' He paused. Had he been a shade too unctuous? Perhaps too much of his sermon style? He wondered. But then he had found that the slightest memory of the pulpit at a meeting outside church often had the effect of embarrassing his audience. He would embarrass them into silence. He decided to lay it on a little thicker. 'We are a small and a Christian community,' he said. 'All men are equal before God. I think we then should not discriminate between them.' Unfair perhaps, but it nearly worked. There was an uneasy

24

silence; then Miss Cherrington spoke.

'How true. How true,' she said. 'I am sure we all agree with the dear Vicar. We must share and share alike. But there still remains the problem of among whom do we share our money. I mean, it is quite obvious that our list includes the dear Vicar's son and Mr Davies's son, who were officers in the Army, and Mr Thomas's son Roger, who was a sergeant. Cases like that are simple. Then, I think, obviously we must include the doctor's niece, who was in the W.A.A.F. But what about all the border-line cases – the Red Cross and the Land Army, and, for that matter, the Home Guard. Where are we going to draw the line?'

'Oh, come,' said Joseph Stanley Thomas, suddenly taking interest in the discussion. 'I was in the Home Guard myself, as everyone knows. I know we did a lot of tiresome work, especially when the aerodrome was bombed. But we were never seriously inconvenienced. I never missed a game of golf for that matter, even when the bombs dropped on the fairway. It added to the fun of the game. Home Guard,' he snorted. 'After all, none of us in the Home Guard were on active service.' Joseph looked round the table. He had been in charge of a platoon; John Davies had been his lieutenant, and his brother Henry had been in the same company. He was glad he had got back at Evan Morgan with the phrase 'active service'. Then he made his slip. 'Why,' he said, 'we must keep this thing within reasonable bounds. If we widen the scope of our welcome, we shall end up by welcoming back our conscientious objectors.'

He stopped speaking and no one said a word. Everyone looked uneasily and blankly in front of him. All except Evan Morgan. For Evan Morgan's son Rees had been an objector, and the village of Llanddewi had not yet given up discussing whether his objections had been conscientious or not. Rees had been a difficult, awkward boy. His mother had died when he was in his early teens, and he had lived alone in the big Manor House with his father – cut off from the village in many ways, and with few sympathetic contacts with his father. Indeed, Evan Morgan had made no bones about the fact that he was disappointed in his legal son, Rees, and quite openly preferred his natural son, Mervyn.

Mervyn Morgan was a few years older than Rees. They had both gone to the County School at Barry. Mervyn had been good at games, popular, an attractive, open lad. Rees had been sullen, thwarted, brooding; no good at games and only tolerably good at his bookwork. He seemed to have spent all his school days in that pimply stage which most schoolboys get over in a year or so. He was short-sighted, and Evan Morgan had often in the years immediately before the war regarded his gawky, bespectacled, pimple-blotched son with a distaste bordering on loathing, and wondered what the future held out for him. The war had deferred that issue. Mervyn had joined up at once in the Navy, and had spent much of it travelling around the world in a cruiser. He had been de-mobbed fairly early, and with no hesitation at all Evan had offered him the management of his shop in Llanddewi – a small shop, but with a large country connexion, and the headquarters of all his enterprises. He would of course, take a while to settle down, but it was obvious that he was going to do well. If only he had been born on the right side of the sheets, and Rees had been the bastard, how much easier it would all have been!

When war was imminent, Rees Morgan had realized the money his mother had left him, and bought a market garden of five acres between Cowbridge and Bridgend. He had registered as a market gardener, hoping to be deferred military service as being in a reserved occupation. In this he was unsuc-cessful. He had been registered as a con-scientious objector and spent the first few years of the war doing agricultural work in Pembrokeshire. Was his action dictated by conscience, or by cowardice? The village could not decide, which is not surprising, as Rees's motives were confused to himself. The

Vicar had preached once, and once only, on the subject, but he also was not clear on the moral issues involved: his Christian charity conflicted with his loyalty to State and the cause of the war – he had not succeeded in doing more than further befogging the minds of the village. Only Joseph Stanley Thomas had known for certain what he thought: Rees Morgan was a rotter – a coward and a rotter. And then, a year before the war ended, Rees Morgan had surprised everyone – including his father and himself – by volunteering for military service. It was true that the war ended without the boy seeing more of the horrors of war than the inside of military training establishments in England. He was demobilized from an artillery O.C.T.U. where he had done surprisingly well.

Puzzled, and wondering whether the boy's curious war history was in part a result of his own neglect and dislike of him, his father had welcomed him home with more warmth than he could quite explain. After all, the boy was his own blood, he said to himself, and if he had been a conscientious objector at first he had had the courage to realize his mistake. In fact, Evan Morgan told himself, it needed some courage to be an objector – more courage than to fool around in the Home Guard patrolling the beaches of the Bristol Channel. He had offered the boy the management of the shop in Barry, and had been delighted when he had accepted it with alacrity. He had been even more delighted when Rees had announced his intention of living over the shop in a little flat – particularly delighted now that he would soon be marrying again himself. There would be no real place for either of his sons in the Manor House when Janet Anderson was installed there as the second Mrs Evan Morgan. Mervyn was already disposed of. He had married the doctor's niece on one of his last leaves, and Evan had bought him the little cottage on the road leading to Sealands Farm.

Evan Morgan had gone even redder in the face than he normally was when Joseph Stanley Thomas had made his unfortunate remark about conscientious objectors. But he was no fool, and had seen how furious Thomas had been when he had said what he did about Nigel Thomas not being killed in action. Perhaps that had been a mistake. But what did it matter? He and Joseph Thomas would go on fighting and bickering as long as they lived, just as they had ever since they had known each other. He swallowed his pride. There was no point in dragging the meeting on and on, though he would gladly postpone his interview with Ellen.

John Davies's voice broke the strained silence: tactful, helpful, thoughtful as ever. 'Yes,' he said. 'There are a lot of complicated questions involved in who should be on our list. I don't think we can settle them here and now. We shall have to meet again before next Friday. I wonder, Mr Chairman, if we could all think over these various border-line cases and draw up a final list when we next meet?'

'An excellent idea.' Miss Cherrington wanted to get home to her supper.

'Is that everyone's view?' It was everybody's view that they should not prolong the meeting. The Vicar sighed with relief and adjourned the meeting. After a few moments of sitting round the table, the members of the Llanddewi Welcome Home Committee got up and left. Joseph Stanley Thomas walked out with his brother and across the market square to the Bell. Evan Morgan wished the Vicar a brisk good night and also crossed the square into the inn. Miss Cherrington mounted her bicycle and rode off to her house, wobbling from side to side with that same air of uncertainty that she had maintained through thirty years of persistent cycling. It was a cold, dark evening. Miss Cherrington drew her scarf tighter round her neck and thought of the cauliflower-and-cheese pie she had ready for her supper. It would not take long to warm up. And after she would have a glass of port. One must be prepared to deal with the chill humours of the autumn. It was true that Dr Wynne Roberts had cautioned her against too much alcohol, but she had never paid attention all her life to cautions or warnings she did not wish to observe. She bicycled out of the village and along the dark avenue of elms that led along the sea-road to her house.

The Vicar and schoolmaster were left behind. They stood at the door of the hall staring across the square. A gust of wind blew leaves across the square and tore at the ragged edges of the posters on the wall. The lights shone cosily from behind the leaded window-panes of the Bell. Three or four people stood at the other side of the square waiting for the Barry bus to come in. The smell of frying fat came on the wind across the square from the fish-and-chip shop behind the Village Hall.

'I'm glad that's over,' said the Vicar.

'I wish next week was over.' John Davies's voice was low and serious.

'You mean the Welcome Home party, John?' The Vicar spoke a question, but his voice told that he knew the answer to it.

'No, Hugh. Not that. That's easy. You know what I mean.' He paused. 'It's meeting Bryn again. You meeting David. Both of us, all the village, meeting our boys again. What are we going to tell them?'

The Vicar hesitated, and when he spoke he had dropped his voice conspiratorially, although there was no one within earshot.

'You mean, of course,' he said slowly, 'about Daphne?'

'Hugh, she was a good girl – a good girl. I swear it. It wasn't her fault.' John Davies spoke earnestly, pleading.

'I know. I know.' Hugh Morris put his hand on the schoolmaster's shoulder. 'John, we've been over all this so many times. Must we go over it again? Can't it rest? Must Bryn and David know? It is only you and me and your wife and the doctor who know the truth. It was hushed up at the time; everyone was satisfied. Of course,' he added doubtfully, 'it was during the war.'

'You can't hush up a thing in a village, Hugh. That's the devil of it. You don't seriously believe that only the four of us know that – well, that my daughter's death was what it was?'

'You may be right,' the Vicar admitted reluctantly. 'But who is going to go to the trouble of starting up malicious rumours at this late hour? Why, Daphne has been dead over a year.'

'Who? I wish I knew who, or was sure that I knew who.'

Hugh Morris stared at him. 'You mean–?' he began.

'They've started again, you know,' said John Davies shortly.

'The anonymous letters?'

'Yes. I had one this morning. Usual filth.'

Hugh Morris groaned. 'This is too much,' he said. 'I thought that they had stopped with the end of the war.'

'Oh, no. They start up again every time her interest in other things flags.'

'Her interest? But are you sure? How can you be sure?'

'I'm virtually certain,' said John Davies. His voice was cold and bitter. 'But I know it isn't the sort of certainty that the police can act upon.' He paused. 'Some day, Hugh, I think I am going to take the law into my own hands. After all, other people do and get away with it – don't they? I mean, people even get away with murder.'

'Murder. My dear John, you mustn't let your mind keep running away back to these things. Daphne's death was an accident.'

There was a pause. The Barry bus swept round the corner and across the square. Its headlights raked the Village Hall and for a brief instant lit up Hugh Morris and John Davies as they stood outside the door of the little committee-room under the hall. In the glare of the headlights their faces were white and stern against the grey stone and green ivy of the wall. Then the bus swung away and they were plunged into dark shadow again.

John Davies spoke slowly: 'Don't you think,' he said quietly, 'that a successful murder should always look like an accident?'

CHAPTER 2

THE WAY HOME

I

'I had a difficult time keeping my temper tonight, Henry,' said Joseph Stanley Thomas. They were sitting in the little parlour behind the bar in the Bell.

Henry picked up his tankard and had a drink of beer. 'Aye,' he said. 'But it was difficult for you. I'm sorry.' He knew better than anyone else just how deeply his brother felt about Nigel's death. 'You've got to keep a close grip on yourself, old man,' he went on. 'I know it's damned hard for you – but you just must. It'll pass in the end. Why, it's nearly three years now since Nigel was killed.'

Henry Thomas remembered that night vividly – the night of Nigel's death, the night the news had come through. Ben Anderson had taken the telegram down himself, but he had been afraid to deliver it out to Sealands Farm alone. He had knocked up Henry and together they had gone out to the farm to break the news to Joseph. To their surprise, it had been surprisingly, horrifyingly easy. The

34

telegram had not been explicit, and Joseph Thomas had assumed that his son had died in an aircraft crashing on taking off or landing. 'I suppose it was bound to happen some time' was all he said, and then: 'Poor Nigel. I hope it was quick.'

It was only next day when Joseph had driven up to Buckinghamshire to the inquest that he realized the tragedy of his son's death. Then he had drunk himself into a stupor at the Catherine Wheel in Henley, and when his wife, his brother, and his brother's wife had come up to join him, they found him late next day in bed, crying. Nigel's death seemed to have precipitated his feelings towards his wife. For years they had lived in a state of mutual and hostile tolerance – he for Nigel's sake, although Nigel had known very well the state of affairs, and she because Sealands Farm was as good a base as any other, and Joseph Thomas was generous with his money. 'Your mother and I don't get on very well together,' he had once explained rather shyly to Nigel. 'But then such a lot of married couples don't hit it off in these days. The more's the pity.' He had wanted Nigel to marry and be happily married, although, if the truth be told, he sometimes consciously dreaded the thought of Nigel's marriage. Nigel had been very interested in Janet Anderson. They had seen a lot of each other at one time, though there had been nothing definite, and on his last leave his father had begun to wonder what if anything were the relations between the two. His mind swung from dread at losing Nigel to hope that in Nigel's happy marriage he would somehow wipe out the shame and disappointment of his relationship with Bella.

Henry Thomas came back from serving beer in the bar.

'Have another drink, Jo?' he asked.

'Thank you, I will,' said Joseph. Henry poured his brother out a large whisky, and added a very small amount of soda-water to it. Then he said: 'Henry. You've always given me good advice, though, granted, I haven't always taken it. But I want your advice now. I've a mind to divorce Bella.'

'Divorce Bella now? After all these years?' Henry had advised his brother to do this fifteen years and more ago, but he had resolutely refused, for Nigel's sake.

'Why not?'

'I was only thinking, you know,' said Henry, 'that after all these years it would look a little odd. I mean, isn't there something about condoning an offence, or something of that kind. I know nothing about these things. Only read the papers. And could you get the evidence at present?'

Joseph chuckled. 'I have the evidence all right,' he said.

'You have?'

'Oh, yes. Bella has been very discreet in her love affairs – most of the time. But you can't hide these things all the time. It was the summer before the war. Bella went to Llandrindod Wells to watch the golf finals. I was supposed to be going to Oxford to see Nigel, but I changed my plans and went to a Farmers' Union conference at Shrewsbury. I was coming out of a side-road at Brecon when I saw Evan Morgan drive past in a car with Bella.'

'Evan Morgan?'

'Yes. They were laughing and talking and didn't see me. I followed the car and found they were staying together in a little hotel between Builth Wells and Llangammarch Wells. No,' he said grimly, 'I don't think there will be any trouble about the evidence.'

'I'm surprised. I never knew there had been anything between Evan and Bella.'

Joseph Thomas nodded. 'I've plenty of evidence,' he said. 'Plenty of other evidence. It has afforded me a morbid satisfaction to collect it. Bella leading her life, as she thought, carefully hidden away from me – and all the while I knew about it. I used to be very amused at her accounts of shopping expeditions to Cheltenham and Gloucester, when I knew she was spending the week-end in a man's flat in Chepstow.' He laughed mirthlessly.

Henry Thomas took a deep draught of beer. 'If you've got all this evidence,' he said, 'and are bent at last on using it, why do you pick on Evan Morgan? Won't it cause a great stir in the village?'

'That is what I want to do, Henry. I want to create a stir. I can't be more hurt than I am. I want to hurt others. I know it sounds unpleasant, and I'm not sure that it isn't unpleasant. But I want to be unpleasant, for a change. I want to hurt Evan Morgan.' There was a wealth of intensity and feeling behind the words. 'I remember the bastard when he was an errand boy,' he went on. 'He was a dirty, lucky twister then. He's a twister now. I hate him.'

II

The door of the Bell opened for a moment. It threw a beam of light across the market square which did not illuminate the two figures still standing talking earnestly under the clock outside the Village Hall. Evan Morgan stepped out from the light and warmth without noticing the Vicar and schoolmaster. He crossed the square and walked slowly up the little village High Street. He savoured the smell of fish and chips from the Fish Bar around the corner, and nodded a brief good night to the three lads loafing on the street corner, their hands stuck in their pockets, cigarettes in their mouths. He passed his own shop, closed and shuttered, and out of long habit he tried the main door and the little door behind that led to the office. He gave an approving glance at the two windows with their goods neatly and interestingly arranged. Very good. Mervyn was a good lad. If only Mervyn and Rees could have been the other way round. But then, now there might be a chance of more sons.

He felt better for the two whiskies he had drunk quickly and in rapid succession in the public-house. The uneasiness and choler which he had felt during the meeting were allayed, even if they had not entirely left him. The trouble was he knew exactly the reasons for his temper and uneasiness. Joseph Thomas always seemed to ruffle him in the same way. But the man himself was only the outward and visible cause. What were the real reasons? It was not jealousy of Joseph's success and talent as a farmer. Was it then jealousy because of Nigel's brilliant career in the Royal Air Force when compared with Rees Morgan's inglorious period of conscientious objection? Or was it fury at the treatment which Bella had meted out to him? For Bella was one of the few women who had told Evan she had finished with him. Usually it was the other way round – it was he who had the job of bringing affairs to an end, and, he prided himself, he was good at it. But with Bella, no. It was made quite obvious that he had served his purpose for a short while, and then she had cast him away. It rankled. And when he thought of her husband, he couldn't help thinking of Bella's treatment of him.

Not that he liked bringing to an end his many associations with women. Despite the temporary warmth engendered by the whisky, he was not relishing his prospective interview with Ellen. But then that was different. Ellen was not an affair. Ellen had been, in a way, part of his life, it was many, many years ago that he had seduced Ellen Williams when he was an errand boy and she a pupil teacher in the village school. She had been faithful to him ever since. And in his odd way he had been faithful to her. All through the years of his married life he had kept up his association with Ellen, and after his wife's death he had always come back to her, whatever other affairs he might have had. Ellen was always there, always in the background. There was, of course, no doubt that when his wife died she had wanted to marry him. But Evan had no desire to marry again, until, now a man of fifty, he had fallen in love with Janet Anderson. It was, he supposed, absurd if you thought of it in one way: a man in the early fifties, with two sons in the middle twenties, falling in love with a girl also in the mid-twenties – a girl who was a contemporary and friend of his sons. But there it was – it was true. Evan Morgan was never surer of anything than that he wanted to marry Janet. That was why he had to speak plainly with Ellen. It would be very difficult, he realized. That was why he had needed the second whisky. But then, he said to himself, Ellen was sensible. He persuaded himself that what he wanted to happen, would happen.

Miss Ellen Williams was standing in the drawing-room of the Manor House, her back to the fire, smoking a cigarette. She was just over fifty, but, with a little too heavy use of paint and powder, tried hard to look a woman of the late thirties who, if pressed, would admit to the early forties. Somehow she always succeeded in looking what she was not – a tart.

'Well, Evan?' she said as he came in.

'Well, what?'

'Why did you most especially want to see me tonight? And why here? Why couldn't we have met in the pub for a drink? And what is this most special piece of information you have to give me?'

He decided to go straight to the point. 'I wanted you to be the first to know, Ellen dear,' he said, 'that I am going to get married again.'

She did not conceal the fact that she was taken completely by surprise. 'To whom?'

41

she said quickly.

'To Janet Anderson.'

'To Janet Anderson? You mean she agrees?'

'Why, certainly.' His pride was touched. 'I should be a fool to tell you I was getting married to her before I had asked her, wouldn't I?'

She saw he was nettled, and on the defensive. 'But, Evan, dear, you can't be serious. You really are a fool sometimes. A defenceless fool.'

'What do you mean?'

'Just this. Why are you marrying her?'

He coloured. 'I happen to be in love with her,' he said. 'And she with me.'

She laughed. 'My dear Evan,' she said, 'Janet Anderson, if she has said, as you tell me, that she will marry you, is doing this for one thing only. Your money – your money and property. I should have thought that you, of all people, were shrewd enough to see that.'

'Is it not obvious, my dear Ellen,' said Evan, 'that anyone who marries anybody with money and possessions will be said to be doing it for them, and not for love?'

'Let us be brutally frank, Evan. What else can Janet see in you? A man old enough to be her father. A lecherous old man bolstering up his age with young girls.'

She had gone too far. The fury in his eyes told her that. 'Certainly, if you wish, let us be brutally frank,' he said. 'I had intended to avoid the essentials of this matter. You may be brutally frank yourself. You are also being very stupid. I could, I suppose, hardly expect you to be impartial; but I did expect you to understand.'

She did not care now what she said. 'But I don't understand,' she said, 'why now, at fifty, you are prepared to pay the price of marriage to achieve ends you found easy before?'

He paused. 'I'm sorry, Ellen,' he said. 'Janet is different. This is not another affair. There it is. We've had good times together, old girl. But now they are over – must be over. I'm changing my way of life.'

He turned his back on her and went towards the windows – the French windows that looked out into the garden. She caught hold of his arm and swung him around. 'Listen,' she said. 'You are talking as though I were one of your girl friends whom you were paying off. I'm not one of your miserable affairs. You can't pay me off. I'm part of you. We've been part of each other for too long. It can't change now. And there's Mervyn. The infatuation of a chit of a girl can't change our lives; shan't change our lives; won't change our lives.'

He shook himself free. 'Don't shout,' he said, 'and don't dramatize yourself. It has changed. However unpleasant it is – you must realize this. We can't go on as we have. You'll have to give me back the key you have of this house, for example. I'm sorry, Ellen,' he said quickly, his voice softening. 'I'm sorry, old girl. You've got to get used to this new fact, and I know it isn't pleasant for you. Everybody changes – every man Jack and Jill of us. We all change. You can't count on anybody. I've led a fairly free and gay life, I know, but I'm settling down at last. I'm going to be the model married man. I shall set myself up here with Janet and bring up a large family. Where are you going?' he asked.

Ellen was putting on her coat. 'Stay a while,' he said. 'Stay and have some supper. Surely we can still be friends?'

She looked at him coldly. 'I don't know what has come over you,' she said. 'It's probably something physiological that I don't understand. Change of life or something of that nature. I doubt whether you are responsible for what you are doing.' She paused, eyeing him critically. 'But whatever it is, I shall deal with it. I shall see you are brought to your senses.'

Then he lost his temper. 'Get out,' he said. 'Get out, and don't come and see me again until you've recovered your temper and your common sense.'

She stood at the door, her hand on the knob. Her hands were trembling. Her face was a curious mixture of rage and fear. Then

44

she spoke deliberately and slowly. 'I hear,' she said, 'that Bryn Davies is expected back next week.'

He took three steps across the room towards her and stopped. 'What the devil do you mean?'

'My meaning is obvious,' she said. 'When Bryn went away, Janet Anderson was his girl. They were practically engaged to be married.'

'That's not true. And even if it were, I'm not interested. It was all years ago. Many things have happened since then. The war is not just a halt of five years; we don't all begin at the end of it exactly as we started at the beginning.'

'Bah!' she said contemptuously. 'You sound like some cinema cliché. Time marches on. Is that what you are telling me?'

'Yes,' he said. 'The chaps who are coming back must realize that things have changed.'

'Many things have happened,' she said softly. 'Including the death of Bryn Davies's sister.'

He understood in a moment. 'Ellen,' he said. 'Listen. You wouldn't ... you wouldn't bring all that up now. I mean, that's all dead and buried.'

'Yes. Daphne Davies is dead. Daphne Davies is buried. But I'm not dead and buried, not yet – although you might wish it.' She waved aside his protestations suddenly.

'Leave Janet Anderson alone,' she said. 'I warn you: if you don't there will be trouble.'

'Bryn Davies will be reasonable. He's probably quite forgotten Janet. It was years ago they were friendly. He was young then. Since then he's been all over the world – seen all sorts of people.'

'And you have stayed at home making love – first to his sister, then to his girl. Quite so. He will not have forgotten his sister. And if he has, I shall make it my business to remind him – unless, of course–'

'Ellen, so you would try and blackmail me?'

'Blackmail? What a word to use among friends! A little firmness. That is a better name. I warn you, Evan. If you go on with this crazy plan to marry Janet, I shall make all the trouble I can. I know you and what's good for you. You are not going to make a fool of yourself, and of me and of Mervyn. I was never more serious in my life.'

She closed the door quickly behind her and walked as fast as she could out of the house, down the stone-flagged path across the garden. When she reached the door set in the outer wall she paused, hoping Evan would come after her and call her back. But he did not come. She wondered whether she had gone too far. For a moment she thought of running back into the house, flinging herself into Evan's arms and sobbing her heart out. But would that work? She decided not. At fifty one she still had many cards to play, thank goodness, but the weak, sobbing, defeated girl was not one of them. 'I'll leave that role to Janet Anderson,' she muttered furiously to herself, and went out into the road banging the garden door behind her.

Across the street the dark mass of the Andersons' house loomed up. The Post Office was in the two ground-floor rooms. A bright light shone out from one of the rooms where, behind uncurtained windows, the telephone exchange was housed. Ellen Williams walked across the road and stood in the shadow looking into the room. Mrs Anderson was at a table at the side of the room sorting letters. Janet Anderson sat at the telephone key-board, laughing and talking into a hand microphone. She turned towards the window and Ellen stepped back deeper into the shadow. Janet's face was smiling – a happy, carefree face. Ellen looked at her carefully and critically for the first time in her life. She had taught her at school and remembered her as a cheeky, rather ugly girl. Now she was a woman, and there was no denying she was a pretty woman – a very pretty woman. Her complexion was good and she used little make-up. Ellen turned away from the lighted window and walked quickly away. Her face was grim and her mouth set in a hard line. There was no one to see her as she brushed aside the tears which coursed in ugly channels along the heavy make-up of her face.

In the drawing-room of the Manor House Evan Morgan poured himself out a glass of whisky. He noticed that his hand was shaking and he laughed shortly. He took the glass over to the fireplace and sat looking into the flickering flames. Then, abruptly, he got up, kicked viciously at the logs in the grate, and went over to his desk in front of the big French windows. He dialled a number and then, when he heard the voice at the other end, his whole body seemed to change – to relax. It was as though he was throwing away the cares of his life. He smiled and his face was softer and kinder than it had been all day. He sat down at the desk and drew the receiver towards him. 'Hello, darling,' he said. 'It's Evan...'

III

The two young men came out through the swing-doors from the dining-room into the great reception lounge of the Airport Hotel at Basra. Outside the double hotel windows it was hot and sticky; the Iraqi workmen unloading a lighter in the glare of searchlights sweated and swore in the thick treacly evening air. Inside in the dry, false, air-conditioned atmosphere, it seemed to be cool.

'I call that a jolly good dinner,' said Bryn Davies.

'So do I. Quite up to the standard set at Karachi last night. And both well above what we shall, alas, be eating in a day or two at home.' David Morris made a grimace.

'Yes. I wonder if the food situation is quite as bad as one assumes it is from the papers and from the letters one gets.'

'I don't know. Being away so long, it's difficult to do more than make a guess.'

'Do you feel, as I do,' said Bryn, 'that you have everything at home out of perspective? I mean it isn't the war and fighting that has done that, but just the separation – the separation of years and distance.'

They were walking down the length of the lounge and paused at the double swing-doors that led from the cold, metallic clean air within to the dark, thick heat outside. 'What shall we do?' It was David Morris who asked the question.

'Let's have a drink. I liked the beer we had in the bar before dinner.' They beckoned to one of the many white-clad boys standing around the walls, and two bottles of beer were brought – ice-cold and fresh to the taste. A mist of condensation formed on the outside of the glasses as the beer was poured out, and its fierce coolness burnt their throats

49

and tongues as they drank. Bryn Davies put down his glass and looked at the labels on the bottles. He laughed. 'This is a curious place,' he said. 'Here we are crossing the world from Singapore to South Wales, and we rest here, halfway round the world, eating caviar from Russia at dinner and now drinking rice beer from Eritrea. It makes me feel more than ever cut off from the world – just like the real temperature and humidity of the night air of the Persian Gulf is cut off from us by the glass walls and the air-conditioning plant.'

'I've got that feeling too. A sort of dis-embodied feeling: as though one were suspended between life and death.'

'Fortunately, not between life and death,' said Bryn. 'But between life and life. That's it. Nobody knows we are here; nobody knows us here; nobody cares about us here. We have no responsibilities, no cares.'

'You sound as if you envy our temporary isolation from the world.'

Bryn hesitated. 'I think I do,' he said slowly. 'Yes; I think I do. It's not that I don't want to get back. I do; of course I do. And whether I want to or not, I have to go back. But it won't be easy. I was trying to explain this to a few soldiers I was talking to before we left Malaya. They wouldn't understand – wouldn't understand that time doesn't stand still. They thought everything was going to be exactly the same as when they left home

– their wives, their children, their jobs; that they could put the war years behind them and snap back into 1939 again – just as though five years had not gone by.'

'Perhaps you exaggerate,' said David. 'We may not find things changed as much as you fear.'

'I shall,' said Bryn. 'My father's retiring, you know. I don't know what he will do without his school. Of course, he has his garden and he reads a lot; but it will be a great change for him. Then my mother is ill. I don't know what's the matter with her – I'm not even sure that they know at home – but they are worried, and so am I. And Daphne is dead.' He stopped. 'I'm sorry, David,' he went on. 'I didn't mean to remind you.'

The other laughed bitterly. 'I need no re-minding, Bryn,' he said, 'nor ever shall. She is often in my thoughts; more often in the last few weeks since I knew I was going home than perhaps at any time since she died. You know we were fighting in the Arakan when the news of her death came to me, and some-how I was able to put her out of my mind by throwing myself into the work we were at. Death and tragedy seemed so much a part of the day's work then, that I thought less of it than I do now, as we move back to a life where sudden death is a remote contingency, fortunately.'

'You didn't think of asking to go home on compassionate leave at the time? I often wondered. I was at the Tactical Training Academy on the Deccan at the time. You didn't write to me.'

'No, I didn't write, and I don't think I could have got home,' said David. 'After all, I doubt whether I had grounds. We weren't engaged, not legally, officially. Daphne thought it silly to bind ourselves together for four years or longer. We didn't know when the regiment went overseas how long we should be separated. Anything might happen, she said.' He paused. 'And she was right,' he said. 'It did.'

'Poor David.' Bryn spoke feelingly. 'Daphne was a fine kid. A chap couldn't have had a finer sister. It makes me sick sometimes to think of the things we did together, that we can never do again, like walking along the cliffs to St David's Castle in the teeth of a September gale, the wind almost tearing our hair out by the roots; and picking blackberries in the Castle ditches; and walking at night to Cowbridge; and collecting mushrooms from the meadows behind the church.' He paused. 'But what's the use?' he said. 'We've got to get over it. My father and mother are not going to get over Daphne's death – not really. But you and I, David, we are young. We can't spend our time worrying about the dead.'

'That's just the point. I do worry.' David

paused. 'Has it ever occurred to you,' he said, 'that there may be something to worry about? That there was something very curious about Daphne's death?'

Bryn Davies put down his glass and stared across the table. 'What exactly do you mean?' he asked.

'It's probably nothing,' said David. 'Probably nothing at all. But we were told so little at the time; leastways, I was. Just that Daphne had died suddenly of blood poisoning. An infected wound not treated in time.'

'You mustn't let your imagination run riot with you. That's a very ordinary sort of thing. Just what could have happened. Just what did happen. My father was most explicit about it all.'

'So was mine. So explicit in one letter that it was as though he were setting forth some official communiqué. And then hardly mentioned it at all afterwards. There is something we haven't been told, Bryn. I'm sure there's something.'

'I expect there are a lot of things we haven't been told,' said Bryn feelingly; and the edge on his voice was not lost on David.

'A lot of things?'

'Oh, never mind, never mind. They won't improve by talking.' Bryn spoke abruptly.

'I don't agree,' said David quickly. 'It's an odd thing, now. I haven't said to a soul what I've just said to you – you know, that I was unhappy about the circumstances of Daphne's death. Or should I say, puzzled. I haven't had anybody I could talk to, of course. We've been separated – you and I – most of the time that we have been in India and Burma with the Regiment. But suddenly now – talking to you – speaking out loud the suspicions I've had bottled up in me for so long – why, it seemed to cure them.'

'That is because you were worrying about something that didn't exist. You've been building up a thing for yourself about a perfectly ordinary accident.' He paused. 'With me it's different.'

'It's Janet, I suppose,' said David shyly. 'Janet Anderson.'

Bryn nodded his head. 'Yes,' he said. 'When we left home, Janet and I were – well, like Daphne and yourself. We had actually thought of getting married before I went overseas, but in the end decided against it. Like you, we were never formally engaged, but we understood perfectly that if we felt for each other at the end of the war as we did then, we should get married.' He paused. 'My feelings are the same,' he said.

'I see. And Janet's are not. Is that it?'

'I don't know. That's the devil of it. I don't know. She doesn't say so. She doesn't say anything. We used to write to each other very frequently, of course. Then our correspondence lapsed a bit. You know how it is:

when you are out in the jungle in Burma there just wasn't anything to write about. I expect it was mainly my fault, but our correspondence just died. I haven't heard from Janet for over six months; she even forgot my birthday this year. I just hear brief bits of news from my mother and father that Janet is well, that Janet spoke to them, but no more. In fact, even they haven't mentioned her for some while. I'm puzzled. I wish I knew what was happening.'

'Well. It's only a matter of a few days now. I suppose we shall both be in Llanddewi by this time next week, if nothing happens to the aircraft and the demobilization machinery is only reasonably swift.'

'Yes. I suppose you are right. There's not much point in inventing troubles or meeting them here at Basra – halfway round the world. When do we set off for Cairo?'

'I looked at the notice board. Another early start. We have to report at the airfield at two o'clock.'

David looked at his watch. 'And it's now nine-thirty,' he said. 'What shall we do?' He glanced at the big lounge full of soldiers and airmen on their way home to be demobbed. 'Play cards? Drink? Or get a few hours' shut eye?'

Bryn yawned. 'I'm for a little sleep,' he said.

They walked up the wide, carpeted stair-case and along the softly lit corridor towards their bedroom. A houseboy leered at them furtively out of one of the dark doorways as they passed. 'Sahibs, sahibs,' he whispered hoarsely, 'you want good jig-jig?' They laughed, and he took their laughter for acquiescence, running after them, plucking at Bryn's sleeve, grinning lecherously. 'Me good jig-jig wallah,' he said. 'Sahib, me very good jig-jig boy.' They turned into their bedroom, and shut the door firmly behind them. The boy squatted down on the mat outside, convinced that his services would be needed later on. He had a wide experience of the sahib in transit.

David Morris turned on the fans and took off his bush-shirt. 'It will be a good thing to get back to Llanddewi from one point of view, anyway,' he said. 'I shall feel cleaner. "Jig-jig, sahib," he mimicked. ' "Sahib, you wanta da company; me very good boy; me show you good High School Girl." Bah! I'm sick and tired of these lecherous cries that have pursued me through every town and cantonment and camp in India. It makes one think there are only three things that fill up the life of the average soldier in India – work, and drink, and bed.'

'And in Llanddewi, it's different?' Bryn Davies's voice was mocking.

'In Llanddewi, of course it's different.' David Morris turned on the taps of the bath,

56

and the rest of what he was going to say was drowned in the swirl of brown Tigris water that filled the bath.

CHAPTER 3

PREPARATIONS ARE MADE

I

Ben Anderson paced up and down the little living-room behind the Post Office. His wife sat by the fireplace in a rocking chair. 'For goodness sake, Ben,' she said testily, 'stop walking up and down. Go out into the garden, or go for a walk – if you must walk.'

'Well, stop rocking yourself backwards and forwards,' he snapped.

Margaret Anderson sighed. 'It's no good getting angry with each other, Ben,' she said.

He stopped his restless pacing and slumped down in his armchair on the opposite side of the fireplace. 'You're right,' he said. 'I'm sorry; it's my nerves. I didn't sleep a wink last night. After Janet told us what she proposed to do.'

'I'd been afraid of something like this for some while.'

'You had? You didn't mention a thing to me.'

'No, Ben. I didn't. You're so hot-tempered.'

He made a cross gesture with his hands. 'You should have told me. You really mean that you knew Janet has been – well, has been seeing Evan Morgan.'

'Yes; for some while.'

'You should have told me. I'm her father. I would have done something about it.'

'What would you have done? That is what I was afraid of. Really, Ben, when you once get an idea into your head, you don't wait to think. Do you remember what you did when you heard two men in the Bell saying that the anonymous letters were written by us in the Post Office?'

Ben coloured. 'It was a damned lie. They could have been had up for slander.'

'And you could have been had up for assault,' she retorted. 'Indeed, you would have been if Sergeant Bill Williams hadn't known that nobody in the Bell would have given evidence against you.'

'That's past history. The present story is much more serious. Tell me, Margaret: you don't think seriously that Janet and Evan Morgan are going to get married?'

She sighed. 'I don't know what to think. All I knew was that they were meeting each other. They were always having phone calls. It's a wonder you didn't notice that.'

Ben Anderson's mouth was set grimly. 'They can meet each other and they can talk on the phone,' he said. 'I can't stop that. But they won't get married.'

'What do you mean?'

'Just this. I am not permitting my daughter to make a fool of herself with one of the most unprincipled men in Llanddewi – one of the biggest scoundrels in the Vale of Glamorgan.'

'Are you sure she is making a fool of herself? After all, Evan has a great deal of money. The Manor House...'

'Are you gone crazy as well? Every penny he's made has been through selling short weight or inferior goods to poor, gullible people. His morals are worse than his business methods, for all that he is a church warden. I tell you I will not have my daughter added to a long list of women who have been his wives or mistresses or whatever you like to call them. I can remember him starting in the shop when he left school – years ago. He was chasing after Ellen Williams then. He...'

'Ben, Ben.' She laid a restraining hand on his arm. 'Ben, you really mustn't go on like this. You'll work yourself into a frenzy and do something which you will bitterly regret.'

He shook off her arm impatiently, almost rudely. 'I will do something, anyway,' he said. 'Mark my words, Margaret. Janet shall not marry Evan Morgan. For if she does it will be something we shall all regret – all of us.' He stumped out of the room, banging the door behind him.

Mrs Anderson sighed. She put fresh coal on the fire, and stood for a moment looking into the mirror above the fire, patting her hair absentmindedly. Then she took off her apron and went into the stone-flagged passageway that separated the living-room from the official part of the Post Office. She paused for a moment outside the door of the exchange. The door had a glass panel and through this she could see Janet seated at the telephone exchange. Then she went into the little room that served as head-quarters of the Post Office and telephone exchange for Llanddewi. Janet turned and smiled at her, and her mother smiled back. 'Had a busy shift, my dear?' she asked.

'No. Just average. Not really much doing.'

'And now? What are you going to do now?'

'I think I shall just skip across the road to the Manor House and have a talk with Evan. We want to get our arrangements fixed up quite quickly.'

Her mother turned away. 'Must it be so soon, Janet,' she asked. 'Can't you wait a little while?'

'Why? Why should we wait?'

'Oh, I don't know. Your father doesn't take kindly to all this.' She waved her hands in a gesture of despair.

'No, Mother dear,' Janet shook her head. 'If we delay things we shall have endless discussions in the village and here at home. I know my marriage to Evan Morgan isn't going to be in the least popular. Let's get it over. People more easily get used to things they don't like, that have happened, than to things that are going to happen.'

'My dear.' Her mother hesitated. 'You are sure in your own mind, aren't you?'

'Yes; of course I am. I know exactly what I am doing.'

Her mother sighed, and she went on quickly: 'Don't worry, Mother, please. It will be all right. A year from now you will be wondering why you worried at all.'

'I'm not worrying about you, my dear,' said her mother. 'I'm worrying about your father.'

'It was obvious that he wasn't going to approve. I'm sorry.'

'But it is worse than that, my dear. It isn't just his not approving. I've just had a long talk with him.' She paused. 'Your father is a strange man, Janet. He is usually so very calm and quiet – he appears to so many people a retiring, shy man whose interests are watching football matches and collecting fossils in the cliffs. But when he does get roused he seems to become more violent than ordinary people. I'm very much afraid that he will go and have a talk with Evan, that he will say some very strange things, that they will quarrel – it might even come to blows.'

Janet shook her head. 'I wish that Evan didn't cause such violent likes and dislikes,' she said. 'I'm worried on his behalf. But I hope Dad won't go and make a fool of himself – and me. You see, my mind is quite made up; nothing Father or anyone else says or does can stop me from marrying Evan. No, nothing.'

Her mother caught her hand and squeezed it, half affectionately, half nervously. 'Oh, don't say that, my dear,' she said. 'Don't say that. It is as though you were defying Fate.'

II

Mervyn Morgan sat in the little office behind the shop in the High Street and gazed with pleasure, through the glass door. He could see the shop neatly stocked with everything from lawnmowers to eggs, the assistants moving about busily, and beyond, through the shop-windows, he could see the street. He was pleased with himself – and had cause to be. The outbreak of war had found him just finishing school at Barry and wondering what to do. He had supposed he would be offered a job somewhere in his father's business and that he would spend his life as a sort of junior partner to Rees who, as his father's legitimate son, would inherit the main interest in the business. The war had been a godsend to him; uncertain of his future and longing for change and adventure, with nothing to lose, he had joined the Navy and had a career of very conspicuous success. He served in many parts of the world, was commissioned and mentioned twice in dispatches. Wounded in a supporting action in the Mediterranean, he had ended the war with a stiff leg. On leave in Llanddewi following his convalescence in 1944, he had spent a great deal of time in the company of Phyllis Wynne Roberts, the local doctor's niece, who was a W.A.A.F. officer stationed at St Athan Aerodrome nearby. A week before he was due to return to his unit, they had got married by special licence in the Registry Office at Cardiff and spent a hurried honeymoon in the Seabank Hotel at Porthcawl.

After he was demobilized, Mervyn was surprised and delighted to be offered the management of the Llanddewi shop. He had thrown his energies and not inconsiderable administrative ability into the running of the business, and it was clear his father was satisfied and was prepared to leave more and more of it in his hands. The future seemed a rosy one. He thought of Phyllis, in their thatched cottage on the edge of Sealands Farm. She was expecting a baby –

their first child. He hoped it would be a son who could carry on the name of Morgan down the years. He himself would see that the boy, if boy it were, should be handed on a fine and flourishing business. There was only one snag at the moment – Rees. Not for the first time he cursed the twist of Fate that had made him the bastard and Rees the legitimate son.

His thoughts had taken him away from his contemplation of the shop, and he did not notice his mother until, with a brief knock, she opened the office door and came in.

'Hello,' he said, jumping to his feet. 'What brings you here at this time?' He glanced at his watch.

'I'm just on the way back to school,' she said. 'But I had to see you for a few minutes. Have you seen your father today?'

'No; I haven't. He's been in Barry and Cardiff. But I'm expecting him in this afternoon. We are going over some business matters.'

'There will be some other things to go over. He'll have some surprising news for you.'

'In what way?' He caught the grimness in her tone.

'Your father is getting married to Janet Anderson.'

'I don't believe it.'

'He told me so last night. Wanted me to be the first to know. Very considerate of him.'

'But I had no idea – no idea that such a thing was possible.'

'Neither had I. A mere schoolgirl. It's only yesterday I remember boxing her ears for being rude to me in class, and for writing rude things on the blackboard. I'd like to box her ears this minute. The impertinent hussy.'

Mervyn had slumped down in his chair. 'This tears it, doesn't it?'

'It certainly would,' she said. 'Remember, your father is only fifty, and he seems very hale and hearty. He might well raise up a large family from that rudely healthy schoolgirl – several sons to take a share in his business.'

'And to live in the Manor House.'

'That is the sort of thing that might happen.'

Mervyn got up and sat on the edge of the table. He lit a cigarette and blew out a cloud of smoke. He looked sharply at his mother. 'What do you mean exactly,' he asked, 'by saying *would* and *might?*'

She looked back at him steadily. 'I don't think these things need happen,' she said. 'And I don't intend they should happen. You and I between us, I think, can stop this absurd marriage. But there isn't much time.'

For a few minutes after the door closed behind her, Mervyn sat staring glumly at the table. Then he stubbed out his cigarette and

walked out into the shop. There was a jaunti-
ness in his step, and a warmth and confidence in the smile he gave the girls behind
the counter.

III

The nurse came into Dr Wynne Roberts's
surgery. 'There's only one more person in
the waiting-room,' she said. 'Mr Davies –
Mr John Davies. He's been there for some
time really, but he insisted on waiting until
the last. Said he was in no hurry.'

'I see.' The doctor did not look up from his
papers. 'Show him in, Nurse, please, and
then you can leave us. I shan't need you
again tonight.'

John Davies came in. He and the doctor
exchanged greetings perfunctorily, each
avoiding looking directly at the other.

'Sit down, John. Have a cigarette.'

John Davies sat down in a worn leather
armchair by the fireplace. 'I'll smoke my
pipe,' he said. The doctor remained at his
desk. He shuffled his papers, putting some
into a file cover, clipping others together with
a glider clip. 'It's cold out tonight, isn't it?' he
said after a while. 'Touch of autumn in the
air.'

'You didn't send for me to tell me about
the weather, I imagine, Wynne.' John Davies

smiled. 'Let me have it. It's bad, isn't it?'

The doctor nodded. 'Yes, John. It is bad. I am sorry.'

The other adopted a tone of forced reasonableness. 'Now Wynne, let's forget for the moment that we are old friends,' he said. 'You're the doctor. You tell me the report – just as though I were an ordinary patient. It'll be better that way.'

Wynne Roberts looked at his papers. 'Just as you wish, John,' he said quietly. 'I don't know which is the more difficult. But here goes. The report of the specialists and the hospital X-ray merely confirm my diagnosis. It is a cancer, as we had both guessed.'

The other said nothing for a while. Then he asked briefly: 'Inoperable?'

Wynne Roberts nodded. 'I'm afraid so. Inoperable, incurable. That is to say, in our present state of knowledge. There will be a time, of course, when we can deal with these diseases, but not now, alas.'

'An operation would do no good?' John Davies spoke as though he were asking himself the question.

'John, an operation would be murder. Surgical murder. We should be condemning Ruth to death by the surgeon's knife. I couldn't recommend it, and I don't think many surgeons would undertake it.'

'Then the sentence is...?'

'Putting it that way makes it worse. I'm

afraid Ruth hasn't very long to live, John. These things are always difficult to estimate. I should say about three months. That is also the figure the specialists in Cardiff gave. But it is only a guess. And, of course, if we sent her into the hospital in Cardiff and used all the latest treatments on her, your wife would live longer – say, two or three weeks or even a month longer; perhaps more.'

'I don't want that,' said John quickly. 'I don't want that. I don't want her kept alive for the sake of living; just a living corpse. That would be cruel.'

The doctor paused. 'I think I agree with you on the whole, John,' he said. 'Of course, she won't be in pain,' he went on quickly. 'We can see to that, thank goodness.'

'No,' said John. 'She won't be in pain. That's a good thing. It is we who live who will be in pain.' Wynne Roberts looked up sharply and the schoolmaster went on quickly: 'Now, Wynne, there is one thing more you must do for me in this matter – for us. Keep it from her. Tell her what you like; tell her anything, but don't let her know she is going to die. We've kept one thing from Ruth already – I mean, the real facts about Daphne's death. Let us keep this from her as well. I don't think I could stand it if she knew the truth.'

Wynne Roberts spoke slowly: 'But if she knows it already – or suspects it?'

68

'How could she?'

'Ruth is a very shrewd woman; and a brave one.'

'But a sentence of death for something you haven't done takes more than human bravery to sustain.'

The doctor got up from his desk and walked over to the fireplace. 'Look here, John,' he said. 'I know this is a great blow to you – perhaps the greatest you have had in your life. But you mustn't get things unbalanced as a result. We are, all of us, all of us,' he repeated, 'sentenced to death the moment we are born. The moment we are conceived. That is the only certainty in this life: that we shall cease living, that we shall die. It doesn't require more than human bravery to sustain that fact – to recognize that we are human. That is what a doctor has to tell himself all the time.'

John Davies shook his head. 'You are doing your best, Wynne,' he said. 'Thank you for it. You are a good friend. But it won't work. You see' – he hesitated – 'I'm afraid.'

'You're afraid?'

'Yes; I'm afraid. I'm not afraid for Ruth. You say she won't suffer any pain, and we will see she doesn't know the truth. I suppose that even if she did, she would carry on with her cynical bravery to the end. No; I'm afraid for myself, and for Bryn, who is coming home, as you know, in a few days. What sort of welcome is this going to be for him? Death! The death of his sister, the death of his mother. The sudden death of his sister; this lingering death of his mother.' His voice was hoarse. 'I knew in my heart the news you were going to tell me,' he went on. 'That is really why I came here late and lingered in the waiting-room until everyone had gone. I didn't want to hear from you the truth. I'm afraid of the truth, Wynne. That's what it is. Afraid for myself, and afraid of myself.'

IV

Miss Mary Cherrington was in her little greenhouse-cum-conservatory watering her cacti when the doorbell rang. She went to the corner and peered through the glass and the creepers at the front of the house. Satisfied that the caller was welcome, and, moreover, that she need not remove the fine, shapeless leather hat that she wore for the garden and the hens and the pig, she went through the house and unlocked the front door – first the large heavy lock, then the chain from its groove, then the little bolt, and finally the Yale lock.

Rees Morgan stood on the doorstep; he was dressed in an old green trilby hat and a dirty raincoat. His shoes had not been cleaned for days. His socks hung in untidy loops around the tops of his shoes. He smiled rather ruefully and took off his hat. 'I hope I haven't got you out of bed, have I, Aunt Mary?' he asked kissing her on the cheek. He always called her Aunt Mary, although she was no more than his godmother.

'Certainly not, me dear boy, certainly not.' He followed her into the hall, and she went on talking: 'It's only nine-thirty.' She gave the grandfather clock a glance. 'I never go to bed before ten o'clock. In fact, always at ten. Ten o'clock promptly.'

They had gone into the drawing-room as she spoke. Miss Cherrington stirred up the remains of the fire and went across to the corner cupboard that served as her serving-cellar. The two cats stretched out in front of the fire got up and walked over suspiciously to Rees. They smelt at the turn-ups of his trousers and at his shoes, and, satisfied with their investigations, rubbed themselves against him.

'Now what shall it be, Rees?' asked Miss Cherrington over her shoulder. She blinked amiably through her spectacles into the cupboard. 'I have made a very good cowslip cordial this year, but my last year's sloe gin is probably the best value. The cats prefer the sloe gin, and their taste in these matters is excellent.'

Rees laughed. 'I'll take their advice, of course,' he said. Two glasses of sloe gin were poured out and a thimbleful was poured into the little saucer by the fireplace. Rees sipped the smooth, fiery liquor. 'Your good health,' he said, and added appreciatively: 'It's very good, Aunt Mary. Very good indeed. You don't mind if I smoke?' he asked.

'Certainly. By all means. And now,' she said, 'why have you come to see me?'

He lit his cigarette and temporized. 'Just for the pleasure of seeing you,' he said.

'Rubbish, dear boy. Now, what is it?'

'I came down to see my father, but he is away, and the house is shut up. I went across the road to the Post Office thinking they might know where he was, but I came away with a flea in my ear. Ben Anderson was very upset about something. When I asked if by any chance he knew where my father was, he said, "In Hell for all I care," and shut the door in my face. Have Ben and Father been quarrelling?'

'I don't know. They were never on very good terms, of course,' said Miss Cherrington. 'And temperamentally they are very opposite characters. But something special must have occurred. Very special. Ben Anderson is usually so good-tempered and masks his feelings so well. A deep man.'

'I wanted to see my father tonight.' He paused. 'You see, Aunt Mary, I have made a great decision.'

'You are always making great decisions, it

seems to me. Not to fight; then to fight; not to enter your father's business; then to enter it.'

'And now,' he interrupted, 'not to stay in it.'

Her eyebrows went up. 'Is that wise?' she asked.

'I haven't paused to think whether it is wise,' he said. 'I just can't go on in that shop in Barry – or, for that matter, in any part of my father's business or in anything to do with shops and business at all.' He went on quickly, his voice quiet but intense: 'I'm fed up with it. It's just not my line at all. You know the sort of thing: "Good morning, Mrs Jones. So warm for the time of year, isn't it?"' he mimicked. '"Of course, your rations? Really, you don't say so. Mrs Evans had three eggs in the Co-op on her book. And twice the ration of cheese and cooking fats. We must see what we can do about it." It's no good. I'm not made that way.'

Miss Cherrington stared at him. 'And just what way are you made, Rees dear?' she said.

'I think I know at last what I really want to do,' he said. 'I want to be a schoolteacher. I want to go to a university or a teachers' training college – anything will do. And then I would like to go and teach. Teach at a school in the country – somewhere in West Wales: Fishguard or St David's or Tregaron.

What do you think?' he asked eagerly.

'If it is really what you want to do, if you are sure, then by all means do it.'

'What will my father say?'

'I think he will be cross. He thinks you've wasted enough time already.'

'I know he does but it isn't fair. Everybody has wasted time; the last six years, if you like to put it that way. But the war wasn't any of their fault.'

'That may be so. But you know your father has violent views on so many subjects. He is quite capable of cutting you off with the proverbial shilling.'

'I think I might be able to get a grant,' he said.

'And I could perhaps help you a little.'

He blushed. 'That's not why I called here this evening,' he said in confusion.

'I know that,' she replied. 'And I didn't only mean financial help, although I might be able to do that. As you know, I have made some arrangements for you in my will. I was thinking of my nephew,' she said, 'Sir Richard Cherrington. He is Vice-President of Fisher College in Cambridge. I think he might help. The only thing is that he doesn't seem very useful in getting people into the University these days. The last time I wrote for his help he sent me back a long letter saying he wasn't a tutor any more, and all about Admission Committees and quotas and one man in ten getting into Cambridge these days. I wrote and told him I was not pressing the claims of ten men – just one man. But he wasn't helpful. Still, we must see what we can do.'

'It's very kind.' He paused. 'I do think my father will be cross with me when I leave. You see, it isn't only that I'm fed up with the shop. I'm afraid that I've also made a great mess of the accounts.'

'You've done nothing illegal, I hope?' Her voice was abrupt.

'Oh, no. It's not that. It's just inefficiency. I seem to have got all the books into a first-class muddle, and it is bound to be found out when they start the quarterly balancing. When Mervyn hears, I expect he will laugh at me. Something else he will be able to hold over me.'

She looked at him sharply. 'You are telling me the whole truth, aren't you, Rees?' she asked. 'There's no reason why you should conceal anything from me.'

He avoided her direct gaze. 'I've told you all that,' he said. 'I want to clear out at once. This evening I thought I couldn't stand it any longer. That's why I came down to see my father. I wish he'd been in. It would all have been over by now.'

'You are still afraid of your father, Rees?'

'No. I'm not any longer afraid of him. I used to be, as you know. But I've got over my fear. Now I just hate him.'

Miss Cherrington looked up quickly, surprised by the depth of feeling in his voice. For a moment she caught an echo of his mother's voice. How long was it, she thought, since she had sat in that very room and said the same thing: 'I hate him, Mary, and wish he were dead.' But it was she who had died, the poor creature, and Evan had lived on.

'I don't care if it is wrong to say so,' went on Rees fervently, 'but it is the truth. I hate him. I hate him. I hate the whole lot of them. I hate Llanddewi. The sooner I get away from here, the happier I shall be.'

Mary Cherrington smiled and got up. She put a hand on his shoulder. 'There's nothing like a little alcohol to bring out the half-truths, is there?' she said. 'The half-truths that in our dramatic moments we would like to believe.'

'But I mean it, Aunt Mary. I really mean it.'

She brushed his words aside. 'There,' she said. 'Who would have thought that my sloe gin was quite so powerful? Even Sir Toby and Lady Macbeth are stupefied.' The two cats were lying stretched in front of the dying fire, fast asleep. 'Now run along,' she went on. 'It is ten o'clock – my bedtime. And you have to catch the last bus back to Barry.' She saw him to the door. 'And come and see me again,' she said, 'when your

76

mind is really made up. We'll have another talk.'

He was soon out of sight around the bend of the drive. She locked the door carefully – the Yale, the little bolt, the chain, and the great lock. She stood in the hall as the grandfather clock struck ten. But she did not go to bed. She retraced her steps to the drawing-room, and sat down at her desk. She took up her pen and began writing. Through the house a variety of clocks announced that they, if a little later than the grandfather in the hall, now thought that Miss Cherrington's bedtime had come. Musical tunes and cuckooings rang out up and down stairs. When they had finished the house was quiet – save for the scratching of pen on paper, and the contented breathing of the cats.

CHAPTER 4

THE RETURNING WARRIORS

I

Dr Wynne Roberts fussed with the papers on his desk, arranging and rearranging them into new piles. He kept his eyes averted from the woman sitting in the leather armchair between his desk and the fireplace. After a while he looked up, and was reminded again of the scene of a few days before. Only then it had been the husband who was sitting in the chair; now it was Mrs Davies herself. He wondered now, as he had wondered in expectation of these two interviews, which was worse – talking to a dying woman or to her husband.

'You make it very difficult for me, Ruth,' he said. His voice was kind, sincere, warm. 'You must remember that I stand in a twofold relationship to John and yourself. I am your doctor; but I count you both among my lifelong friends. You, perhaps, have been more my friend than John himself; but I've known you both for nearly thirty years – ever since I first came to Llanddewi as junior partner to old Dr Evans Pritchard. Do you remember him? Surely he was the last doctor in the Vale always to wear a top-hat and a black frock coat.' He paused, and his face broke into a smile. 'I'm not trying to change the subject, you know.'

Mrs Davies laughed. The tension was broken. 'There is no reason why our friendship should not stand the strain of this,' she said. Wynne Roberts looked at her admiringly; she was calm and cool – the master of the situation. 'We've disagreed over many things in the past,' she went on, 'but we won't disagree over this. Look, Wynne.' Her voice was urgent. 'I'm not afraid. I'm not afraid of the truth. John came to see you a few days ago to get the specialist's report, didn't he?'

'Well.' His tone was defensive.

'He came home and told me that it was satisfactory, or fairly satisfactory. That I had to be at home under observation for three or four months, and that I then might have to go to hospital for treatment.' She paused, and the doctor said nothing.

'That is not what you told him, is it?' she said. 'That is, perhaps, what you agreed to tell me, to save my feelings. But what you don't seem to understand, Wynne, is that it isn't my feelings that must be saved. It's John's feelings we must save, not mine.'

He looked at her, surprised. 'John's feelings?' he asked.

'Yes, John – not me. It's the living who suffer most when those they love are ill, desperately ill. Surely, Wynne, you must know that by now. Death is worse to those that see it happen and survive it, who live on into a world that is suddenly and for ever empty, than for those who die.'

He said nothing, and she went on. 'I'm going to die, of course, Wynne, aren't I?' She shook her head impatiently. 'You can't conceal it from me,' she went on. 'Neither could John.' She smiled, and her voice was tender with the love and affection and companionship of a lifetime. 'John never could conceal anything from me,' she said. 'After he had seen you, he came home – drunk. That has happened so very seldom that I know it always means something is wrong. He had been trying to muster up enough courage to see me by drinking in the bar of the Bell. But it didn't work. He told me what you had agreed to say, and then he began crying. The big baby. Then, of course, I knew. It gave it away. John has only cried when I've been in pain. I guessed then the truth he was afraid to tell me, the truth he was afraid of – afraid of himself living through the months when I shall be dying and the years afterwards – without me.'

She stopped speaking and there was a long pause. Wynne Roberts looked out through the window into the garden. He said nothing. There was nothing he could say.

'How long have I got, Wynne dear?' she asked.

He did not move his head or look at her. 'About three months,' he said. His voice was scarcely louder than a whisper.

'And there's no hope at all? An operation?'

Wynne Roberts turned from the window and faced her. This is what makes it worse, he thought. The faint hope that shone through the façade of fortitude and almost inhuman reasonableness – the hope that defied all science and certainty – the wish to live. He shook his head. 'My dear Ruth' – he spoke slowly – 'I don't have to say that everything that can be done will be done, do I?' He talked on. Suddenly the refuge of words seemed safer than silence. 'If only we knew more about this damned disease,' he said. 'If only medical science were more advanced. There will come a time when we shall be able to deal with cancer just as well as we now deal with malaria and smallpox and the rest of them. But not at the moment. That's what is so damnable.'

'We won't tell John, of course,' she interrupted.

'Won't tell John? What do you mean? He already knows.'

'We won't tell John that I know,' she said. 'He doesn't want me to know, and we'll let him think he has been successful. That may make the weeks ahead more bearable for him. I don't want him to suffer more than he has to, the poor dear.'

'You don't want him to suffer?' The doctor passed his hand across his forehead. 'My God! I have never heard anything so noble, so self-sacrificing, so–' Words failed him.

She brushed his sentimentalism aside. 'Rubbish!' she said brusquely. 'You've never been married, Wynne, or you wouldn't talk like that. And, anyway, it is very easy to be noble when you are under sentence of death.' She paused. 'Now that we are really getting down to things,' she went on, 'there is another thing you can tell me. Daphne. Tell me about Daphne – about Daphne's death. The truth, I mean, of course.'

He stiffened and his face went grave. She smiled. 'You see,' she said, 'you have suddenly gone on the defensive. There's no need to, Wynne,' her voice pleaded. 'I'm not trying to worm your secrets out of you. I know the truth here again – or I think I do. It was no ordinary case of blood poisoning, was it?' She paused. 'She was going to have a child, wasn't she? She was trying to get rid of it? Isn't that the story? Why didn't she come to me, Wynne, at the very first? Why didn't she? Why don't children trust their parents? That's what I ask myself. What have I not done in her upbringing that made her not want to tell me all? Or if not me, at least you?'

'But–' he began.

'Bah! I know what you are going to say.' She brushed his protest aside. 'These things can and should be arranged these days. You know, Wynne Roberts, that you do arrange them yourself. I would consider you the poorer doctor if you didn't. We do progress in some ways – though very slowly. When I was a girl we were always reading about these illegal operations – as the newspapers insist on calling them. But my daughter–' She hesitated. 'Why didn't she come to me?' she repeated. 'But then she was always so proud, so headstrong. She took after me, I suppose,' she added as an afterthought.

He made as if to say something, but she went on: 'Then she did it herself?' She talked on as though there was no one else in the room. 'I wonder. I very much wonder? If anyone helped her, I bet it was Ellen Harper Williams. That's what they are saying in the village, isn't it? But if so, why?' She paused. 'Because the child was Evan Morgan's child. That's what I think.'

Wynne Roberts spoke slowly: 'There isn't a shred of evidence,' he said. 'You're making all this up. I'm surprised at you.'

'H'm. You are only surprised because I have put into words the thoughts you have had,' she said shrewdly. 'Come along. Isn't that so?'

He avoided the direct question. 'There is

83

no point in dragging up all these things now,' he said. 'You have enough to worry yourself about without adding to your suffering. Daphne is dead, and nothing that you or I can do, Ruth, will bring her back.'

'Yes,' she said. 'Daphne is dead, and you tell me that I shall soon be dead. But John is alive, and my son Bryn is alive – we expect him back tomorrow, by the way; he and David Morris are at the demobilization place at the moment.'

'Bryn doesn't know,' said Wynne Roberts quickly. 'I mean about Daphne – the real facts about her death. He needn't know, need he, about Daphne or about you?' His voice was pleading. 'I'm very fond of Bryn,' he said. 'He's a grand boy. Well, he's my godson; perhaps I am partial. But we are going to hear great things of him one day. I am sure of that. The important thing is to let him adjust himself to the post-war world as quickly and as easily as he can. It won't be easy – we both know that, after five years in the Army. But we ought not to make it any more difficult for him. He is not going to have much of a welcome home, whatever we do – his sister dead, his mother seriously ill, and by all accounts his girl – I mean Janet Anderson – no longer interested. Don't let us pile on the agony for the boy.'

'Of course not, Wynne. I'm with you there.' She got up and began putting on her

84

coat. He helped her and they stood for a moment looking out through the window into the garden. A light autumn wind was stripping the leaves off the elms and blowing them in gusts across the lawn. Next-door a bonfire had been lit and the acrid smoke drifted across and in at the open window.

'My last autumn,' said Ruth Davies quietly. She put her arm in his, and they stood close together. 'I feel a curious sense of power, Wynne, now that I know I am going to die,' she said. 'I mean power to do what otherwise one would be afraid of doing. One has given to one suddenly the power to do the greatest good, the greatest evil – and take no rewards, no punishments. The greatest punishment meted out by the English law is death by hanging, isn't it? Have you ever thought, Wynne, that the only people to whom that sentence is no deterrent are those already sentenced to death?' She turned to him and smiled. 'But you don't understand what I mean. Nor, perhaps, do I fully understand myself. I'm getting light-headed.'

'You must rest, Ruth,' he said. 'You must rest. And you mustn't think too much about these things.' He wanted to say something – he was puzzled, disturbed – but he did not know what to say. The moment passed.

'Dear Wynne, you are always a great help,' she said. 'I've always been able to say things to you that I couldn't to anyone else.' She turned at the door. 'You are coming to my party, aren't you?' He hesitated, and she went on quickly, 'Yes, you must. It's only a little domestic party for Bryn and David, a sort of private welcome home. Just a few people.'

'You are very kind,' he said quickly, turning away. 'Very kind. But I really don't think I can come.'

'You must, Wynne. Really you must. I shall be most disappointed if you don't. You see,' she said, 'it isn't as though it will be an ordinary party. It will be the last party I shall ever give. It's an occasion.' She paused, and then said quietly: '"Mrs Ruth Davies at home for the last time."'

And, thinking back over that strange interview in the weeks to come, Dr Wynne Roberts was bound to confess that these last words, with their curious tone of triumph and resignation, had given him an uneasy and inexplicable foreboding. Was it only that he always felt it was a challenge to Fate to say that anything you did was 'the last'? Was it that fifty years of medical practice and a scientific education had not completely eradicated the primordial superstitions we all have? He remembered in the anxious, desperate days that followed the party how he had on that earlier occasion stood looking out through the window at the swirling autumn leaves, and, without turning round, had said softly, 'Very well, then, if you insist,

I will come to your last party.'

II

The demobilization arrangements went off quickly. David Morris and Bryn Davies arrived at the station at Llanddewi before they were expected. There was no one to meet them. Their heavy luggage was following by sea; they had with them only the light suitcases which they had been allowed to bring in the aircraft.

The two men had been cheerful on their journey from the demobilization centre in the Midlands to Cardiff, but as the railway wound its way along the coast from Barry westwards they settled into a gloomy silence. There seemed to be nothing left to say to each other. They stared out of the windows at the familiar countryside as it rolled past them. Bryn thought of how much the re-membered landmarks had meant to him when recollected in tranquillity on the sandy, dry plains of Northern India or in battle in the green, choking, steamy jungles of Burma. In the eager freshness of his memory, the Bristol Channel had been so blue, the fields so green, the lanes quiet and tree-shaded, and the mountain wall of Devon and Somerset across the water boldly etched in purple shadow against the southern sky. But now, on this blustery afternoon in late September, the sea was a dirty grey and the opposite coast was shrouded in rain-cloud. The grey drabness of the landscape seemed to penetrate the compartment, and their spirits sank. It would be absurd to suggest that a premonition of disaster had invaded them for a moment. All our attitudes to life depend on the balance we maintain between those cheerful factors which lead to elation and optimism, and those depressing factors which lead to pessimism and despair; and it is a specific of human nature that with the best will in the world we cannot with certainty control this balance. With whatever urgent cogency our reason assures us that all should be well, some submerged intuitive apprehension anchors us in defeatist gloom. Both Bryn and David were deliberately thinking in the last stage of their long journey from Singapore of the delights of reunion and reassociation that awaited them. The more furiously and consciously did they do this, the more surely did their spirits sink.

The little train drew up alongside the single platform at Llanddewi. It had started to rain, and the rain beat down on the flagstones on the platform, on the drably painted railings, on the slate-roofed station buildings. 'Well, here we are.' David Morris broke the silence. 'The moment we have been waiting for so long is here.' A porter sheltered in the wait-

88

ing-room door, his collar turned up against the rain. He was unknown to them, and the new, unsmiling face mirrored their melancholy. They had caught an earlier connexion at Cardiff, and though telegrams had been sent, no one had expected them by this train, and there was no one to meet them. 'I don't suppose Llanddewi can rise to a taxi,' Bryn had speculated gloomily. They asked the porter, to be told that the only cars available at the village were hired out that afternoon for a funeral. Bryn Davies had shrugged his shoulders, and turned up his coat collar.

'I'm afraid there's nothing for it, then,' he said, 'but to foot it ourselves.' They set off down the pot-holed road from the station to the village. When they got to the main road they parted, Bryn turning inland up the hill, David continuing through the village and up behind the market square to the Vicarage on the road down to the sea. They had parted with few words. 'A funeral,' Bryn had said with a short, sardonic laugh. 'Some welcome! I'll be seeing you.' And he had shouldered his bag and walked off.

III

The Reverend Hugh Morris was taking off his shoes when his son arrived. He peered incredulously as the door of his study opened and David came in. 'My dear boy,' he said. 'This is splendid. We weren't expecting you until a later train.' They shook hands warmly, and David's gloom began to dispel under the warmth of his father's welcome. 'Miss Rodgers! Miss Rodgers!' the Vicar called out to his housekeeper. 'Mr David has arrived – and he's very wet.' He came back and said solicitously to his son: 'You must change out of your wet clothes, my boy, and then we'll have tea and hot buttered toast by the fire.'

Tea with his father by the study fire was so familiar and unchanged a ritual that David began to forget the present. The reassuring past of the days before the war was being re-created for him. Every thing was the same – the basket of logs, the old plated muffin-dish in front of the fire, the desk untidily covered with papers, the John Speed map of Glamorgan still above the fireplace – appearing crookedly placed because of the sloping walls – the faded photographs of College groups above the yellow roll-top desk, the photographs of himself as a schoolboy actor. And his father – the same, though looking a little older; his feet in their worn carpet slippers stretched out to the blaze, slumped into the faded chintz-covered armchair.

After tea he left his father in the study and wandered round the house peering into all the rooms, nostalgically remembering events and people. His bedroom was much as he

90

had left it, although the Vicarage had housed evacuees during the war. He changed his clothes. Miss Rodgers had put everything back as it had been and in the big cupboard by the fireplace were still piled together all his books and games from childhood, his stamp collection, his cigarette cards, his birds' eggs, his trays of fossils – relics of the changing tastes of a young schoolboy. Lovingly he picked up the finest ammonite in his collection. What a find that had been – on a ledge of rock just washed by the sea in the cove by Sealands Farm. What a labour of love it had been chipping it out of the soft limestone, hurrying lest he should be cut off by the rising tide, yet careful not to break the corrugated ribbings of the tight, spiral shell.

Abruptly he shut the door of the cupboard and walked across to the window. He looked down into the darkening garden. The neat lawn shaded by beech trees was being covered with falling leaves. It needed brushing and the path needed weeding. From the garden he could see that the garage roof needed retiling and that the thatch on the roof of the little summer-house-cum-tool-shed where he had slept before the war on hot summer nights was also in need of repair. He saw all these things and noted them mechanically, but they meant nothing to him. David was remembering that afternoon at Sealands Cove. The touch of the dead fossil had revived a dead love. It was walking back along the narrow strip of dry beach, hurrying before the rising tide, that he had realized clearly, vividly, and for the first time, that he was in love with Daphne. He had seized her in his arms and kissed her passionately, the big ammonite the while in the haversack on his back. 'I love you, Daphne,' he had said. She had replied simply, directly, 'I love you, David. But we can't stay here. We shall get cut off by the tide.' And they had hurried on to the Llanddewi village beach, hand in hand, rejoicing in their newly declared happiness.

That had been the summer of 1939 – the summer before the war, before the October in which he was supposed to go up as an undergraduate to Jesus College, Oxford. And now ... and now. He went downstairs and out into the garden. His father was still by the fire in the study and Miss Rodgers was washing the tea-things in the kitchen. It had stopped raining. He walked across the lawn, and out through the wicket gate that led down to the church. The old church at Llanddewi, built in stone in the eleventh century by the conquering Normans on the site of a wooden Celtic church, is set in a hollow. Nothing now remains of the original pre-Norman foundation except three broken Celtic crossheads and an ogham inscription. David stood at the head of the flight of steps leading down to the grey limestone church in the hollow, and surveyed the sea of tombstones that marked the resting-places of thirty generations of the people of Llanddewi. In the far corner of the churchyard, where stood a ruined chantry, its crumbling walls covered with ivy, someone was at work. The gravedigger, of course. David remembered that there had been a funeral.

He walked over to the man. Munnings, the old sexton, had been one of his childhood's friends and heroes. In his spare time Munnings had been gardener at the Vicarage and had made things out of wood for David: tops, catapults, a bow and arrows, whip-handles, a boomerang that had worked – whatever had been necessary and seasonable for the cycle of boys' games. He remembered how frightened and excited he had been one day when the boomerang had circled around Miss Cherrington's hat as she crossed the Vicarage lawn on her way to tea. And it was Munnings who had taught him to play cricket. Munnings would be another link with the pre-war past – a reassuring, comforting link.

But as he got towards the chantry, he stopped. The gravedigger was not Munnings. It was someone David did not know. He looked up from his work of filling in the new grave and straightened his back. He was a middle-aged man with gingery hair. His dun-coloured corduroys were tied with string beneath the knees.

'Good evening,' said David.

'Evening.' The man spoke with a strong Welsh accent, unlike the ordinary people of the Vale of Glamorgan.

'I thought from a distance you were old Munnings,' said David jerkily.

The man looked at him keenly before he spoke. 'Are you a strange one to these parts, then?' he said. 'But how is that? You knew old Munnings, but you didn't know–' He stopped. 'P'raps you been away, mun. Is that it?'

'Yes. Yes. I've been away. Has old Munnings gone away?'

'Yes; he's gone away.' The man pointed with his shovel at the earth-filled grave. 'We buried him this afternoon,' he said. 'Gor, mun, it was a fine funeral. A fine funeral. As good as those we used to have up in the valleys before the war, and before the depression, when living was living, like, and dying was dying. Lots of flowers, as you can see.' He pointed to the wreaths and sprays that were for the moment heaped on a neighbouring grave. 'And everybody was there, from old Colonel Vaughan downwards. All the chapel folk came too. He was a much-respected man in these parts was old Munnings. It's a great thing to have church and chapel at your funeral, don't you think?'

David turned his head away. He did not

answer the rhetorical question. Another link with the past had been snapped. Abruptly he wondered if there was anything more sinister than a strange coincidence in the fact that Munnings had been buried on the day he and Bryn had returned to Llanddewi. Daphne dead; Munnings dead. Was he exaggerating, taken in by an excess of sentiment masquerading as an emotion? He pulled himself together. Surely if there were any significance it meant only this: the past is dead; bury the dead and leave the dead buried.

'Have you been here long?' he asked the gravedigger abruptly.

'Three years,' he replied. 'I couldn't work down the mines any longer' – he tapped his chest – 'so I came down here to do some gardening work. And then, when old Munnings got took ill last year, I did his work for him. And now I've buried him.' He pronounced the word as though it rhymed with hurried.

'Tell me,' said David, 'if you know where Miss Daphne Davies is buried.'

'Over there.' The gravedigger pointed. 'Over there by that old yew tree. Why do you ask?'

David hesitated. 'I knew her, very slightly,' he lied, 'before the war.'

'A nice girl. She was a nice girl. I used to see her a lot when I was doing the garden for Mr Evan Morgan at the Manor House.'

'Did you?' David looked intently at the gravedigger.

'Yes,' said the other. 'She used to come and see him a lot. They do say – mind you, I'm not saying it – that Evan Morgan was the cause of her trouble. But, there, I don't hold much with gossip myself. Maybe it is all lies. Gossip often is.'

David's face had gone white, but in the gathering evening the gravedigger saw no change in him. Nor did he know that David's heart seemed to be pounding away faster than ever before. The young man contrived with great difficulty to make his voice sound as casual as he could. 'She was in trouble was she?' he said.

The gravedigger noticed nothing – not even the deliberate offhandedness. 'Oh yes,' he went on. 'Of that there is no dispute. That is a matter of common knowledge, in a manner of speaking. She was going to have a baby, like, and tried to get rid of it. Something went wrong, poor kid, and blood-poisoning set in. Now if she had only come to me,' he went on, 'I could have told her the name and address of an old widow lady up in the valleys who'd have done the trick. Very useful she has been to me more than once. Very useful indeed.'

But David Morris was already out of earshot. He walked across the churchyard hardly looking where he was going. His face in the light of the lamp by the lych gate was the grey-white colour of wood-ash; his hands were clenched. He took the steps up to the street two at a time. He did not notice, leave alone recognize, Miss Ellen Harper Williams, who was standing at the top of the steps. She looked after him, and then back across the churchyard at the gravedigger. Then she began walking over to where the gravedigger was now piling flowers on the earth he had heaped over Munnings's grave. Her lips were moving, and her face showed that her half-articulated thoughts were unpleasant ones. She threaded her way slowly, purposefully, among the tombstones and across the darkening churchyard.

IV

Sir Richard Cherrington lay in his warm bath in Fisher College, Cambridge, luxuriating in the thoughts that flood one with joy when a large piece of work is at last satisfactorily completed. For years he had been engaged on a corpus of the Bronze Age statues of the West Mediterranean; the war had interrupted it, but at last the final footnote had been checked, rechecked, and completed, the final polish put to the text, the underlines to the illustrations revised, and the whole thing delivered to the printers. The day before he had driven over to Bletchley and deposited the manuscript with the United University Press. Feeling in need of a celebration, and his own College being empty of congenial spirits as usual in the first fortnight in September – he had no one for companion in this deadest moment of the academic year except a pimply mathematician who thought only of the distance of the stars, and a nervous young philologist who talked interminably about his commonplace experiences in the war – he had gone on to the Yellow Barn and indulged himself in those pleasures of food and wine, which, after the pleasures of scholarship, meant more to him than anything else, certainly than the conversation of his fellow men. A lobster thermidor, a *suprême* of chicken with mushrooms and asparagus tips, an excellent piece of Brie, and a *soufflé prâliné,* with a half-bottle of Chablis, and a half-bottle of Chambertin, a glass of Armagnac afterwards, and Cherrington had driven back to his College rooms satisfied with existence. That was all one could expect any more, he thought to himself: occasionally to be satisfied with existence. We are animals pretending to be gods, he thought, as the hot water swirled around him. Animals pretending to be gods, our pretences caught out at every turn. But could scholarship be explained in animal terms? Was there not here something not animal, something transcending brute nature, something of the spirit – the eternal, unsatisfied quest for truth?

Cherrington got out of his bath and began to dry himself – slowly, methodically, as he did everything. No; scholarship was just another animal pleasure. Curiosity and the urge to collect. It was the squirrel collecting nuts, the small boy collecting stamps. What difference from the scholar collecting bronze statues? It might all be a form of constipation. But did the squirrel arrange the nuts in new patterns? Did the small boy deduce any new facts from his stamps? Cherrington sighed. True; but what was the difference? 'Only one of degree,' he said firmly and out loud, addressing his large cat, Voltaire, who sat on a pile of towels on a table by the window, visually in contact with his master, but sufficiently far away to avoid being splashed with his bath-water. Voltaire purred, not because he had understood Sir Richard's remark, nor because he found his tall, naked, slightly bellied form attractive to look at, but because it was breakfast-time. Cherrington's gyp had brought in the breakfast dishes from the kitchen; Voltaire had sniffed at the covers by the fireplace and hoped for kidneys.

Cherrington seized a silver dredger of talcum powder and drowned himself in a shower of white mist. The fine particles drifted over to the window and irritated Voltaire, who jumped down and walked leisurely through the bedroom and back into Sir Richard's big keeping-room. He gave the breakfast dishes another olfactory examination and was disappointed; a second smelling suggested they were, perhaps, only sausages, and post-war, bread-filled sausages did not take a high place in Voltaire's estimation.

What next, Cherrington thought, now that the statues are disposed of? There were only three weeks left before Term began again with its long round of lectures, classes, discussions, committees, councils, boards. How quickly, he meditated, as do all dons in September, how quickly the Long Vacation sweeps away: how quickly; and with so little done! But first, a complete holiday, which to him meant a few days of rest somewhere within easy reach of southern England where the food was good and there were some material remains of the prehistoric past to walk to. He thought of the possibilities as he finished his bath and put on his dressing-gown. Burgundy with the hillsides of the Côte d'Or a rich purple in the September sun; the valley of the Dordogne and lying on the riverside meadows under the tall poplars; the Isles of Scilly – he thought of the peace of being put ashore for the day on an uninhabited island, and the sunsets over the Atlantic.

He walked into his keeping-room, drank a glass of iced pineapple juice, and glanced through the post, neatly set out beside his coffee cup. An invitation to tea and croquet from a College widow, some offprints from Spain, a reminder from the Society of Antiquaries that he should return a book to their library, book catalogues from antiquarian booksellers in York and Brighton, an appeal for money to restore the tower of a church in Suffolk – and a letter from his aunt. This was more interesting. He opened it and read. Dear Aunt Mary! How much to heart she had taken the paper-economy drive; every envelope was made to do tremendous service before it was eventually consigned to the waste-paper basket or burnt. He slit the economy label with his paper knife, and spread out the sheets of thick paper covered with his aunt's large scrawling handwriting.

'My dear Richard,' she wrote. 'You have not mentioned any plans for September, and I wondered if you would like to come and spend a few days with me. It would be nice to see you, and I am sure you would enjoy a few days' peace at Llanddewi. But, of course, I have a special reason for asking you. It is this: Llanddewi is being plagued with anonymous letters. I know that anonymous letters occur from time to time in all communities, even, I believe in university circles – and my source for this is not only Miss Sayers. During the war we had a particularly violent outbreak of poison-pen writing here. We perhaps didn't pay too much attention to it then – there were other things to do, and some of us regarded it as one of the hardships of war. But the war is over, and I have come to the conclusion, very reluctantly, that they ought to be stopped. There is no harm in an occasional anonymous letter, particularly if one knows who they are from; it is helpful sometimes, if hurtful, to know what one's acquaintances really think of one. But I believe that our poison-pen writer in the village is really dangerous and may stir up trouble. I spoke to the dear Vicar a few days ago – you remember Hugh Morris, of course – and we are not anxious to go to the police; not unless we have to. In any case, the police is Bill Williams, and I have little opinion of his intelligence.

'We wondered – I wondered would be more truthful – if you would come down and deal with the situation?

'What we want is advice and action. It is not so much a problem in detection, because you see, my dear Richard, I know exactly who writes these letters and why. In fact, it is all too painfully obvious. I would like your advice on what to do.'

And there was a brief postscript: 'Although it is not quite Michaelmas, I believe I can get a goose from Sealands Farm, and, as you know, I still have claret and burgundy in my cellar to satisfy even you for many a long night.'

Sir Richard put down the letter. Dear Aunt Mary, he thought, she always knows that the way to the heart is really through the stomach. He made up his mind at once. He would drive down to South Wales, spend the inside of a week there, and then take the car on to Southampton and across to France and so back to Cambridge in time for Term. But first, breakfast. He turned on his electric kettle and, filling his coffee-mill with beans, began grinding them vigorously. Voltaire sat watching him with that apparent interest which makes cats so companionable to human beings.

CHAPTER 5

THE PARTY

I

Mrs Davies's party was not a great success. Several of the invited guests had been unable to attend; Mrs Thomas of the Bell excused herself on the grounds that she had to be busy preparing for the official Welcome Home Party, but her husband and her son Roger were there. Bella Thomas of

Sealands Farm sent a message through her husband that she had a migraine and could not come. Colonel Bryn Vaughan had refused on the ground of official business, and Mrs Mervyn Morgan wasn't there – well, with the baby only a matter of days off, she could hardly have expected to be there, unless one was prepared for it to be born at the party. Still, everyone else was there: David Morris and his father, Dr Wynne Roberts, the Andersons from the Post Office – Ben, Margaret and Janet (they had handed over the exchange for the day to an assistant) – Evan Morgan and his two sons, Mervyn and Rees – the latter very sulky – Miss Ellen Harper Williams, Joseph Stanley Thomas, his brother Henry and his son Roger, Miss Mary Cherrington, and old Mr Rendle, the solicitor from Cowbridge who had handled everyone's affairs from Llanddewi for so long that it was inconceivable that any party or any occasion, marriage, funeral, or christening, could take place in the Vale of Glamorgan without his genial presence, his high-pitched, precise voice, his dry humour, his long but very amusing anecdotes. Indeed, it seemed that Mr Rendle alone in the whole party seemed unaware of any undercurrents of feeling. Or if he was aware of them he showed no signs that he had appreciated the tenseness that spread through the gathering. There was plenty to eat and drink. Ruth Davies had always been an excellent cook, and her husband had mixed a cold punch of cider, tea, and brandy which should have been guaranteed in normal circumstances to lift the company from its everyday preoccupations to that temporary plane of rosy well-being which is the only justification for parties. But to forget the humdrum necessities of the present is not always to shift to a plane of well-being; sometimes the most miserable facts of existence are brought forward with a greater clarity. Mrs Davies's last party was soon plunged in that most desperate of conditions – alcoholic gloom, and there seemed little that she could do about it by bright conversation or her husband by diligently keeping the guests' glasses full. John Davies began to suspect that by some fatal alchemy the ingredients he had so carefully put together in the cup – the cider, the tea, the brandy, the sugar, the lemons, the spice, and the sprigs of borage – had in some perverse way transmuted themselves into that least welcome of beverages – the cup that inebriates and dispirits.

Dr Wynne Roberts was the first to leave, saying that he must not keep his evening surgery waiting. Once he had gone the party began to break up. Henry Thomas hurried away to take over the bar of the Bell from his wife, Ben and Margaret Anderson said they must get back to the Post Office to do their shifts of duty, the Reverend Hugh Morris had a meeting – or said he had a meeting. Mr Rendle and Evan Morgan left together, saying they had some private business to transact.

David Morris was the last to leave. Bryn Davies walked with him to the front gate and down the road leading to Llanddewi. They stopped a few hundred yards down the road by an old barn which John Davies had bought and converted into a workshop and garage. 'Coming down to the pub for a pot of beer?' David asked, but Bryn shook his head. 'I don't think so, thank you,' he said. 'I'm doing a job of work on the car. Fitting a portable radio.'

David seemed to pay no attention to what Bryn was saying. He looked abstractedly up and down the road, then he turned and said abruptly: 'Is it true, Bryn, I mean, true what Joseph Thomas has been telling me? About Evan Morgan and Janet. That they are getting married?' He hurried on. 'It sounds absolutely incredible – just stark crazy.'

Bryn Davies spoke slowly. 'I wish it were only a rumour,' he said. 'I wish to God it were. But it's true, I'm afraid. Only too true. I've talked to Janet – talked to her several times in the last few days since we got back. But it is no use. I realized at once, of course, that she had lost all interest in me. I think I

106

knew that long before I got home. We are quite friendly, of course. It would be stupid if friends quarrelled because they had changed their minds. And over all this she has changed her mind; she is determined to marry Evan Morgan. She says she loves him, and wants to settle down as his wife in the Manor House.'

'Does she know Evan Morgan's record?' David spoke hotly.

Bryn sighed. 'But do we?' he asked. 'Do we really?'

'What do you mean?'

'Well,' Bryn went on, 'we know that Mervyn Morgan is his illegitimate son by Ellen Harper Williams. I think we've known that since Mervyn was passed off among us at school as his nephew, and since we were old enough to know what illegitimacy was. There's no dispute there. But the rest of it – all the stories of Evan Morgan's love affairs; how much truth, and how much Llanddewi gossip is there in them? You know there's been a great spate of anonymous letters in the village in the last few years. My father was telling me about them. He says he is quite sure they are written by one person – Ellen Harper Williams.'

'But–' Dave interrupted.

'No; wait,' the other went on. 'It doesn't matter whether they are or not. The fact is that the anonymous letters exist and have existed. Don't you think they may be responsible for much of the malicious gossip?'

David was silent a moment and then he said: 'Anonymous letters and gossip don't only deal in lies. You know, no smoke, and the rest of it.'

'But everything they say is not necessarily true,' Bryn went on quickly.

David Morris hesitated. 'I've a right to say this to you, Bryn,' he said. 'You mustn't misunderstand me. It's this. They are saying in the village that Daphne was going to have a baby. That she died trying to get rid of it. That Evan Morgan was the father.'

For a while Bryn Davies said nothing. When he spoke his voice was wooden. 'I know,' he said slowly. 'That is what is being said.'

'You know? How do you know?'

'I received an anonymous letter yesterday setting out just what you have told me. A neat, typewritten affair, full of filth.'

'What are you going to do about it?'

'I showed it to my father.'

'What did he say?'

'He said that if we could be certain the letter was written by Ellen Williams, he would murder her.'

'But he didn't deny that what the letter said was true?'

'He said he didn't know,' said Bryn Davies. 'And then he broke down. I couldn't go on questioning him. But I've been speaking to Joseph Stanley Thomas. You know that in the old days he was a particular friend of mine. I used to go shooting with him a lot, and it was he who taught me to play golf.'

David Morris dropped his voice and spoke conspiratorially, 'Has he told you about his scheme?'

Bryn nodded. 'He suggested we should have a game of golf together tomorrow and talk it over. Will you go?'

'Yes.'

'So shall I, at least for the game of golf. But the idea is all a little childish.'

'Childish?'

'Well, you know what I mean. It's like a schoolboy prank, or a pack of undergraduates taking it out of someone they didn't like.'

'I don't quite agree.'

Bryn Davies said nothing, and David went on: 'I had an insane impulse at your mother's party today,' he said. 'A completely insane impulse. It was when we were looking at the war trophies you had set out on the hall table – the paperweight made from the Messerschmitt fighter that was shot down over your head in the desert, the jungle knife you killed those three Japanese with – you remember? Well, I thought how easy and how useful it would be to add a man like Evan Morgan to the long list of these we have killed during the last five years.'

Bryn Davies looked at him sharply. Their eyes met. 'You know as well as I do, David,' he said, 'that you are talking nonsense. The war is over. There is all the difference between what we had to do in Burma and Malaya in time of war and what we can do in South Wales in time of peace.'

'I know. I know,' said David impatiently. 'I will remember. I do remember. Murder is no longer our profession. The object of our operations is no longer the destruction of the enemy.'

There was an edge to his voice which made Bryn Davies suddenly very alert. 'It isn't,' he said. 'We've got to get used to that fact – the fact that killing a man who has done no evil in the heat of battle is one thing, and a good thing, but that killing a man here in Llanddewi – an evil man who has done endless harm – killing here in a calculated manner is murder.'

David said nothing for a while. Then he spoke quietly. 'Yet he deserves it,' he said, 'if he murdered Daphne.' As he spoke he turned on his heels and walked down the road towards the village. Bryn Davies watched him disappear into the gathering darkness. Then he went into the garage and began tinkering with the car. His face was grim, but as he worked he whistled softly to himself.

II

When Evan Morgan said that he had to take Mr Rendle off for a business talk, Janet Anderson elected to leave the party and walk back to the village alone, but as she walked down the road towards Llanddewi a car drew up at her side and a door was flung open.

The driver of the car was Joseph Thomas. 'Jump in,' he said. 'I'll give you a lift down to the village.' She got in murmuring, 'It's very kind of you, but you shouldn't have troubled. Such a short way.'

He made no attempt to restart the car. 'It isn't only that I want to give you a lift down to Llanddewi,' he said. 'I want to talk to you. Seriously. And I got no chance at the party.'

She said nothing, and he went on, 'I'll come to the point straight away. I want you to give up this idea of marrying Evan Morgan.'

For a moment she was too surprised to say anything. Then she burst out: 'What impertinence! It's none of your business what I do.'

'But it is. Believe me, it is,' he said. 'I've always had the greatest affection for you, Janet. I think it began even before you and Nigel used to see a lot of each other. I used to hope that you and he – well, that you and he might have got married. But that was not

111

to be. That is a dead hope.' There was a note of bitterness in his voice that silenced her. 'After Nigel's death,' he went on, 'I began to hope that you might become interested in me. I thought, of course, you would want a younger man. There had been Nigel, and there had been, I believe, Bryn Davies. Isn't that so? You're still interested in him?' he questioned.

She answered in spite of herself. 'I like Bryn very much,' she said, 'but only as a friend, of course.'

'H'm. When I heard about this proposal to marry Evan Morgan, I realized that older men had a chance with you. Although it was dreadful news, it has actually given me hope, and that is why I must talk to you now. That is, if you are seriously prepared to consider marriage with a man much older than yourself who could give you not only love, but a home and a settled comfortable secure way of life. I assume you are not in love with Evan Morgan and not seriously committed to marry him?'

Janet did not know what to say. The situation was in so many ways tragi-comedy. If Joseph had been passionate she might have thought the whole situation ridiculous and unfortunate and been able to deal with it. But he seemed so calm, so businesslike, so determined and reasonable. 'You sound like a man making a business proposition,' she said. 'Are you suggesting yourself instead of Evan? You must be joking. You're not even in a position to make such a proposal.'

'I'm not really at this stage making a proposal, my dear,' he said. 'I'm just telling you that I want you to give up the idea of Evan. Give yourself time to think. Think of me if you can. And I hope, by the way, that in a short time I shall be in a position to make a proposal to you – if you give me any encouragement.'

'What do you mean?' Her curiosity got the better of her sense of the ridiculousness of the situation.

'I think you should know that I have decided to divorce Bella,' he said slowly.

'I see. I'm sorry.' The words were perfunctory.

'And I think I should tell you here and now,' he went on, 'you will be bound to hear sooner or later – that the co-respondent who will be cited will be none other than the man you propose to marry.'

'Evan?' She could not conceal the apprehension in her voice.

He nodded his head.

'It isn't true,' she said quickly. 'It isn't true. I don't believe a word of it. You are only saying this to hurt me.'

'I'm afraid it is true. And believe me, I do not want to hurt you in any way.'

Without another word he started the

engine and drove on in silence until he drew up outside the Post Office. As she got out he said 'I'm sorry, Janet; but you had to be told. Believe me, I love you too much to let you marry Evan, and will do all in my power to prevent it.'

III

The Reverend Hugh Morris had paid little attention to the meeting which had taken him from the Davies's party. It was in any case hardly his direct concern, being only a sub-committee of the Parish Council meeting to consider suitable sites for the proposed new Parish Cemetery. He listened to the arguments for a while; they were almost all the same, whatever the speaker, and however cloaked. Every speaker wanted the cemetery as far as possible from where he himself lived. The Vicar had tried to reason with them, saying that death could not be staved off by concealing from everyday sight the resting places of the dead. He had quoted Donne at them: 'Every man's death diminishes me because I am involved in mankind; and therefore, never send to know for whom the bell tolls; it tolls for thee.' The sub-committee thought it a religious text and were a little embarrassed.

After a while he excused himself and

walked back through the village. He paused at the top of the stone steps that led down from the street level to the circular churchyard. By the poor street lights the tombstones stood huddled round the church, close-packed between the wall, the church, and the river. He went down the steps and stopped halfway across the churchyard. Here was his wife's grave, and around her, in vault and grave, her Vaughan forebears back to the Norman Conquest. And all around about her the Evanses and Davieses and Morgans and Morrises of the village – right back, he supposed, to the first Christian burials of Welsh people on this spot long before the Normans had come. And before that – on the hill, by the Vicarage was a barrow with burials supposed to be as much before the Christian era as the present moment was after it. The silent testimony of the departed. And now the first Christian cemetery at Llanddewi was too full.

He paused again at the far end of the cemetery by a grave that had not yet had a headstone put on it. It was the grave of Daphne Davies – Daphne, who might have become David's wife and reared up grandchildren for the Vicar, children who would one day come to rest in the new cemetery.

Did David know how Daphne had died? Why she had died? And when he knew, what would he say and do? Hugh Morris crossed the river by the narrow metal bridge at the end of the churchyard and climbed the hill to the Vicarage. He paused under the shadow of the ruined gatehouse of the now-destroyed medieval monastery of Llanddewi and looked across the valley and the church-yard to where the village clustered around the hilltop and sprawled down the hill to the sea and out to the country. And then suddenly he decided he must do something which he had shirked since Daphne's death. He must see Evan Morgan and learn the truth. He must see Ellen Harper Williams and learn the truth. But what if it confirmed the rumours which were current in the village – the stories which he had listened to reluctantly when Miss Rodgers had told him. What would be the right thing to do if he felt that they had virtually murdered Daphne? What was the responsibility of a man, be he priest or layman, convinced of the guilt of a man or woman whom he yet knew could not be convicted of murder?

He shook his head impatiently and climbed on towards the Vicarage, the Donne sentence still in his mind. *Every man's death... I am involved in mankind...* He looked across the valley again; the smoke curled up from the thatched and slate roofs, grey wisps in the darkness, and in the distance the Manor House on top of the hill... *It tolls for thee.* He shivered and walked into the Vicarage.

IV

Across the valley in the village school a figure detached itself from the shadow of the trees around the playground and crossed to the shed where the gardening tools were kept. It disappeared behind the shed to the back door of the school. A key was fitted into the lock, the door swung open, and closed again carefully and quietly. A few minutes later, had anyone been listening carefully in the playground, they would have heard the distant muffled but regular tapping of the typewriter in the Headmaster's study. Only there was no one within hearing distance – no one except the figure at the typewriter to hear the little bell that rang at the end of each fateful line; in its way tolling the death of four people in the village of Llanddewi.

CHAPTER 6

A BODY IN THE DARK

I

It began raining as Sir Richard Cherrington drove through Cardiff. He had had a pleasant drive from Cambridge across the south Midlands and over the Cotswolds in the September sunshine. But now a steady drizzle had set in, and it was already dark when he got to Llanddewi. Idly he wondered why there were few lights in the windows of the houses as he drove by. As he drove into the Market Square with its Butter Market and old Town Hall – relics of Llanddewi's prosperity in Elizabethan times – he saw the reason for the apparent emptiness of the village. The Town Hall was all lit up, a group of people were hurrying up the steps out of the rain, and across the square, fastened from the top of the Butter Market to the Town Hall entrance, was an illuminated and beflagged sign which said 'Welcome Home'. All the letters of the legend were alight except the H of 'Home,' and a young man on a ladder was trying to replace the bulbs and reaspirate the greeting.

Sir Richard stopped the car and spoke to a police constable. 'It's for our returned warriors, sir,' was the answer to his query. 'Sort of welcome party for them, only not many of them 'as turned up yet. Too shy, I expect.'

Cherrington had a sudden thought. 'Is my aunt in there, by any chance?' he asked, 'I mean, Miss Mary Cherrington?'

The policeman peered at him closely, unable to accept at once the fact that the grey-haired old gentleman could be the nephew of someone who looked very little older than him. 'Your aunt, sir?' he said incredulously, and then answered Cherrington's question: 'No. She's not here. She was here this afternoon arranging the flowers and that, but she went home.' Cherrington thanked him and drove off across the square and up the narrow street which led past the church and to the west.

As he turned the corner by the church, Cherrington's headlights picked up a figure that crossed the road quickly in front of him – a short, thick-set figure in a mackintosh and a black trilby hat. It was the Reverend Hugh Morris – Cherrington remembered the Vicar well. Indeed, in his young days Sir Richard had been most attracted by Mrs Morris – Miss Vaughan as she then was. He had been piqued at the news of her marriage to Hugh Morris, whom he had always considered a dull sort of dog; genuinely moved to hear of her death, he made to stop and greet Morris, but the Vicar walked quickly into the churchyard. He had glanced a moment at the lights of the car, blinking at them, and in that brief glance Cherrington thought he caught a strange, preoccupied look. There was something more too than preoccupation, than absent-mindedness, in that look. It was as though the Vicar had received a great shock and could not focus his mind or his eyes on the immediate moment.

Cherrington shrugged his shoulders and drove on, mounting the hill on the other side of the river past the church. He encountered one or two groups of people hurrying in to the village. At last the houses and cottages ceased and he was back on the high land that ran along behind the coast. The lighthouses at Nash Point and the lightship at Breaksea flashed at him, their intermittent beams marking out the north side of the Bristol Channel for ships coming up to Barry and Cardiff. He drove on and soon came to the turning to his aunt's house.

Tresaeth House was in a sheltered hollow of its own. The drive wound down from the main road through thick shrubberies of rhododendron, fuchsia, and laurel. Tresaeth Cove was a small, landlocked beach protected on each side by projecting cliffs awash at high tide, and could only be approached by the private drive to the house. The Cherringtons had lived here ever since Mary Cherrington's grandfather had built it from the profits made when some of his fields in one of the north Glamorgan valleys had become the centre of a coal mining village. Sir Richard brought his car to a standstill at the front door and rudely blew all his car horns – the ordinary klaxon for the English roads, the cuckoo horn which made him so popular with his colleagues' children, and the special mocking trumpets he kept for motoring in France. This strange fanfare penetrated his aunt's slight deafness, and he was soon welcomed and brought into the house.

'My dear boy,' said Miss Cherrington, 'I am delighted to see you.' The twenty years that separated their ages would never persuade her to treat him as a contemporary. 'You can unpack later.' She brushed aside his protestations. 'The first thing is a drink. After a long journey, a drink is essential. Introduce yourself to the cats. They are the same ones as when you were here last, but you will have forgotten them.'

'I never forget a cat,' began Cherrington, but she went on: 'The fat gentleman who belches is Sir Toby, and the thin female who moans and groans so much in her sleep is Lady Macbeth.'

Cherrington bent down and tickled the

cats with the practised skill of a cat-loving bachelor. Then he walked round the room. He had forgotten to buy cigarettes; his case was empty. He looked hopefully in various boxes, but they were filled with his aunt's trinkets, stamps and drawing-pins and clips and old emergency ration cards. Miss Cherrington came in wheeling a trolley on which there was a bucket of ice and a bottle of champagne.

'I say,' said Sir Richard. 'Champagne, eh? We are going the pace.'

'There's a lot in the cellar,' said his aunt. 'And this is the only time to drink it. Will you open this bottle for me, please?'

Cherrington lifted out the bottle, wrapping a cloth around it carefully. He undid the wires and began to ease off the cork. 'I was looking for a cigarette,' he said. 'Don't you stock any now you have given up smoking yourself?'

'I'm afraid I've run out.'

'I thought you might have some of those nice Turkish cigarettes whose stubs I see in the ashtray.'

'No. No; I haven't. Those must be old ones that have been overlooked.' She took up the ashtray and emptied the stubs into the fireplace. The champagne cork leaped out with a loud pop. 'That's a good sound,' said Miss Cherrington.

The glasses filled. Sir Richard lifted his and

bowed. 'Here's to you, my dear Aunt Mary,' he said. 'And here's to crime ... may it never cease ... and may it never cease to be detected.'

II

There had been very few in the evening surgery, and Dr Wynne Roberts had finished early; finished, in fact, in time, as he thought, for him to get across to the Town Hall and hear the formalities of the Welcome Home. A pity. He would have liked to have an excuse which kept him away. The telephone rang as he was changing out of his white coat. The nurse lifted the receiver and spoke into it. Dr Roberts listened hopefully.

'Yes. Yes. This is Dr Roberts's surgery. Yes. The Doctor is here... Would you please say that again?... Just a minute, please.' She put her hand over the receiver and spoke in a whisper to the doctor. 'Mrs Thomas of Sealands Farm is very seriously ill. Would you please go out to her at once?'

'Who is it speaking? What is the matter?'

'I don't know.'

'Here give me the phone, Nurse.' He picked up the receiver. 'Hello. Wynne Roberts here. Who is that? Mr Thomas? Is that Mr Thomas of Sealands Farm?... Hello. Hello.' He shook the receiver and shouted into it: 'Hello. Who's there?' He put it down with a snort. 'Cut off,' he said. 'That's very peculiar. Very peculiar.' He walked across the surgery and then turned round sharply. 'Nurse,' he said, 'what's the Sealands Farm number? 141, isn't it? Would you get it for me while I put a few things in my bag?'

He busied himself with his bag, then went out into the hall and put on a raincoat. He came back and spoke crossly. 'Can't you get the number, Nurse?' he said.

'I've dialled the number all right,' she replied. 'It's ringing, but there's no answer.'

'No answer. But there must be an answer.' His voice was irritable.

She shook her head. 'It just goes on ringing.'

'How odd. Who was it spoke to you first?'

'I don't know. It was a man's voice.'

'Mr Thomas? Mr Joseph Stanley Thomas, I mean?'

'I don't know, Doctor. I've only spoken to him once or twice.' She hesitated. 'Yes; it might have been his voice.'

'H'm. And there's still no reply?'

'Still no reply.'

'Well, if there is, tell them I'm on my way. I'll be there in five minutes if the car starts.'

When she heard the engine of the car, she rang the Post Office. Mrs Anderson replied. Yes, the number 141 was in order as far as they knew in the telephone exchange. The nurse rang again. The ringing tone went on quietly, relentlessly, unanswered.

III

Police Constable Roderick abandoned his vigil under the steps of the Llanddewi Town Hall and, benefiting from a break in the rain, walked back to the Police Station, which was a converted house on the outskirts of the village on the road down to the Town Beach. Had he waited a few minutes longer he would have seen Dr Wynne Roberts come out of his house in a great hurry, throw his bag into the back of his car, and drive off quickly along the Barry road. As it was, he had just got into the Police Station and was shaking out his rain-cape when he met Bill Williams, his Sergeant, hurrying out of the charge room. He was obviously very excited and his hair was ruffled.

'Thank God you're on the spot for once, man,' said Sergeant Williams. 'Thought we should have to look all round the village for you.' His voice and manner conveyed a sense of great urgency.

'Something's up, I suppose,' said Roderick.

'The hell it is. Something mighty big. The biggest thing that's ever happened in Llanddewi. It's out at Sealands Farm. We've just had a telephone message to say that Mrs Thomas has hanged herself.'

'Bella Thomas hanged herself? Well, I'm damned. You wouldn't think she was that sort, would you?'

'It's no good thinking anything at the moment. We've got to get out there – and quick. Get the motor cycle and combination out. I've telephoned Headquarters and they are sending out Harris – Inspector Harris. He's going to meet us at the farm.'

IV

Half an hour later four men sat in Inspector Harris's car and talked. It certainly was a queer do. Dr Wynne Roberts had been the first to get out to Sealands Farm, only to find it locked, and no answer to his repeated knockings and shouts. He had then driven to the thatched gamekeeper's cottage, where his niece, Fay Morgan, lived. Fay was alone resting on a sofa in front of the living-room fire.

'Someone's been pulling your leg,' she said. 'Mrs Thomas has been away for a few days. She's gone off to London to stay with her sister – or that is what she has given out,' she added maliciously. 'There's no one in the house tonight. The cowman and the maid are off at the Welcome Home dance in

126

the Town Hall – that's where Mervyn is. And Mr Thomas himself went off earlier.'

It was at this moment that Sergeant Williams and Constable Roderick drove up. Wynne Roberts went back to the farmhouse with them and, while they were discussing what to do, Detective Inspector Harris arrived in his car. 'It's obviously a hoax,' said Harris when he had been told the facts. 'Obviously a hoax, because the two stories don't tally. The doctor's message was that Mrs Thomas was ill; the message you received at the Police Station, Williams, was that Mrs Thomas had hanged herself.' Nevertheless, they decided it was their duty to look over the house. Fay Morgan told them where the back door key was kept, under the flat stone in the copper in the wash-house. They examined the house from top to bottom. There was no one there, and there were no sounds or signs of any disturbance.

'Would you recognize the voice that telephoned you?' Harris asked Williams.

Sergeant Williams shook his head. 'I doubt it,' he said slowly. 'The man said so little and spoke oddly, like. As though he was perhaps trying to hide his voice. But there was something familiar. I mean, it was an ordinary voice.'

'An ordinary Vale of Glamorgan voice?'

'Yes. That's it. It was a local voice. I think

127

it was.'

Harris turned to the doctor. 'And you didn't hear it at all – even supposing it was the same voice?'

'I'm afraid not. My nurse answered the phone and by the time I got to the receiver I was cut off.'

They separated and drove back to Llanddewi. The doctor went back to his house. The constable, Roderick, was dropped at the Town Hall. Sergeant Williams went to the Police Station in Inspector Harris's car. The two men were met in the hallway of the police station by Mrs Williams. She was very distraught.

'Thank God you've come,' she said. 'Come into the charge-room at once. It's young David Morris.'

Sergeant Williams hurried into the charge-room, his wife and Inspector Harris close on his heels. David Morris was slumped down in a chair by the fireplace. He had a glass of brandy and water in his hand. As the policemen came in he smiled weakly and tried to get up.

'Hello,' he said, putting a hand to the back of his head. 'It's still very sore.' A spasm of pain screwed up his face. 'I still can't think straight,' he said.

'What's the matter? What's happened?' It was Harris who spoke.

'It's Evan Morgan,' said the young man,

touching his head again.

'He attacked you?' asked Sergeant Williams.

'No, no, he's dead … he's dead. Dead, I say. Murdered.' He paused. 'I didn't kill him,' he added simply and quickly.

'Where is he?' Inspector Harris's voice was imperative.

'In the Manor House.'

'You must come with us.'

They got into Harris's car – the three of them, Inspector Harris, Sergeant Williams, and the young man. Nothing was said as they drove through the village. The Manor House was in complete darkness. David Morris led the way to the front door. 'In here,' he said. They went into the main living-room of the house. 'The lights don't work,' said David Morris, 'and the telephone wires are cut. That's why I couldn't get through to you.' Sergeant Williams shone his torch on to the centre of the room. Evan Morgan lay sprawled across his desk, his legs crumpled up under the chair in which he had been sitting. Sticking out of his back was the wooden handle of a dagger or knife. He was obviously very dead. Harris stepped forward carefully and felt his pulse and heart. 'Matter of form,' he mumbled to Williams. 'Been dead some while, I should say.'

Sergeant Williams nodded his head. He shone his torch around the room until he made sure there was no part of it they had not seen. Inspector Harris turned to Morris. 'And now, young man,' he said, 'sit down and tell us your story.'

It was then they heard a muffled cry. It came from the inner room. Carefully and with as little noise as possible, they opened the door at the back of the room. Williams shone his torch into the inner room. On the floor was a figure securely trussed up with ropes and gagged. The figured groaned as the torch played on it; its legs twitched. The Sergeant bend down and shone his torch on the face of the bound figure. 'It's Bryn Davies,' he said, adding by way of explanation to Harris. 'You know, the local schoolmaster's son – John Davies's son.'

As he spoke there was a faint, despairing noise behind them. They turned to see David Morris stagger and fall to the ground. They were at his side in a moment.

'It's all right,' said Williams. 'He's only fainted.'

Harris stood up and mopped his forehead. 'Cripes!' he said. 'What the hell next? Two bogus phone calls, and now here we are with a corpse on our hands, one man fainted, and another bound and gagged – and all in the bloody dark.'

Bill Williams swore loudly. 'As you say,' he said, 'here we are: the two of us – all in the bloody dark.'

CHAPTER 7

A CLEAR CASE

The news of the murder of Evan Morgan had not arrived at Tresaeth House when the Cherringtons sat down to breakfast. Miss Cherrington's faithful Fanny, who had done for her for years, cycled up from the village about ten o'clock every morning, except on Sundays, and departed again every day at tea-time. It was she who brought out the letters and the newspapers, so that there was nothing to excite Sir Richard and his aunt as they faced each other. Cherrington had risen early and gone for a walk along the cliffs towards Llanddewi. The rain had stopped in the night; it was a fresh, clear morning – a light breeze was blowing from the west. The hills of Devonshire and Somerset were a clear grey-blue across the water. It was a peaceful, quiet scene.

Sir Richard was helping himself to sausages from a chafing dish when his aunt said, 'I'm afraid that I have dragged you down here on false pretences.' Her voice was hesitant.

'You mean there are no anonymous letters? There never were? You invented them?'

'No. Not that. But there is no mystery about them.'

Cherrington sighed. 'It would help, you know, Aunt Mary,' he said, 'if you started at the beginning and told me the whole story.'

'There's not a great deal to tell,' she replied. 'I think I gave most of the facts in my letter to you. They began – the letters I mean – during the war, and have been going on at intervals ever since. I've found out that several people have had them: the Vicar, Dr Wynne Roberts, John Davies, the schoolmaster, and Mrs Davies – these I know about and there may be very many more.' She smiled ruefully. 'Some of them are just abusive, or quite unfounded in their accusations. One letter accused me of embezzling the funds of charities and making money out of flag days – silly things like that. But some, I'm afraid, have been founded on fact. They accused me of getting more food than my ration allowance from Morgan's grocery shop, or getting special supplies of butter from Sealands Farm. All too true, I'm afraid.'

'What form do these letters take?' Sir Richard asked.

'They vary. Sometimes they are very ingeniously constructed – letters cut out of newspapers and pasted on to a sheet. Sometimes they are in a disguised hand – a childish, uncouth hand, like someone writing with his left hand to conceal his normal writing. But most often they are typewritten. I'll show you one.'

She got up and went to her desk, returning with a folded sheet of plain, unheaded note paper on which was typewritten in capitals this message:

DO YOU THINK IT A GOOD THING THAT THE WELCOME HOME FUND MONEY ENTRUSTED TO YOU SHOULD BE SPENT BY YOU ON EXTRA RATIONS TO WHICH YOU ARE NOT ENTITLED? THERE IS ALWAYS WELCOME UNDER THE COUNTER FOR THE RICH.

Cherrington read it through twice. 'H'm,' he said. 'May I keep this?'

'Of course. But, as I said, there is no longer any mystery. I always had my suspicions.' She paused. 'Do you remember Ellen Harper Williams?'

'Why, yes. The assistant schoolteacher.'

'That's right. Well, she lost her house during the only bombing raid we had here that really touched the village of Llanddewi. It was in the middle of the war, and I have no doubt that they were really trying to get the aerodrome. Anyway, they dropped a stick of bombs across the end of the village. Ellen Williams's cottage was blown to smithereens. She had great difficulty in finding anywhere

133

to live afterwards – she never was popular in the village. In the end, I was persuaded to help her. I converted the loft above the garage into a flat and she has lived there ever since.'

'You are telling me all this, Aunt Mary, because you think she is the authoress of these poison-pen letters. Is that it?'

She nodded. 'I think so. Maybe it was having her house destroyed that deranged her mind. I don't know. But I've had my suspicions for a long time that it was her. Now I know. Three days ago she said to me, "When is Sir Richard coming and how long is he stopping in Llanddewi?"'

'Well? What does that prove?'

'I had told nobody you were coming.'

'Are you sure? Not even Fanny?'

'No. Or at least not until after Ellen Williams had spoken to me.'

'Then how did she know?'

'That is just the point. I wrote my letter to you late one evening and left it on the hall table with my other letters to be posted next day. It was sealed of course. Ellen Williams picked up my letters, and before I knew what was happening took them off with her to post on her way to school. She often does that with my letters, and I catch the earlier post.'

'I see. And she opened the letter.' He rubbed his chin meditatively. 'You make it very easy for her to do so don't you, with your economical use of old envelopes? Those adhesive economy label things are just gifts to nosy parkers.'

'Maybe. But I think it proves it, doesn't it?'

Sir Richard hedged: 'It proves she could have opened your letter. That she had the opportunity,' he said. 'That's all.'

'Bah!' Miss Cherrington snorted. 'She has been opening letters and all sorts of things for years.'

Cherrington said nothing for a while. Then he asked: 'Well, what am I supposed to do? You sent for me to solve your poison-pen mystery. Now it appears that it is solved. What next?'

'I want you to stop her writing any more.'

'You want me?' His voice was incredulous. 'How?'

'Frighten her. Anything you like. But this business must stop.' Miss Cherrington's voice was suddenly hard.

'You realize I must talk to the police?'

Miss Cherrington sighed. 'I suppose so,' she said reluctantly. 'I suppose so. If it has to be, it has to be.'

His aunt's words were in Cherrington's mind as he drove down to the Police Station. He was met at the door by Constable Roderick – a bewildered, subdued Roderick who had been up all night and still had no very clear idea of what the events of the night had meant. His face lightened momentarily

135

when he saw Sir Richard. Cherrington had been told by his aunt to ask for Sergeant Williams, whom he remembered from previous visits.

Roderick shook his head. 'The Sergeant is very busy at the moment, sir, I'm afraid,' he said. 'Very busy indeed. I don't think he will be able to see you. Unless,' he went on, 'it's anything to do with the murder.'

Sir Richard looked steadily at the young policeman. 'Did I hear you mention the word "murder"?' he said.

'Yes, sir. I thought perhaps you had come to give us some information.'

'Murder? Murder here in Llanddewi?'

It was at this moment that the door of the Police Station opened and Colonel Vaughan came out with Inspector Harris. Vaughan looked tired, but he recognized Cherrington at once. He had known Richard as a young man; they had kept up occasional contacts in later life; as an amateur archaeologist, he had unbounded admiration for Cherrington's work.

'Hello, Cherrington,' he said. 'What are you doing here?'

'Good morning, Vaughan,' said Sir Richard. 'Good to see you again. I'm here to see Sergeant Williams about some anonymous letters, but I gather you have something more important to think about at the moment.'

'We have. But just a moment.' Vaughan

hesitated. 'Did you say anonymous letters?' he asked.

Cherrington nodded.

'Come inside.' Vaughan spoke briskly, and led the way into the Police Station. They went through the charge-room into the Sergeant's office. A very tired Sergeant Williams was sitting at the table. 'Here we are, back again, Williams,' said Colonel Vaughan. 'Sooner than you expected us. By the way do you know each other? Professor Cherrington ... Sergeant Williams ... and of course Inspector Harris.

'Professor Cherrington was saying something about anonymous letters.'

'It's just this,' explained Sir Richard. 'My aunt – you know, Miss Mary Cherrington up at Tresaeth House – wrote to me last week saying there was an epidemic of anonymous letters in Llanddewi and would I help her to find out who was responsible.'

'Do you know anything of this epidemic of poison-pen writing?' The Chief Constable turned to Sergeant Williams.

'No, sir,' he said. 'Not a thing. But then,' he added ruefully, 'I should be the last to be told. So often in a village people think the police are here to prosecute them and not to protect them.'

'I have one here,' said Cherrington, and handed over the letter his aunt had given him. Harris took out another sheet of paper

137

from his dispatch-case and compared the two. He took out a magnifying glass from his pocket and ran over the two letters.

'Well?' Colonel Vaughan asked abruptly.

'No doubt at all,' said Harris. 'Of course, we shall have to get one of our experts to go over them carefully, but as far as I can see, these were both done on the same machine.'

'Could I ask where you found the letter you are comparing with mine?' said Cherrington. 'I mean, a moment ago you seemed to know nothing about these poison-pen letters. Or am I speaking out of turn?'

Colonel Vaughan got up. 'I think,' he said, 'that we should take Professor Cherrington into our confidence. Especially as he is going to be about in the next few days. He is already well known in Llanddewi, and has a flair for nosing out other people's secrets. What do you say, Inspector? He may be of very great help to us.'

'It's for you to say, sir.' Harris spoke without enthusiasm.

'Good. Now, could you run over, for Sir Richard's benefit, what we know so far?'

Harris picked a file of papers out of his bag. 'It's like this, sir,' he began wearily. 'We believe that this anonymous letter' – he pointed to the one he had earlier taken out of his bag – 'was sent by a murderer. By the murderer of Evan Morgan.'

'So there has been a murder?'

'You didn't know?'

'No. The papers get up to Tresaeth rather late, and no phone messages had got there before I left.' Cherrington smiled.

'I must begin at the beginning,' went on Harris. 'Or the beginning as far as we are concerned. It all started with two telephone calls. Two bogus telephone calls. One to Dr Wynne Roberts saying that Mrs Thomas of Sealands Farm was dangerously ill. The other to the Police Station here saying that Mrs Thomas of Sealands Farm had hanged herself. The police rang me up and we all went out to the farm – Sergeant Williams and Constable Roderick, whom you met at the door, and Dr Wynne Roberts and myself. The house was shut up; nobody there. We have since learnt that Mrs Thomas is staying with her sister in London and is very well. All this was at seven o'clock.'

'A hoax, in fact.'

Inspector Harris nodded crossly. 'Exactly,' he said. 'We all got back to Llanddewi about seven-twenty and found waiting here in this Police Station a young man, David Morris, the Vicar's son. He was in a distraught condition – shock, you know; he was, in fact, suffering from slight concussion. He told us that Evan Morgan was dead, that he had been murdered in his house; and we went back with him to the Manor House. Three of us: Sergeant Williams, myself, and Morris. I suppose we got to the house at about seven-thirty. All the lights in the Manor House were out; we found Evan Morgan there lying across his desk, stabbed through the back. In the inner room we found another young man, Bryn Davies, the schoolmaster's son, securely tied up with a rope and gagged.'

'Good heavens above,' said Cherrington. 'And how do these two young men explain their presences?'

'It is a curious story, and that is where the anonymous letters come in,' said Harris. 'They both say that they received through the post an anonymous letter asking them to go to meet Evan Morgan at the Manor House at seven o'clock last night.' He paused. 'Here actually is one of the letters,' he said. 'There are no fingerprints, I am afraid, but perhaps you would be so good as not to touch it, just the same.' Cherrington stood up and looked down at the letter spread out on the table. It was brief, and said:

PLEASE BE AT THE MANOR HOUSE AT SEVEN ON FRIDAY EVENING BEFORE THE WELCOME HOME DANCE YOU WILL HEAR SOMETHING TO YOUR GREAT ADVANTAGE. PLEASE TELL NOBODY AND DESTROY THIS LETTER.

Cherrington sat down again. 'I see,' he

said. 'Rather like a secret assignation in a schoolboy thriller.'

'Quite so,' said Harris. 'But this was no schoolboy joke. Whoever sent these letters meant business, and his business was death.' He paused. 'David Morris did as he was told. He destroyed the letter and told no one. Bryn Davies was suspicious of the whole thing and spoke to David Morris about it. They then discovered that they had had identical letters; this is the letter Bryn Davies received. They therefore decided to go to the Manor House together. According to their statements, they got there just before seven o'clock. It was all dark. Bryn Davies had a torch, and by its light they saw that the front door was open. Puzzled and suspicious, they went in, and found Evan Morgan dead, just as I have described him to you. Davies says that they didn't touch the body, but perhaps here their accounts are a little confused.'

'It's really only what one would expect,' put in Sergeant Williams, 'when you think what they had just seen.'

'Anyway,' went on Inspector Harris, 'the next thing we have been told is that when they were waiting there in the dark wondering what to do, they heard a noise – from further in the house – from an inner room. Obviously a few minutes passed while they were groping their way in through the front door and into the room where they found Morgan's body. They had realized something serious had happened to the electric lights – by the way we have found that they had been switched off at the main by the back door. Well, then, these two chaps heard this noise from an inner room, and rather boldly, I must admit, they went towards it.'

'Foolish and dangerous, I admit,' said Colonel Vaughan. 'But I admire them. Both, of course, are trained Commandos.'

'Again the accounts are a little confused, not unnaturally,' said Harris. 'But it appears that David Morris was knocked on the head. He doesn't remember any more until he came to some ten minutes later. Bryn Davies was overpowered, gagged, and bound. As I've said, the next stage in the story is when we arrive back with David Morris and find Davies still gagged and bound on the floor.' He paused, and glanced over his notes. 'I think that is all there is to tell at the moment,' said the Inspector.

'Have you been able to fix the time of death?' asked Cherrington.

'That's the devil of it,' said Harris. 'The man who planned this murder was damned clever. We know Evan Morgan was dead when Morris and Davies got there at seven o'clock, but we don't know how much before, within limits, he was killed. Dr Wynne Roberts didn't get back from Sealands Farm with us until seven-twenty or so; it was well after half-past when we got him to the Manor house, and all he was able to say was that Morgan had been dead between half an hour and an hour. That doesn't help us very much. Of course, that will be one of the first lines we shall pursue: to find out when he was last seen live.'

'I see. And the weapon?' said Cherrington. 'You say he was stabbed in the back?'

'Yes.'

Cherrington hesitated. 'Would it take a great deal of skill and strength to do that?' he asked.

Harris shook his head. 'I don't think so,' he said. 'It wouldn't be easy, but it wouldn't be difficult provided you had some knowledge.'

'The sort of knowledge any soldier would have?'

'Yes; or any medical student or anyone trained in first aid. It would of course require some strength. As I see it, the murderer came in through the French windows and found Evan Morgan seated at his desk with his back to the window – and, well, there you are – just drove this dagger into his back. There would be no struggle; probably not even a cry.'

'H'm,' said Cherrington thoughtfully. 'And to return to the weapon. What was it exactly?'

'Now, that's very interesting,' said Harris. 'Our man has taken it off for detailed examination, so we can't show to you. It was one of these murderous knives which they gave troops in the Far East. What did you call them, sir?' He turned to the Chief Constable.

'I described it as a sort of *kris* or *kukri*,' said the Chief Constable. 'You know, the native knives of the Burmese, Malays, and Gurkhas; but that wasn't a proper description. This wasn't a native knife. It was an imitation issued to jungle marauding parties – particular troops engaged on special missions. Long blade–What did you say, Harris?'

The Inspector looked at his notes. 'Blade seven inches long,' he said, reading from his notes. 'Handle three and a half inches long.'

'We don't have to look far for the ownership of this particular knife,' he added. 'It belongs to Bryn Davies.'

Sir Richard's eyebrows expressed his surprise, and asked the question that Harris's remark had begged. 'It has his initials on the handle,' said Inspector Harris, 'and he admits it is his. He brought it back as a souvenir from the war, as you say. Both he and David Morris were demobilized from the Far East. Bryn Davies says he last saw it at a party in his home about a week ago. His father and mother gave a sort of welcome home party, and there were a few war souvenirs on view.'

'On view to whom?'

'As far as I can gather, to a great number of people.'

'Well,' said Vaughan, 'I gather there were various friends of the Davies family there. I was asked to go myself – John Davies is a very old friend of mine – but I couldn't go.'

'So that you didn't know of the existence of this dagger until last night,' said Cherrington.

'I did not know of the existence of this dagger,' said Vaughan, 'until I saw it late last night in Evan Morgan's back. But I get your point. The murderer doesn't necessarily have to be someone who was at the Davieses' party. That is a thought.' He paused. 'And in any case,' he went on, 'we have another clue. Haven't we, Harris.'

'Yes,' said the Inspector. 'And we hope it is an extremely important one. It was raining last night, and the ground was soft. When we came to examine the Manor House we found a man's footprints outside the windows – the French windows of the room in which Evan Morgan's body was found, and these footprints were directly outside them. It only started raining about half past six yesterday, and these were certainly there by soon after seven-thirty. They're size nines. We have casts of them, of course, and photographs. But one thing we can be sure of at once. These footprints were made neither by David Morris nor Bryn Davies. And there is another thing. There are rose bushes either side of the french window, and low down on one of them we found some strands of cloth – as might be torn from a man's trousers.'

'Or a woman's skirt or anybody's overcoat,' said Cherrington. 'And not necessarily last night.'

'Quite so, sir,' said Harris. 'That is quite true. But it fits in with our theory.'

'You have a theory, then?'

'Yes. I think myself it is all very plain – a very clear case. Someone wanted to get rid of Evan Morgan, someone who had a very good reason; and you need a very good reason for murder, to my way of thinking. This someone laid a very careful plot to implicate these two young men – Morris and Davies. He sends them the anonymous letters and thus ensures they are there at the Manor House at seven. Meanwhile, he has murdered Evan Morgan and with the knife stolen from the Davieses' house – perhaps at the party last week. He gets the police and the doctor out of the way at the vital time by a clever but obvious ruse. He plunges the Manor House into darkness, and lies in wait for Morris and Davies. In the darkness he deals with them. Then he gets away. Very clever indeed.'

'Except that he conveniently leaves his

footprints in the wet earth of the flower-bed, and perhaps some of his trousers on a nearby rose bush, so that you will have no difficulty in finding him.'

'Ah, that is just the point,' said Inspector Harris. 'You can't expect a complicated scheme like this to go through without a hitch. Maybe he was waiting outside the window for a suitable moment to attack Evan Morgan. Perhaps Evan Morgan turned round and the murderer stepped back into the rose bushes. He couldn't plan everything.'

He paused, and no one spoke. Then Colonel Vaughan said: 'You don't seem very convinced by our suggested reconstruction of the crime, Cherrington. To tell you the truth – I'm sorry about this, Inspector – but there are one or two things that puzzle me. Granted the murderer wanted to implicate Morris and Davies, why knock them out? Why not leave them to find the body and make the most of explaining to the police why they were there?'

'What surprises me much more in this strange story,' said Cherrington, 'is the character of the murderer. These anonymous letters that my aunt has been telling me about – it appears very probable that they were written by a woman. And we all know – this is one generalization from books on the psychology of crime that perhaps we can accept – that the role of poison-pen writer is more a feminine one than a masculine one.' He paused. 'This letter that summoned the young man to this strange assignation is obviously of the same style and form.'

Colonel Vaughan pursed up his lips to express his doubts. 'You are not suggesting,' he said, 'that the murderer is a woman?'

'No; not necessarily,' said Cherrington. 'But I suppose it could be, couldn't it? The dagger could have been driven into Evan Morgan's back by a woman?'

'It's possible,' Harris admitted reluctantly.

'But that is not my point,' said Sir Richard. 'We must remember it could be a woman. All I was meaning is that we don't get a certain clear picture of the murderer or murderess from the anonymous letter or the fact of the stabbing. But surely, a person who can overpower and deal with two returned warriors, two grown men trained in self-defence and in the techniques of personal armed and unarmed combat and the rest of it...' He paused.

'Exactly,' said Harris. 'That is the point. A vigorous, strong man. I think we do have a clear case. We know the sort of man we are looking for. A powerful sort of chap. We have his size in shoes. I hope we shall find a tear in his trousers. And I very much doubt whether he will have a satisfactory explanation of where he was between six-thirty and seven last night. I am glad you agree with us, Sir Richard.'

Cherrington drummed with his fingers and said: 'I don't think that I do agree with you.'

CHAPTER 8

THE WILL AND THE WAY

I

It was at this stage of their discussion that there occurred a very welcome interruption in the person of Mr Rendle.

Mr Rendle had had an unusually disturbing morning. Precise in speech, he lived a life which was, if not unvarying in habit, at least most carefully planned to avoid variations and surprises. Before he retired to bed each night, Stephen Rendle went carefully over his engagement book for the following day. The evening on which Evan Morgan had been murdered, he had contemplated the book with considerable distaste. He had looked at the first entry for the next morning: 'Saturday, September 15, 11 am. Evan Morgan. Will. Manor House, Llanddewi' had been the entry. It was not the work to be

149

done that worried Rendle. In fact, the work was nearly all done. The will was drafted. It only remained for himself and his clerk to take the documents over to Llanddewi and for them to be signed and witnessed. That was not what was worrying him. What kept him staring at his engagement book, a frown on his face, was whether at this late hour he should still try to persuade Evan Morgan to alter his will in any way. In these intimate country legal practices it became, sometimes, so difficult to know when one was speaking as a lawyer, when as a friend. Stephen Rendle was a shrewd man, and knew very well that what really disturbed him was not so much the new proposals in Evan Morgan's will, but that he was marrying Janet Anderson. Again, it was not that Stephen Rendle disapproved of marriage. His confirmed bachelor disposition and his wide experience as a lawyer had not concealed from him that marriage was, as he described it to himself in his less charitable moments, a necessary evil to most members of human society. But the forthcoming marriage of Janet Anderson, the daughter – and the most charming daughter – of parents who had been old friends of his and of Evan Morgan, was what disturbed him; and the more so since Joseph Stanley Thomas had asked him to commence divorce proceedings against Mrs Thomas, citing Evan

Morgan as co-respondent. Rendle looked with distaste at the second entry in his engagement book for the following morning, which said: '12 noon. J. S. Thomas.' Could he, the legal friend of both parties, be handling two such matters? He thought not, and fell into an embarrassed sleep.

His doubts were resolved, the next morning when he opened the *Western Mail* and read the brief account there of the sudden death of one of his clients. Such a thing had never happened to him before; indeed, Mr Rendle reflected, such a thing must be happily rare in the experience of most lawyers, that his client is murdered a few hours before an appointment. With a vague hope that he could be of some assistance – after all he was the dead man's lawyer – Rendle set out for Llanddewi alone. His entry to the Manor House barred by a policeman, he walked through the village to the Police Station.

Colonel Vaughan, Inspector Harris, and Sergeant Williams were old friends of his. He was introduced to Cherrington, whom he knew only by name.

'A bad business. A very bad business,' said Rendle. 'Violence is always a bad business. But there, we see so much of it in our professions, do we not, gentlemen?'

Colonel Vaughan said nothing in reply; and then he asked: 'I suppose you came over because Evan Morgan was a client of yours?'

Rendle nodded his head. 'Why, yes. That is so. You might say I am watching my client's interests, or the interests of his estate. I am myself one of the executors of his estate. The Manager of Barclays Bank at Cowbridge is the other.' He hesitated. 'You have no idea who committed this crime?' he asked shyly. 'I assume it is a crime. I have only read what is in the *Western Mail*.'

Inspector Harris spoke briefly. 'I think there is no doubt that Evan Morgan was murdered,' he said. 'By whom we don't know yet. But we have some clues.'

'Good. Good.'

'I expect you can help us a great deal,' said the Chief Constable. 'Very glad you turned up when you did.'

'But how can I help you?'

'We wondered who benefits by Evan Morgan's death. You have his will, I assume.'

'Ah.' Mr Rendle put his fingers together and looked around the room. 'Sir Richard is helping you in this investigation?' he said. 'Pardon the question, but professional etiquette, you know.'

'He is. You can speak freely in front of him.'

'Quite so. No offence intended of course, Sir Richard. But this is a confidential and complicated matter. The police, I know, are entitled to this information, but it must go no further. Morgan, as you know,' he went on, 'was, by our standards here in the Vale of Glamorgan, a rich man. He owned land, houses, shops, securities, as well as, of course, the goodwill of his own very extensive business here in Llanddewi and the branch shops up and down the Vale. He was an unusually acute – one might almost say he was a ruthless – businessman. At his death his estate was to be divided into three portions; one portion to his son, Rees Morgan, who you know manages his shop in Barry, the second to his – er – natural son, Mervyn Morgan, who manages his shop here in Llanddewi, and the third share to Miss Ellen Harper Williams, who was – er – how shall I put it, we are all men of the world here – a great – er – friend of his since his wife died.'

'She was the mother of his son, Mervyn, as I expect you know,' Colonel Vaughan added by way of explanation to Cherrington.

'So that three people benefit by Evan Morgan's death,' said Inspector Harris, 'Rees Morgan, Mervyn Morgan, and Miss Harper Williams.'

Rendle nodded. 'At a guess I should say that each of them will get twenty to thirty thousand pounds. And all this is apart, of course, from the charge and goodwill of the various shops.'

'There is no doubt, then,' said Vaughan,

'that very good motives for murder exist.'

'Three very good motives,' put in Cherrington.

'Certainly two – if you exclude the woman,' said Harris. 'And the footprint was certainly that of a man.'

Cherrington turned to Stephen Rendle and asked quietly: 'You said, Mr Rendle, "was to be divided". I wondered why you didn't say "will be divided or "is divided". Am I splitting hairs?'

'Not at all. You are very acute.' Stephen Rendle smiled appreciatively at Sir Richard. 'The estate will be divided, when probate has been granted, in the way I have described. That was Evan Morgan's intention for many years. I have told you the terms of Evan Morgan's will at the time of his death. But if his death had occurred a little later, the terms would have been very different.'

'I see. Yes of course,' said Vaughan. 'You mean that Evan Morgan was getting married and that his wife would automatically get the greater part of his estate.'

'Not only that. I naturally told Evan Morgan,' said Rendle, 'that it was his duty to change his will when he married again. It was advice I would have tendered to any of my clients in the same circumstances. He asked me to draw up a new will providing for his wife and for any children that might be the issue of the marriage. His proposed treatment of the original beneficiaries was, I thought, a little sharp for one who was, comparatively speaking, a rich man. They were to receive payments of one thousand pounds each only, but there were complicated arrangements regarding the position of his two sons in relation to the businesses. Mervyn Morgan's position in the shop here at Llanddewi was safeguarded for at least five years. Things like that.'

'You drew up this new will?'

'I did indeed,' Rendle tapped his bag. 'After very considerable discussions, I may say. I have it here in my bag. It isn't signed, and has, of course, no legal value. But it was to take effect immediately. It specifically mentions Miss Anderson as a beneficiary. Evan Morgan was hoping – had been hoping, I suppose I should say – that he and Janet Anderson would be married soon, but if not, if there was to be a long engagement, he wished for these new testamentary dispositions to take effect at once.'

Rendle hesitated, and then decided to continue: 'I put the new form of will in my bag last night at my office because I was coming over to Llanddewi to see Evan Morgan this morning. I had an appointment to see him at eleven o'clock this morning – for the purpose of signing the new will.'

'I see,' said Colonel Vaughan. 'So that means there were three people who stood to lose a lot if Evan Morgan lived until eleven o'clock this morning. One of them is a woman.' He hesitated, and then went on slowly, 'I was wondering,' he said, and paused.

'You were wondering,' said Cherrington, 'which of the two men wears size nine in shoes.'

II

Cherrington accepted with alacrity the invitation of the police to go back with them to the Manor House. They drove in Vaughan's car – the three of them, Vaughan, Harris, and Cherrington – to the main gate of the Manor House. It opened on to the top end of the High Street, opposite the Post Office. They went in and up to the front door. As he walked along, Cherrington took stock of the position. The main path led past the French windows to the front door. It was joined by another path from the side gate, which also continued around the house to the back. They entered the house. The front door gave on to a hall with a stair-case and three doors – one leading to the right to the dining-room, one through to the scullery at the back of the house, and one on the left to the living-room. Inspector Harris led the way into the living-room. 'It's in

156

here,' he said, 'that the murder was committed.'

The body had been taken away, but there were still photographers and fingerprint men busy at work. Cherrington noted the large desk in the middle of the room and the chair between it and the French windows. A chalk outline marked where the body had lain across the desk.

'Was there much blood?' asked Cherrington.

'Hardly any.'

'The murderer's clothes would not have been splashed?'

'Chances are they would not have been.'

'And there would not have been any struggle?'

Harris shook his head. 'There need not have been. If he – the murderer, I mean – came in through the windows, he would be behind his victim. One blow – a well-directed, violent thrust with the dagger – and Evan Morgan would have slumped across the desk. It would have been all over quickly.'

'And the French windows haven't yielded any interesting fingerprints?' asked Cherrington.

The fingerprints man stopped in his work and turned round. 'Far too many, I'm afraid,' he said. 'There are fingerprints everywhere – on the doors, the desk, the mantelpiece, the telephone.'

'That's an odd thing, isn't it?' said Cherrington. 'When Morris and Davies were in here, horrified by their gruesome discovery last night, why didn't they telephone?'

'Wires cut,' said Harris briskly. 'I'm afraid we have to hand it out to our murderer. He had carefully arranged that the telephone wires were cut, the electric light off, the local doctor and police summoned away from the locality.'

'One has the impression,' said Colonel Vaughan dryly, 'of someone sitting down and writing operation orders for the murder – You know the sort of thing, I mean, Cherrington – all down to the last detail. I can imagine it all starting off in the usual military style. Object of exercise: the murder of Evan Morgan without the slightest suspicion falling on myself. And ending with list of equipment necessary: one dagger, pair of gloves, one coil of rope, etc.' He laughed grimly.

'The murderer wore gloves, I suppose, all the time?'

'Yes. The fingerprints on the dagger are blurred, and there are no prints in the scullery on the electric main switch, which had been thrown over.'

'What I want to get straight in my mind,' said Cherrington, 'is the attack on Morris and Davies.'

'Yes?' Inspector Harris's voice only sounded mildly interested. 'Their account is that they heard a noise coming from the office or scullery – anyway, from the back of the house somewhere. They set out to investigate.'

'How?'

'According to their accounts, and as I said earlier, they are a little confused, David Morris went first holding the torch. They went out through this door' – he pointed to the back of the room – 'into the room Evan Morgan kept as a kind of office and junk room, and shone the torch around. Nothing suspicious, apparently. Then they very cautiously opened the door from office to scullery. David Morris was holding the door open, and Bryn Davies, thinking the murderer, if he was still there, might escape another way, walked back through the living-room into the front hall and through the other door into the scullery. It was, apparently, as Morris was creeping cautiously into the scullery that he was struck on the head. This must have been, I suppose, a few seconds before Bryn Davies came through the door from the hall, and was himself attacked.'

'The murderer was very lucky in his timing,' said Cherrington.

'You mean he was lucky that Morris and Davies separated for a moment and he was able to deal with them singly?'

'Exactly. Most fortunate for him. Especially

as they were tough Commandos back from the war,' said Cherrington.

They walked into the office, and after a glance around Cherrington opened the door into the scullery. Will you walk through the living-room and into the hall and come back into the scullery through the other door, Inspector, please?' he said.

Harris did so and Cherrington stared at his watch. 'Forty seconds,' he said when the Inspector joined them again.

'Of course, Bryn Davies might have been much slower,' said Harris. 'He might have been walking stealthily, so as not to make any noise – and remember, it was dark.'

'Or, again,' said Cherrington, 'he might have been much quicker. He might have been hurrying – hurrying to cut the murderer's retreat through the hall.'

'Exactly,' said Colonel Vaughan. 'You see, it doesn't get us much further. I can't see that what happened to Morris and Davies after the murder of Evan Morgan is going to lead us to his murderer. The murderer was there in the house – he got away – and disposed of Morris and Davies who never even saw him.'

They walked round the scullery. 'Back door here,' said Harris. 'It was unlocked when we arrived. Murderer presumably escaped that way. But no footprints. Very puzzling. Perhaps he didn't go this way. Of course, it was raining and the back-yard is flagged. And here is the electric mains switch. The mains had just been cut off.'

'What's this?' Cherrington had picked up an old candlestick holder on the dresser in the scullery. Inspector Harris looked over his shoulder. 'Cigarette ash,' he said. 'Nothing odd there.'

'Did Evan Morgan smoke?' asked Cherrington.

'A pipe,' answered the Chief Constable. 'Always a pipe. I never saw him with anything else.'

Cherrington sniffed at the cigarette ash carefully, and with the end of his finger he cautiously turned over the cigarette stub. 'H'm,' he said. 'Abdulla No. 11. Expensive Turkish cigarettes. And the amount of the ash! Your murderer begins to interest me enormously. A gentleman with a great flair for organization, as you said, and an active strong man. He lies in wait calmly for Morris and Davies when he has just committed a murder and could escape through the back door. Yet, instead of escaping, he stands here, smoking an expensive Turkish cigarette. And then, dusting his hand lightly, he disposes of Morris and Davies, all in forty seconds – or more. What a fellow!'

His sarcasm was not lost on Vaughan and Harris. 'This cigarette ash may be nothing to do with it,' said Harris.

'True,' agreed Cherrington. 'But this house is so clean and tidy. I hardly believe dirty cigarette ash would have been left here for a long time. And it is so conveniently near to the electric mains switch. Out go the lights, and the murderer stands waiting here, smoking quietly, waiting for his next victims.'

III

Cherrington and Colonel Vaughan sat in the inner private parlour of the Bell. Pint pots of mixed stout and bitter beer stood on the table between them, and plates of bread and cheese and ham and chutney. Cherrington had looked with appreciative delight at the generous portions of ham, and the fine Caerphilly cheese when Henry Thomas had brought them in.

'I suppose it's all right to discuss our problem in here,' he said.

'Oh, yes. I think so. Henry is a good, reliable person,' said Vaughan. 'We can't be overheard from the other bar, and Henry will see we are not disturbed.'

'It was only this that passed through my mind,' said Cherrington quietly. 'Our landlord is, as you say, brother to Joseph Stanley Thomas. Do you think it was entirely coincidence that Sealands Farm, his farm, was selected as the rendezvous for the abortive visit of police and doctor? Surely it must have been arranged by someone who knew that there would be no one there?'

Vaughan thought a moment. 'I don't think that follows,' he said. 'It wouldn't have made much difference, after all, if there had been someone at Sealands Farm. The police and the doctor would have been away from Llanddewi at the time of the murder. I regard that as the essential of the rather dangerous telephone manoeuvre.'

'Why dangerous?'

'Well, it's not so easy to hide your voice over the telephone. It's an automatic local exchange – automatic, that is, except for trunk calls – so there was no danger of being overheard at the telephone exchange. The danger was the voice itself. I think it has been proved that the more you try to hide your voice – that is to say, the more conscious you become of the way you are speaking – the less likely you are to conceal some very real feature in the voice.'

'I'm not sure about that.'

'It's true. Believe me, it's true,' Vaughan went on quickly. 'I often notice it around here in the Vale of Glamorgan. A man who has acquired a veneer of an English accent, for example – a set of standard English vowels – when he becomes excited, the veneer often slips away and some of the vowels drop back into the good Vale of Glamorgan Welsh, the vowels and the intonation.'

'You think therefore that there is just a chance of the two bogus telephone calls being traced?' Cherrington spoke thoughtfully. 'Let me see,' he said. 'It was the doctor's nurse and Sergeant Williams's wife who took the calls, wasn't it?'

'Yes. We shall have to see what we can do there. But I don't hope for much from the telephone calls. And I certainly think there is nothing to implicate the owner of Sealands Farm. There are two things,' Vaughan went on, 'that I feel sure have nothing to do with the solution of the case. The fact that Sealands Farm was used as a bait for luring away the police, and the fact that anonymous letters were used by the murderer – even letters of the same style and type as had apparently been used in the village before. I think the murderer knew about the poison-pen letter writing. He knew it had been going on and he used it. Secondly, he knew that Sealands Farm was the place farthest away in the parish of Llanddewi that was still in the beat of the Llanddewi police.'

'Ah!' said Cherrington. 'That's an interesting point. But why do it at all? That's what puzzles me. I mean,' he went on quickly, 'let us suppose for a moment that Inspector Harris's story is right. The murderer arranges for David Morris and Bryn Davies to be there. He arrives, steps on the flower-bed, tears his trousers on the rosebush, stabs Evan Morgan in the back, cuts the telephone wires – presumably after making these bogus calls – plunges the house into darkness, waits in the kitchen until Morris and Davies arrive, the while smoking an expensive Turkish cigarette. Then he knocks both young men out and disappears. Now, why?'

'Why what?'

'Why make the phone calls? Why wait? Why, if you are so clever as to be able to arrange a complicated murder like this, why leave your footprints and your cigarette ash behind?'

'You are making too much of these points. There is a great deal still for us to find out, but I think I can answer some of your queries. The footprints I explain as Harris did – a mistake; all murderers, fortunately, make mistakes, and if the owner of these shoes can't explain what he was doing there after six-thirty yesterday outside the windows of the Manor House, he is, I would say, in a difficult spot. The cigarette ash may prove to be an entirely false clue. It might be the ash dropped by anyone earlier in the day, or even before. It hasn't necessarily anything to do with the crime.'

'That is so.' Cherrington hesitated. 'Then how do you view the whole affair?'

'Fairly simply,' said Vaughan. 'Llanddewi is not the place to breed highly complicated murderers with unbreakable alibis and the rest of it. Rendle has shown us very clearly the motive; three people benefited by Morgan's death. And they had to see that he died before this morning if they were really going to benefit from it. Those three included one woman – Ellen Harper Williams. I rule her out. She'd been Evan Morgan's mistress for over twenty years. I don't believe she would do such a thing.'

'A woman scorned...' Cherrington began, but Vaughan interrupted him.

'I know all that,' he said, 'and also that she might have been the author of the anonymous letters in the past. Nevertheless, even if it were physically possible, I don't think she is our murderer.' He paused. 'That leaves us with two people. Two young men – who both owe part of their parentage to Evan Morgan. My two patricides. Do you know them? Do you know Mervyn and Rees?'

'Not really. I have only a vague memory of them as boys. The years of the war have changed them, I imagine.'

'That is just it. Rees Morgan is a weak chap – a conscientious objector who later joined the forces for a short time. A nice fellow, mind you. I say nothing against him at all. But he is a quaint, non-violent fellow. And so I say that psychologically we have only one fellow who could do the job – Mervyn Morgan. He's our man. There is little doubt about it. As soon as we have got down to our routine investigations – where the rope came from that bound up Bryn Davies, the footprint, and the rest of it – we shall be well on the way to the solution of the case. I don't think it will be difficult and I don't think we shall have to call in Scotland Yard.'

There was a long pause while Cherrington went on munching bread and cheese.

'You are not convinced?' the Chief Constable asked.

'I am not. You see, Vaughan, you have been concentrating on the will. I don't merely mean Evan Morgan's will, although that is relevant, very relevant. I mean the will to murder. The motive and the mental disposition to kill. I grant you that there's a motive sticking out a mile in this case. But you've got to show how it was done. You've got to show the way as well as the will.'

'But the way wasn't difficult.'

'I know what you are thinking,' said Cherrington. 'The way Evan Morgan was murdered. That's no problem. A dagger stuck once into his back and it's all over. Yet not so simple. You think about it. It's not so easy. The murderer was a good anatomist. Then there's another thing. No sign of a struggle.'

'Exactly. But we've gone over all that. The murderer was jolly quick.'

'Quick? Jolly quick? Bloody quick, I should say,' said Sir Richard. 'Have you tried – just think of it – getting through those French windows, standing behind the desk, and stabbing a man? All in a twinkling, without disturbing your victim and without leaving footprints on the carpet. There was no struggle because the murderer was accepted. He did not come in suddenly through the windows out of the dark. He was in the room talking to Evan Morgan – perhaps had per-suaded Evan Morgan to write something at his desk; then while he was doing this he steps behind him, takes out the dagger, and plunges it into the back of the man quietly writing by his side, or in front of him. That is why there were no footprints. But that is all by the way,' he went on quickly. 'I'm really thinking at the moment of what went on afterwards. The phone calls, the business of Morris and Davies being disposed of, the rope – all that, and yes, if you insist, I am still thinking of that cigarette ash.' He rapped with his fingers on the table. 'Dammit, Vaughan,' he said. 'And there's this other confusing thing. Those phone calls. I had been thinking in my mind that they were done before Morris and Davies had arrived. But they weren't.'

'Yes. But what is wrong with that?' said Colonel Vaughan. 'The murderer – call him Size Nines or Mervyn Morgan or what you like – commits his murder, lies in wait for these two chaps he has summoned by anonymous letter, knocks them out, and telephones. Ah, I see. But wait a minute. Wait a minute.' The Chief Constable paused. 'It's the timing that becomes difficult to understand. We shall have to go into that very carefully. Morris and Davies got to the Manor House at seven or thereabouts, and the phone calls were made then. There wasn't time for all that happened – if the calls were made from the Manor House after they were knocked out.'

'And we know that couldn't have been the case,' said Cherrington.

'Why?'

'According to the evidence you collected from them – if I understand it aright – the telephone lines at Llanddewi were cut and the phone therefore out of order when they got there.'

'Ah! They arrived at seven and the calls were after. Yes, I see. But perhaps the murderer went and telephoned somewhere else.'

'But was there time?'

'That must be looked into. You certainly have a point there.'

Cherrington said: 'You have no objection, have you, if I do a little detection on my own? I mean just a little conversation here and there. After all, there's no one under arrest at the moment.'

'Quite so. No; of course there is no objection. You'll keep us informed of anything you find out or suspect you have found out?' The Chief Constable's tone was guarded.

'Certainly.'

The Chief Constable hesitated. 'And I suggest,' he said, 'that you leave your talk with Mervyn Morgan until Inspector Harris has done his job.'

'I will indeed,' Cherrington agreed readily. 'I shall go and talk first to the two principals. I mean David Morris and Bryn Davies.'

CHAPTER 9

THE PRINCIPAL BOYS

I

Sir Richard Cherrington delayed his visit to the two young men he had described as the two principals – David Morris and Bryn Davies – until he had been back to Tresaeth House and talked to his aunt.

He told her the essentials of the story he had learnt from the police – the essentials that she would in due course read in her *Western Mail*. He withheld from her some details such as the clue of the footprint, the torn piece of flannel on the rose bush, the cigarette ash in the scullery.

Then he said: 'Tell me, Aunt Mary, who was it among your friends and acquaintances in Llanddewi who drove seven inches of cold steel into Evan Morgan's back last night?'

His aunt sat unmoved, but she rested her knitting for a moment on her lap. She said nothing, so that Sir Richard, thinking her deafness had prevented her from hearing his question, was about to repeat it when she said slowly and softly:

'I think I know.'

'You do?'

'Yes. I think so.' She nodded her head. 'I'm only guessing, of course, as you realize, but then I'm in a good position to guess – better than most people.' She smiled. 'Certainly better than you or Sergeant Williams, or this Inspector Harris you tell me about. Or Bryn Vaughan,' she went on. 'Yes; of course I may be wrong, but it does seem likely to me. It was done by two people. That is obvious.'

'Two people?' Cherrington's voice was keen, his manner alert. 'That's exactly what I think,' he said. 'You see at once the very improbability of the story told by David Morris and Bryn Davies. They are asking us to believe too much. Then there are the other things – the timing, and the telephone calls in particular, and the character of the men. They are surely the only two who could have planned the whole affair and carried it out.'

She smiled at him. 'But you've got hold of the wrong end of the story,' she said. 'David Morris and Bryn Davies may well be telling a tale that has discrepancies – and I think I know why they are doing so. No; there are only two people in Llanddewi who could have done this thing – Ellen Harper Williams and her son, Mervyn Morgan.'

'You are serious? You really mean this?'

'I'm very much afraid that I do,' said his aunt. 'Ellen and Mervyn had a lot to lose if Evan Morgan married again. Mervyn had a very great deal to lose financially, but Ellen had everything to lose – money, her man, her life. Think of it – being replaced in the affections of a man you had loved and lived with for twenty years by a young girl you used to teach at school.' Miss Cherrington sighed. 'I have sympathy with her,' she said. 'Or, rather, I understand her, and understanding is more than halfway towards sympathy. It needs a fixity of purpose and,' she went on, 'I would say a slight madness to work out a plan to kill someone. Ellen Harper Williams has both. She's never been quite all right since she was bombed out of her house. She planned this affair carefully. I begin almost to believe that the anonymous letters were all part of the plan so that you and others can now be saying, "Someone used the anonymous letters to send one in the same vein." But why not the other way round? Ellen has been sending anonymous letters for years so that when one arrives arranging a rendezvous for murder, you just say that. I believe she summoned Bryn Davies and David Morris to the Manor House. I suspect that the trap she laid was a more complicated one than we know about. I even suspect that they realized something of what had happened – they saw perhaps that they were in a trap, and they did their best to make it all look less suspicious than it must have been when they first got there. I should think they saw they were in a trap and tried to get out of it.'

Cherrington took off his pince-nez and polished the lenses carefully with his silk handkerchief. 'You think she didn't herself stab Evan to death?' he said. 'You think her son is in this too? She could have done it all. Evan could have been stabbed by a woman – a woman with some medical knowledge.'

'Ellen was a nurse in the First World War and ran first aid classes in the village in 1939 and 1940. I think she has the knowledge. Yet I don't believe hers was the hand that killed Evan. You will find it was Mervyn Morgan who actually stabbed his father, but somehow – and this is the devil of it – they will have so worked it that each of them – Ellen and Mervyn – have alibis.'

Cherrington shook his head.

'I don't believe it,' he said.

'But why not?'

'Don't misunderstand me, Aunt Mary,' he said. 'I'm not saying that you are wrong. I'm not saying that Miss Williams and Mervyn Morgan aren't our murderers – the one an actual murderer and the other an accessory before and after the fact. You may be right. But I don't believe it yet, because I cannot see how, if you are right, David Morris and Bryn Davies fit in... And that is my first job. Find out how they fit in to the story.'

II

After tea Cherrington drove down to Llanddewi. He called in the three village shops which stocked cigarettes and came away from each without having bought anything. He drove over to Llantwit Major and again drew a blank in the shops there. But in a small shop near the Duke of Wellington in Cowbridge he found what he wanted – a box of Abdulla No. 11 Turkish cigarettes. He drove back slowly and, deep in thought, to Llanddewi along the quiet lanes in the middle of the Vale of Glamorgan, and drew up his car beside the schoolmaster's house. It was on the hill out of Llanddewi leaving by the minor road to Cowbridge: a square, sturdy, neo-Georgian house with green shutters. John Davies and Ruth his wife were keen gardeners, and in their twenty-odd years had made the grounds of Lampeter House one of the most lovely small private gardens in the Vale of Glamorgan.

Mr Davies was working in the garden when Cherrington arrived. He looked up from staking and tying his chrysanthemums, and took the pipe out of his mouth. Sir Richard began cheerfully: 'Hello, Mr Davies,' he said. 'Do you remember me – Cherrington, Richard Cherrington, Miss Mary's nephew?'

John Davies's face, which had been drawn and serious, broke into a smile. 'Hello, Mr Cherrington,' he said. 'I wouldn't have recognized you. I don't think I would. It's a long time since we've seen you down in the Vale.'

'How is Mrs Davies?' Cherrington went on.

'Well, thank you. Quite well.' The voice was formal, drained of any tone.

'I hope you will give my very kindest regards to her,' said Cherrington. 'I well remember her excellent Welsh cakes – many years ago – and her potato cakes.'

John Davies straightened his back and looked away from his chrysanthemums. Yet he didn't look Cherrington straight in the face. 'Ah!' he said. 'She was a good cook, wasn't she?' Cherrington noted his use of the past tense, but something in his voice stopped him from commenting on it. He was puzzled; puzzled, too, by the way the man seemed to be making that remark to himself.

'But it was really your son I came to see,' went on Sir Richard briskly.

'My son Bryn?'

'Yes. Is he in?'

'He's at home,' said John Davies. 'But I think you will find him down in the garage. The war seems to have turned him into a mechanic – a minor compensation of military life, you might say. He never was one for practical things, but he now seems most useful – cars and radios and sewing machines. He's been fitting a radio into our car. You know where our garage is. Down the road there.' He came with Cherrington to the gate and pointed down the road to Llanddewi. 'We didn't have a car when Mrs Davies and I laid out the grounds,' he said. 'And when we could afford one we just couldn't give up any of the garden. So we bought that old barn. It is really an old cart-shed. Belonged to Sealands Farm. Right on the edge of Joseph Thomas's ground.'

III

Cherrington found Bryn Davies at work in the garage. He saw a thickset man of medium height with thick, dark, curling hair. His face and arms were bronzed, and Sir Richard suspected that the tropical sun had had to work on a skin already swarthy. Grey eyes that faced you squarely and unflinchingly out of an open face; a long nose with a kink in it – Cherrington supposed the relic of some boxing or football accident. What are first impressions worth? Perhaps very little, but Sir Richard's first impressions were of a solid, reliable, trustworthy young man with a good sense of humour. Bryn Davies was dressed in an old pair of dungarees – open at the neck, the sleeves rolled up. He had jacked up one of the back wheels of the car and was changing the wheel when Cherrington came into the old cart-shed and introduced himself.

'I won't shake hands with you, if you don't mind,' said young Davies. 'As you can see, my hands are filthy.' He took a rag out of his pocket and began wiping the grease off his hands.

'And I won't waste your time. You are busy.' Cherrington's tone was brisk. 'I've called for a special reason. Let's get to the point at once. The police have asked me to assist them in their investigation of Evan Morgan's murder.'

Davies nodded. 'Anything I can do to help,' he said. 'I have already given a long statement to the police. Perhaps you have seen that? What can I tell you that I forgot to tell Inspector Harris and Co.?'

'It isn't so much a matter of forgetting things. It is atmosphere,' said Cherrington. 'Could you bear to tell me, in your words, just what happened last night? Not a police statement.'

'Of course. Where shall I begin? When I met David Morris? I met him in the pub – in the Bell, you know.'

'No. Start earlier,' said Cherrington. 'Did you meet him by design or accident? Go back earlier. Tell me about the anonymous letter which the police showed me.'

'I see.' The young man paused. 'Well, the anonymous letter came by the post first thing yesterday morning. When I read it I thought it was a joke – at first. Then I began to wonder what it was all about. I met David Morris for a drink in the Bell yesterday morning, and from something he let slip I got the idea that he too had had a letter like mine. We eventually got round to talking about the letters, discovered we had had identical letters, so we decided that, hoax or no hoax, we would go and see Evan Morgan together. That is why we met again last night in the pub.'

'At what time?'

'It must have been about twenty minutes to seven. I'll tell you how I know the time.' He smiled. 'I had been listening to the wireless at home. I switched off the set when the sports news was over, which must have been half past six, and set off to Llanddewi. I stopped for a moment or two in the garden to speak to my father – he was interested in the football results. Then I walked down at my ordinary speed. It would have taken me ten minutes.'

'David Morris was there when you got there?'

'No. He arrived a minute or two afterwards. We had a couple of drinks.'

'How long were you in the pub?'

The young man hesitated. 'Difficult to say,' he said. 'Ten minutes – perhaps a quarter of an hour. I should think we left the Bell about a few minutes to seven. I heard the Town Hall clock strike seven as we went in through the gate into the garden of the Manor House, and it only takes three or four minutes to walk from the Bell up the High Street.'

'You didn't notice anyone on the way?'

Bryn Davies shook his head. 'I don't think we did,' he said. 'Of course, as you know, it was dark, and drizzling with rain.'

'Yes. And then?' Cherrington prompted.

'I think I've said most of what follows in my police statement.'

'By the way,' said Cherrington, suddenly remembering, 'will you smoke?' He held out the flat box of Turkish cigarettes.

The other shook his head. 'No, thank you,'

he said. 'I don't smoke. Not even cheroots when I was in India and they were so cheap.' He paused. 'You really want me to go over again exactly what happened after we arrived at the Manor House last night?'

'Please, if it doesn't distress you too much.'

'It was an unpleasant experience, of course, I mean, finding Mr Evan Morgan stabbed to death in that way. But there I'm afraid I have had to get used to unpleasant experiences in the last few years.'

Sir Richard nodded his head in understanding and Bryn went on. 'The house was in darkness when we arrived,' he said. 'That was the first surprise. We then thought the letters had been a hoax. We walked up to the front door. It was open.'

'And this would be a few minutes after seven o'clock?'

'Yes.'

'I see. The front door was open. Were the French windows to the living-room – you know what I mean, the windows on the left of the front door – were they open?'

Davies hesitated. 'No,' he said. 'I don't think so. The front door being open puzzled us a little. We shone a torch and then we saw that the door into the living-room – the door leading out of the hall – was also open. We went in rather cautiously and – well – there was Evan Morgan's body lying across the desk.'

'What were your first thoughts?' Cherrington asked sharply.

The young man puckered his eyebrows. 'Do you know,' he said, 'I think our first thoughts were for ourselves. At least, mine were. I didn't think a thing about Evan Morgan. It was obvious he was dead and that we could do nothing for him. I felt his pulse, and I knew it was a matter now for the police and the police surgeon. We tried the telephone – it was dead – wires cut – but all the while I was worried about ourselves. I wondered why it was we were summoned there; and I suspected – I still suspect – some sort of trap.' He paused. 'It was then we heard a noise from the inner room, or from the back of the house, and we went to see what it was. Cautiously, of course, for fear of getting croaked ourselves.'

'You both heard the noise?'

Bryn Davies looked puzzled. 'Oh, I think so,' he said. 'I don't really remember the details. Anyway, we both went into the inner room – the room at the back that Evan Morgan apparently used as a sort of work-room, odd-job room, and the rest of it.'

'Yes?'

'We shone the torch around the room. No one there. Then we decided to go through into the scullery. I suddenly remembered that there was, of course, another way into the scullery.'

'You knew your way about the Manor House quite well, then?'

'Oh, yes. I used to play there a great deal when I was young. With Mervyn Morgan and Rees Morgan – and with David Morris. We were all about the same age. Played hide-and-seek and all kinds of games. We all knew the house very well. I've hidden in all the cupboards in the house – that's to say, years ago, of course.'

'But last night you were playing a quite different sort of game in the Manor House. A game in earnest.'

Again the puckered eyebrows. 'I'm not sure I understand you.'

'I only meant,' said Cherrington easily, 'that last night you were playing hide-and-seek with a murderer.'

'I see. Yes.' Bryn Davies sounded relieved. 'You can, if you like, put it that way. It was a kind of game of hide-and-seek. I doubled back through the living-room and into the hall and opened the door from the hall into the scullery. From then on I remember nothing – except, of course, the blow.' He rubbed his chin ruefully. 'It is still sore,' he said.

'You were knocked out at once.'

'That is so. I suppose I was lucky to get away alive.'

'And you saw nothing of your attacker? You saw nobody once you had opened the scullery door?'

He shook his head.

'Not even David Morris and his torch?'

'No.'

'And that is all really that you can tell us, is it?' said Cherrington. 'I mean, there is nothing else that you noticed. Nothing you thought odd at the time, or have since thought odd, looking back at yesterday's events?'

The young man hesitated. 'No,' he said dubiously. 'No. I don't think so. Of course,' he went on quickly, 'we were darn' fools to fall into the trap that had been laid for us. Fools.'

'I'm not so sure about that. It was surely quite natural to go and investigate a noise. There is one thing, though, that I want to ask you – just a point of detail. It relates to your last few minutes of consciousness in the Manor House last night.'

'Yes?'

'How long do you think it was – how many minutes or seconds, that is – between the time when you left David Morris at the door between the work-room and the scullery and when you arrived at the door between the hall and the scullery? How long did it take you to double through the living-room and the hall?'

'Not long. I went as quickly as I could.'

'A minute, perhaps?'

'It might be less.' He hesitated.

'I see.' Cherrington paused. 'Now, do you think that David Morris was knocked on the head first, or do you think that you were dealt with first and David afterwards?'

'I don't know. It was all so quick.'

'Morris had the torch, hadn't he, so that he would have been pointing it into the scullery – at you as you came in from the hall?'

'No,' said Bryn Davies. 'I had the torch.'

'I see. You had the torch. You left David Morris, took the torch and doubled round into the scullery. H'm. Then another thing puzzles me. Why did the murderer tie you up, but leave David Morris free?'

'Perhaps he had only one length of rope.'

'It's possible. But if he was expecting you both, you would think he would have rope for both. Did he make a good job of tying you up?'

'Yes; very good. I tried my damnedest to get myself loose – that is to say, after I had recovered my senses. My feeble wriggles merely seemed to tighten the knots. He must have been a real expert at the job. I know quite a bit myself about escape tricks and the rest of it, but he was too much for me. Of course he had an unconscious man to deal with instead of the types we were trained on in the south-east Asia war zone. Still, he was good.' He turned to Cherrington. 'That ought to give you a good clue to the murderer, shouldn't it?' he said. 'Someone good with a rope.'

IV

Cherrington got into his car and drove away. He drove slowly down to the village, noting that it was about half a mile from Davies's house to the Post Office and the Manor House, and just over half a mile to the Bell Inn. So much was in confirmation of Bryn Davies's story: it would have taken about ten minutes to get from his house to the centre of the village – that or just under ten minutes. Sir Richard crossed the Market Square, past the Town Hall, and drove round the churchyard, across the little river and up the hill to the Rectory.

The Rector was walking about in the garden in obvious distress. 'My dear Cherrington,' he began at once, with no introduction, 'this dreadful crime. Here in our midst. Somebody – someone well known to us all – some one of *us* – do you realize that? – of *us* – has done this thing. Taken another human being's life. I wasn't able to sleep last night for one moment. The tragedy of it all.' He wrung his hands. 'And the suspicion. We are all of us under suspicion. All of us. It is really quite unbearable. I just don't know what I shall do; nor what I shall say when I next preach.'

'It is about the murder that I have called to see you,' said Cherrington.

The Rector stopped and stared at him. 'You? But why?'

Cherrington hesitated. 'I'm trying to help the police,' he said. 'They want all the help they can get in these investigations, you know. I agreed to help them, and thought my first job was to have a talk with the principal witnesses; I mean Bryn Davies and your son.'

'But they weren't witnesses, man.' Hugh Morris spoke quickly, vehemently. 'You have the facts wrong. They were not witnesses to anything. They arrived after the crime had been committed. How can they be of assistance to you and the police?'

'You forget that they came into contact – close contact – with the murderer.'

'Did they? Did they? Yes; I suppose you can put it that way, if you like. But I implore you not to bother my son at the moment. It has all been a great shock to him – a very great shock. He did not get home until three o'clock this morning. The police were callous, quite callous. They kept my son and John Davies's son there half the night questioning them and making them sign statements. David is unwell,' he went on. 'Do please leave him alone. Come back another time. I assure you he is not fit for further

186

questioning yet.'

A cool but jerky voice cut in to the conversation. 'I think perhaps, Father, that I am the best judge of that.' David Morris had come out of the house quietly and crossed the lawn unobserved by his father and Cherrington.

'Oh, very well,' said his father abruptly. 'I was only trying to spare you. If you think you know better... I shall be in the house if you want me again, Cherrington.' He turned and walked quickly off across the lawn and into the Rectory. Sir Richard watched him go and then he brought his eyes back from the house to the young man in front of him. David Morris was a very different figure from Bryn Davies. Thin and tall, with fair hair and a pale complexion – the first impression was of a nervous uncertainty. For all his years in the Army and his experience abroad, David Morris still contrived to look like a schoolboy – a sixth-form schoolboy just getting out of the pimply stage. He ran his hand jerkily through his hair. 'What did you want to speak to me about?' he said.

Cherrington explained his purpose and credentials, and at the young man's suggestion they went off and sat in the summer-house at the corner of the lawn. 'Let's sit here if you don't think it is too cold,' he said. 'We shall catch the last of the sun.'

Sir Richard took out his cigarette box.

Morris made to take a cigarette and then drew back his hand. 'If you don't mind,' he said, 'I'll have one of my own. I have never got to like Turkish cigarettes.' He took out from his pocket a packet of Players. Cherrington lit a match and held it up for him. The feeble flame in the darkening shadow of the summer-house lit up the boy's face, emphasizing its pallor and lines.

'I shall not worry you for long,' said Sir Richard. 'I just wanted to see you, and ask you one or two small things about last night.' He paused, and then asked: 'You met Bryn Davies in the Bell?'

'Yes. I didn't notice the time when I arrived there, if that is what you want to know. I had been for a short walk.'

'In the rain?'

'It wasn't raining when I set out. I just walked around.' He hesitated. 'If you are in the confidence of the police, you know about the anonymous letters, of course?'

Cherrington nodded.

'I was puzzled. And I went for a walk to try and clear my head. My father will corroborate this. I left just after the news, when the sports news was beginning. I didn't walk very far, out along the road in the direction of the sea; then I turned around and went back to the pub. Bryn Davies was there waiting. We had agreed to meet.' Morris turned suspiciously to Cherrington. 'I have a feeling, you know,' he said, 'that the police don't believe Bryn Davies or me. They suspect me of overpowering Bryn myself.'

'You? But why?'

'Maybe they think I murdered Evan Morgan when I was out on my walk, then met Bryn in the pub and went back to the Manor House with him, and knocked him out, creating the impression there was someone else there. But I didn't, you know. I'm as much in the dark as anyone. I wish to hell I knew what was behind the whole thing.'

'Let us get back to the Bell,' said Cherrington, kindly. 'You got there soon after Bryn Davies had arrived?'

'I suppose so. I arrived after him, certainly. We stayed there about fifteen to twenty minutes, I should think. I know we left just about seven o'clock – a few minutes to seven.'

'And then?'

'But you know the rest. We got to the Manor House. It was dark, the front door was open, also the door into the living-room.'

'Were the French windows open – the ones from the living-room out into the garden?'

Morris hesitated. 'I don't know. I didn't notice. Is it important that I should remember?'

'Not really. Just go on. You went into the living-room.'

189

'Yes.' David Morris put his hands over his eyes. It was a melodramatic gesture, and Cherrington watched him carefully. 'Horrible,' said the young man, and shuddered. 'It was quite horrible.'

'You saw all this – all this horror – in the light of a torch?'

Morris looked up. 'What?' he said. 'Oh yes. Bryn had a torch with him, and we looked round the room. The lights were cut off,' he added, unnecessarily. 'So was the telephone.'

'How long did you stay in the living-room before beginning to search the house?'

'I don't know. I suppose it wasn't very long, but it seemed an age. It seemed absolutely endless.'

'Then you moved into the work-room at the back,' Cherrington prompted.

'Yes. Bryn heard a noise in the back of the house.'

'You didn't hear it?'

He stared at Cherrington. 'I can't remember,' he said. 'Perhaps I did. What is the use of these futile questions? Are you trying to catch me out?'

'My dear boy,' said Cherrington. 'For God's sake take a hold of yourself. No one is trying to catch you out.'

'Then why do the police send you to ask me all over again the questions I have already answered? It's a trap. You're trying to trap me. To see whether I tell the same story. Well, I won't stand for it. Do you hear? I won't stand for it. You are persecuting me and I won't have it.'

He jumped up. Sir Richard put out a restraining hand, but before he could stop him Morris was across the garden and out on to the road. Cherrington walked quickly after him to the gate, calling out his name. But it was no use. David Morris turned up the road away from the village, the road that led to the cliffs and the sea, and was soon lost in the gathering darkness of the evening. Sir Richard shook his head sadly, and got into his car. But he did not drive away at once. He took out a large notebook and began writing. It was only after he had been writing for a considerable time that he put on his car lights and drove away.

CHAPTER 10

TIME, GENTLEMEN, PLEASE

I

Cherrington was sitting at the breakfast table next morning when his aunt came in from answering the telephone and said that he was wanted by the police.

It was Inspector Harris at the other end. 'I have some news for you, Professor,' he said. 'We've found our man.'

'You mean the man who made the footprints outside the French windows at the Manor House?'

'Yes.'

'Good. Who is he?'

The Inspector hesitated. 'I would rather not say any more over the telephone, if you don't mind,' he said. 'We are going to question this man in about twenty minutes' time. Colonel Vaughan is coming over to the Police Station here in Llanddewi. He suggested that we should invite you to come along at the same time – that is, if you are interested,' he added. Inspector Harris's voice still seemed to convey his disapproval

192

of Cherrington's close association with the inquiries.

'Excellent. I will be along as soon as I can.'

But Sir Richard's car was slow in starting, and when he got to Llanddewi the Chief Constable was already there. He greeted Cherrington with a slightly wintry smile. 'We have been having complaints about you, Cherrington,' he said with forced heartiness. Cherrington's raised eyebrows asked the question.

'It is your third-degree methods,' said Vaughan. 'Your interview with David Morris last night apparently upset him a great deal. It also upset his father. The boy complains that the police are persecuting him, and his father rang me up this morning at a very early hour. Couldn't the police use orthodox methods, and what did I mean by employing plain-clothes specialists? Hugh Morris is my brother-in-law, as you know.'

'Well, I'm damned,' said Cherrington. 'Still, I like the phrase "plain-clothes specialists". I am sorry to embarrass you. It was the last thing I wanted to do. And it is all rather strange that the Morrises should have complained. I was very kind and polite, you know. I begin to wonder whether the two men at the Rectory are hiding something from us.'

Vaughan gestured impatiently with his hands. 'You are always wanting to make more mystery of everything,' he said rudely. 'These speculations can wait until we have seen our man.'

'The man who so conveniently left the footprints?'

'Yes,' said Vaughan shortly. 'The Inspector has found that the man who left his footprints outside the French windows of the Manor House was Mervyn Morgan. Harris also asked Morgan what he had been wearing on Friday evening. He produced a suit — a dark grey flannel suit with chalk stripes. It corresponded exactly with the small fragments of cloth caught on the rose bush outside the Manor House windows. There was a tear, but the tear had been mended. In fact, Mrs Mervyn Morgan said she had only just mended it.'

'That's important, isn't it?' said Cherrington.

'Indeed it is. Mervyn Morgan only noticed the tear when he took the suit off on Friday evening. It was then he mentioned it to his wife.'

'Exactly. He mentioned it to his wife. Extremely important point. There is no attempt at concealment.'

'There was no attempt at concealment of the shoes or the torn trousers, if that's what you are getting at,' said Vaughan. 'But there was plenty of other concealment — concealment of material facts.'

'There most certainly was.' Inspector Harris took up the story. 'We asked Morgan some questions about Friday night. According to his account, he left his shop at about six-thirty, went to the Bell for a drink, then on to the Welcome Home party, where he says he stayed until he went home at about ten o'clock.'

'What was his attitude during questioning?'

'You want my frank opinion?' asked Harris. 'Lying all the time. Just brazening out a lie. Yes,' he went on, 'I'm afraid there is very little doubt about it. He is our man. There's everything there – the money, the motive – gain – and we have proof that he was there. It is time we questioned him.'

He went to the charge-room, and in a few moments returned with Sergeant Williams, a police shorthand writer, and Mervyn Morgan. Morgan was a handsome young man; tall – that is, tall for a South Welshman – with curly dark hair, high cheekbones, a broad forehead, and a rather high colour. He was, not unnaturally, ill at ease, as Sergeant Williams motioned him to a chair and explained briefly the presence of Colonel Vaughan and Professor Cherrington.

'We asked you to come along, Mr Morgan,' said Harris chattily, 'to amplify the statement you made to us yesterday. I should warn you of course that your answers are going to be taken down, and that they may therefore be used in evidence.'

'I don't see how I can help you in your inquiries,' said Mervyn Morgan. 'I wish that I could. I told you yesterday what I knew. I was at the Bell and then at the Welcome Home dance.'

'You did not visit your father on Friday night?'

Was there the slightest hesitation in reply? Sir Richard thought he detected it, and an uncertain note of bluster in Mervyn Morgan's reply. 'No,' he said. 'I most certainly did not.'

'Then can you explain to us, please,' said Harris smoothly, 'how your footprints were found in the soft earth of the flower bed outside the French windows of the Manor House when we examined them on Friday night? And how a few strands of your grey flannel suit were torn off by the rose bushes at the side of the window?'

'It isn't true. That is the explanation.'

'But it is true. And you know it is true.'

Mervyn Morgan sighed. 'Very well,' he said. 'I admit it.' There was exasperation in his voice, as though he were cross with himself for having bothered to deny the facts in the first place. 'But it has nothing to do with the murder. I went there early in the evening.'

Inspector Harris's voice took on a new note of authority and firmness. 'Your footsteps were made after it began to rain,' he said. 'The rain began on Friday night just about six-thirty. The ground was already thoroughly wet when you stood outside your father's windows. Come, Mr Morgan. You know you are not telling us the truth. It would help us, would help yourself, if you did so.'

Mervyn Morgan hesitated, and Cherrington felt the tension in the room as they waited for his reply. 'Oh, very well,' he said abruptly, looking around at their faces. 'You win. I was rather stupid to suppose that I could get away with it.'

'Could get away with what?' Inspector Harris could not conceal the note of hope in his voice.

'Why,' began Mervyn Morgan; and then he stopped. A flush spread over his face. 'I say,' he went on, 'I hope you don't think, any of you, that I murdered my father.' There was a silence eloquent of the fact that some of them did.

'Please go on with your story, Mr Morgan,' said Harris. 'You did go to the Manor House on Friday night?'

'Yes. I did go to the Manor House on Friday night. I did step in the flower-bed and peer through the French windows.'

'You only looked through the windows?'

'Yes. I swear that I did not go into the house.'

'Why did you look through the windows at all?'

'Because I saw a light flickering about inside. The house was in darkness when I arrived, but this light was moving about in the living-room, as though someone was shining a torch about. So, instead of going up to the front door, I looked in at the window.'

'What did you see?' Harris prompted.

'I saw two men, one of whom had a torch which he was playing around the room. Then, as he played it on to the desk, I saw my father, slumped across the top of the desk, with the handle of something sticking out from his back.'

'You saw the faces of the men?'

Mervyn Morgan hesitated. 'No,' he said. 'At least, not to recognize for certain. No. I could not say who they were.'

'Nor who you thought they were?' Harris pursued.

'No. I'd rather not. It would be pure guess-work.'

'And then what happened?'

'One of the men swung the torch round in the direction of the window. I thought that I should be seen. So I stepped back. That must have been when my trousers got torn on the rose bush,' he added ruefully.

'Yes; but then? You gallantly went into the house and tried to capture the murderers of your father, I suppose?' Harris's tone was sharp and contemptuous.

'I didn't,' said Mervyn Morgan quietly. 'I was too frightened. I'm afraid I turned tail and fled as quickly as possible to the Town Hall. I got in easily through the side door. I don't think anyone saw me arrive, but they might have done so. That is why I pretended to you yesterday that I was there all the time. A silly thing to do, I suppose, but quite natural.'

'I am sorry you think it is natural to deceive the police,' said Inspector Harris severely. 'Do you know, I think you are still deceiving the police?'

The young man looked up quickly. 'That is not true,' he said. 'I admit that yesterday I was foolish, but what I have told you today is the truth.'

'Is it? I wonder,' said Harris. 'Shall I tell you what I think happened?' He made a sign with his hand to the shorthand writer, who stopped recording the conversation. 'I believe you left the Bell as you say, that you got to the Manor House, peeped through the window at your father, then, when you found he was alone, flung open the windows and murdered him.'

Mervyn Morgan stood up. His face was white. 'So you are now openly accusing me of murdering my father, are you?' he said quietly. 'It is not true.'

'I accuse you of more,' went on Harris.

'We know who the two men were whom you say you saw. We know it from their own confessions – David Morris and Bryn Davies. That comes as no surprise to you, does it?' he went on quickly.

Mervyn Morris stammered in his confusion. 'I – I thought – that is to say, I had an idea it was them,' he said. 'But I was not prepared to identify them in a court of law.'

'You thought you had recognized them,' said Harris, scornfully. 'I suggest to you that you retired to the back of the house when Davies and Morris arrived, that you lay in wait for them in case they should find you, that you knocked them both out, and tied up Bryn Davies with rope.'

Mervyn Morgan's astonishment could hardly have been feigned. 'Is that what happened to them? Say that again, please. They were both knocked out and tied up? But how could that be?'

'You deny that you did this to them?'

'Of course I do. And, Inspector, you know as well as I do that I didn't do it. In fact, that I couldn't have done it.'

'You could not have done it. Why not?'

'One man couldn't dispose of David Morris and Bryn Davies together. That's quite absurd. They would have given such a good account of themselves in the process that the man – whoever he was – would show some signs of it.'

'An absurd story, is it?' said Harris. 'Then how do you account for the fact that they were knocked out?'

'Quite simply. They knocked each other out, I expect, after murdering my father.'

Inspector Harris looked appealingly at the Chief Constable and shrugged his shoulders.

'I should like to ask you one question,' said Colonel Vaughan. 'I know you as a strong, tough fellow. I remember you in the Llanddewi Rugger team before the war, and your Marine Commando training must stand you in good stead. I can, of course, appreciate what you mean when you say you were not prepared to take on Morris and Davies single-handed and dispose of them without being mauled yourself. But there is one thing in your story I find difficult to believe. You say that you fled away, fled into the night from the two men you think you recognized, and whom you believed – whom you still believe – to have murdered your father? That was surely the act of a coward. It doesn't fit into your character. Why did you do it – if you did do it?'

'I suppose, sir, that I panicked,' said the young man. 'You see, I thought I had been trapped, and that the murder was being pinned on me. I thought that was the intention of the anonymous letter.'

'The anonymous letter?'

'Yes. I received an anonymous letter telling me to go to the Manor House at seven on Friday evening.' He fumbled in his pocket, brought out a leather notecase, and gave Colonel Vaughan a folded piece of thin, typed paper. It was a message in typed capitals, just like the one which Bryn Davies had shown the police. In fact, it might well have been a carbon copy of the same message.

'When did you get this?' asked Vaughan.

'Friday morning. I was naturally very surprised – couldn't make out what it was. Thought it was a joke or a hoax. But I went – and, well, you know the rest of the story.'

'Did you tell anyone you had received this letter?'

'No, sir.' The voice belied the answer.

'Not even Miss Harper Williams?'

'No,' said Mervyn Morgan with directness. 'I did not discuss the matter with my mother. I expect you know that she is not very well. She has been much distressed since the news of my father's impending marriage to Janet Anderson.'

Harris turned to Vaughan and Cherrington. 'Have you any other questions to ask Mr Morgan?' he said. Colonel Vaughan shook his head. Sir Richard took his cigarettes out of his pocket and offered them to Morgan. 'Will you smoke?' he said affably.

Mervyn shook his head. 'No, thank you,' he said. 'I only smoke a pipe. Cigarettes are wasted on me.'

'Tell me,' said Cherrington slowly. 'As you walked to the Manor House, went in through the gate and walked up to the French windows – at what moment of that journey did you hear the Town Hall clock strike seven?'

Morgan turned to him quickly. 'You won't catch me out that way,' he said, smiling. 'The Town Hall clock is out of order, and has been for some while.'

'That is quite true,' said Sergeant Williams by way of explanation to Cherrington. 'The clock has not been restarted since the war. There is something seriously the matter with it.'

II

Sir Richard Cherrington drove from the Police Station to the Bell. It was a thoughtful man who got out of his car and went to the front door of the inn – a thoughtful but also an absent-minded man. The door was locked. Cherrington glanced at his watch, which said twenty minutes to one. He tried the door again, and it was not until he had been rattling the latch for a good two minutes that he remembered the geography of Great Britain and Lloyd George and Welsh Nonconformity. He paused, his thoughts on the Welsh licensing laws remaining unspoken for want of an audience, not for want of any urgency or forthrightness. Then he remembered with pleasure that in Wales, fortunately, Nonconformist observances were in many places but a thin veneer over a social habit that was more Gallic and Mediterranean in its essentials than Anglo-Saxon, and he went round to the back of the pub and knocked at the kitchen door.

Henry Thomas opened the door and beckoned him in. He led the way into the private bar parlour, where Cherrington had lunched the previous day with the Chief Constable.

'What is it to be?' Henry Thomas asked. 'Stout and bitter seems to be your favourite tipple, Professor, doesn't it?'

Cherrington nodded. 'It is indeed,' he said. 'But I thought you were closed officially on Sundays? The Vale of Glamorgan is legally Wales, isn't it, although no one speaks any Welsh here?'

'Quite right,' said the landlord. 'This is Wales, if not Welsh Wales. You get my meaning?' He put down a tankard in front of Sir Richard. 'But drink up your beer all the same,' he said, adding in a lowered voice: 'How's the murder going?'

'The murder?' Cherrington temporized. 'I believe the police are busy investigating,' he said.

'And I believe that you are helping them,'

said the landlord. 'Though they do say that the investigation is practically over.'

'Oh, do they? I shouldn't be too sure about that.'

'They do say' – Henry Thomas nodded his head – 'that they are going to arrest Mervyn Morgan.'

'Then you have more information than I have,' said Sir Richard. 'And you may be right. But seeing you have spoken about the murder, I will confess that I have something to do with the police investigations, and that I did call in here today to ask you for some information. Information about Friday night – about the night of the murder.' The landlord said nothing and Cherrington went on: 'Were you serving in the bar that night?' he asked.

'Yes. I were,' said Henry Thomas ungrammatically. 'And I were all alone that night. My missus she was at the Town Hall doing the catering – she's a real one at the catering,' he added.

'So you were here alone on Friday night. You had to serve in all the bars. You have three bars, is it?'

'Three bars, or two, properly speaking, and here. There's the public bar with the dartboard. And there's the smoke-room lounge on the other side – with the bar billiards table. Those two bars, and this little private room which I let my friends use.'

'I see. And I suppose as you had to move about from bar to bar, you couldn't really say who was and who wasn't here on Friday evening at what time.'

'I think I can. First of all I can remember because there were very few people about, most of them being at the Welcome Home party. After all, that's sense, isn't it? No one would come to a pub at all if there was always free drink at the Town Hall, would they? Then I've been thinking over Friday evening because Inspector Harris – now there's a smart man for you – he was asking me if I could remember anything at all of that night that could have any bearing on the murder.'

'And could you?'

'I don't know. The Inspector was interested in what went on from opening time up to seven o'clock and after. The first man to come in that night was my brother, Joseph Stanley Thomas. You know him. He came in here and sat by himself drinking until well after seven o'clock. He gets very depressed these days, and drinks a lot. Never been the same man since his boy Nigel was killed in the war.'

'Your brother was in here drinking the whole time?'

'I told the Inspector I couldn't be certain of that,' said the landlord. 'I went in to the other bars to serve. Naturally, he wasn't under my eye the whole time, so to speak.

And, anyway, no man can go on sitting drinking for ever. He's got to get up now and then – you get my meaning. By the way, it's just across the yard at the back if you should want it. There was no one except my brother here until round about half past six. Mervyn Morgan came in about then. He went in to the public bar, as he always does, and threw a few darts at the board. I know the time because it was just after the sports news. I'd left the wireless set on and they started up some dance music which I can't abide, and I went to turn the set off. It was just then that Mervyn Morgan came in and I drew him his drink.'

'So that at six-thirty or just after there were two people here. Your brother in here and Mervyn Morgan in the public bar. Is that right?'

'It is.'

'And otherwise nobody?'

'Nobody until in comes Bryn Davies. He walks into the lounge bar, and a few minutes later in comes David Morris. They sat drinking and talking for a while, and then they left.'

Cherrington hesitated. 'I suppose it is too much to hope,' he said, 'that you remember the time they left?'

'As a matter of fact, I do. I had been hoping to nip across to see the Welcome Home party for a few minutes. I promised the Missus and

Roger that I might look round about seven o'clock, when the official doings were to begin. So I was keeping an eye on the clock. David Morris and Bryn Davies left here round about five minutes to seven, and Mervyn Morgan left after them, just on seven o'clock.'

'Then you went to the Welcome Home yourself, I suppose?'

Henry Thomas hesitated. 'Well, no, as a matter of fact, I didn't,' he said. 'I didn't like to leave the pub entirely unattended.'

'But your brother was here in this private bar,' said Sir Richard quickly. 'He could have looked after the place while you were away across in the Town Hall.'

'That's what I thought,' said Henry Thomas. 'But when I came in here at seven, he had gone. By the time he came back it was ten past seven, and the opportunity was gone.'

'I see.' Cherrington recapitulated: 'So that between six o'clock, when you opened, and seven-ten, there were only four people in the Bell?'

'Right. And at about a quarter past seven in came John Davies, the schoolmaster, you know. And from then on the pub began to fill – especially after the news of the murder started to leak out.'

'Good.' Cherrington finished his beer and got up to go. Then at the door he turned round sharply. 'Wait a minute, Mr Thomas,' he said. 'Wait a minute. Your clock's ten minutes fast. Now, the times you have told me, and told the inspector, are they the real times, or are they all ten minutes wrong? I mean, did you look at your clock when Mervyn Morgan left, as you say, at about seven o'clock – did it say seven or ten past seven?'

'Why, ten past seven,' said Henry Thomas. 'I always take the ten minutes off to compensate like.'

'So that when you say that David Morris and Bryn Davies left at ten minutes to seven, it was about seven on your clock?'

'Yes.'

'But that is most interesting,' said Cherrington. 'Most interesting.'

'I don't see how,' said Henry Thomas, frowning. 'All pub clocks are fast – five or ten minutes fast. Everybody knows that.'

'Yes, yes,' said Sir Richard. 'I know. I suppose everybody does. But does everybody remember it?'

CHAPTER 11

CIGARETTES BY ABDULLA

When Cherrington arrived at the Police Station on Monday morning, he was confronted with as gloomy and dispirited a pair of men as it could be feared to find.

Colonel Vaughan turned as he came in. His greeting was brief and perfunctory. 'Hello,' he said. 'Got any news or ideas?'

'I was just going to ask the same of you.'

Inspector Harris looked up from his papers. 'We were just discussing,' he said, 'whether or not to call in Scotland Yard.'

The Chief Constable nodded his head. 'That's true,' he said. 'No reflection on Harris and Williams or anyone, of course. But we are beginning to feel that, alone, we are getting – well, not nowhere, but not along any road that looks as if it is leading to any solution.'

'The Chief Constable wanted to ring up this morning, but I persuaded him to give me until teatime,' said Inspector Harris. 'I'm just going through the papers in the hope I can see them in some fresh light, but so far I have had no success. Mind you,' he said defensively, 'we have learnt a few new things.'

'Good,' said Cherrington.

'Not much good though,' said Harris. 'We have questioned everyone remotely connected with Evan Morgan or who could have been at the Manor House on Friday night. The first thing is that we have found when he was last seen alive. It was at five minutes past six by the boy who delivers the evening papers. Apparently this boy goes to the railway station and collects the evening papers off the train that arrives from Cardiff and Barry at a minute or so to six. Then he sets out and delivers the papers – the paper, I should say, for, of course, it is only the *South Wales Echo and Express*. The Manor House is his third call. We have no proof of time. The boy, naturally, doesn't look at his watch when he calls at every house, but he kept to his normal round last Friday, and therefore I think we may take it Evan Morgan was alive at about five minutes past six. The train wasn't late – or anything like that.'

'The boy actually saw him?'

'Oh, yes,' said Vaughan, interrupting. 'None of your detective story stuff of simulated voices while the corpse was there all the time. Evan Morgan came to the door and took the paper from the boy.'

'I see,' said Cherrington. His voice was

thoughtful. 'So we have no one who saw Evan Morgan between six-five, when the newspaper boy saw him alive, and fifty-five minutes later, when David Morris, Bryn Davies, and Mervyn Morgan all claim to have seen his dead body.'

'That's it.' Inspector Harris roused himself from his gloom. 'Fifty-five bloody minutes without a single clue as to what went on during that time. And the medical evidence does nothing, as far as I can see, except to confirm what we know. Time of death somewhere between six-five and seven o'clock.'

'Quite so.' Cherrington stroked his chin. 'But this is news. I mean that Morgan was last seen alive at five past six. It does rather change the complexion of the case.'

'In what way?'

'Well, I had been thinking of the crime as committed somewhere between six-thirty and seven, or perhaps at seven itself. The people I have spoken to – David Morris, Bryn Davies – and the people I have heard about from you, such as Mervyn Morgan, for example, we have been checking their movements before seven o'clock and at seven o'clock; we have been interested in the time from six-thirty to seven-ten. Now it seems possible that Evan Morgan could have been murdered between six-five and six-thirty equally well.'

'Perfectly correct,' said Harris. 'But there

are a few more things we have learnt. We have traced the rope – the rope that was used to truss up Bryn Davies. That was a good piece of investigation by young Roderick. The rope came from Jones the ironmongers' in Barry. They sold it to John Davies.'

'The schoolmaster?'

'Yes. There is no mystery about it. He admits that he had a coil of rope of this kind. He stored it in his garage. Of course, he has no idea when it disappeared from his garage, and the theft would have been easy.'

There was a pause and Cherrington said: 'Tell me your list of suspects.'

'It is little more than a list,' Harris said gruffly. 'First of all, the three what-do-you-call-'ems. The three principal beneficiaries: Miss Harper Williams, Mervyn Morgan, and Rees Morgan. Take Miss Harper Williams first. You know, of course, that she lives in the converted loft of the garage of your aunt's house – Tresaeth House. She says that she went home from school on Friday at about four-thirty and was alone in her flat until a quarter to seven, when she walked down to the Welcome Home dance. She walked down alone, saw no one, got to the dance about seven or just after. You see how damned easy it all is. She could have committed the murder if she had left Tresaeth House just a little earlier than she said she did.'

'I was driving my car along the road from Llanddewi to Tresaeth at about six-forty-five to six-fifty on Friday evening,' said Cherrington. 'I didn't see her.'

'You might not have seen her,' said Harris. 'It was dark and raining.'

'I noticed the Rector, anyway,' said Cherrington.

'When and where?' Harris's question was barked out sharply and crisply.

'I saw him as I was driving along from Llanddewi to Tresaeth. It must have been just after a quarter to seven. He was crossing the road from the village towards the church. He looked a little odd.'

'Odd?'

'Well, a little distracted. He didn't look at the car. Just walked on.'

'It is certainly a little odd,' said Harris. 'We asked the Reverend Hugh Morris for an account of his movements. He told us he left his Rectory somewhere between a quarter and half past six – he doesn't know exactly when. He says he went to the church, where he was until seven o'clock, when he went to the Welcome Home party.'

'He did not tell you that he had been in the village before seven,' said Cherrington. 'You are sure of this?'

'We didn't ask him specifically this point,' said Harris. 'But we did ask him if he had been anywhere near the Manor House that

214

evening before seven o'clock, and he said "No; most definitely not."'

'That does seem a point worth following up,' said Sir Richard. 'But we are interrupting your *exposé* of the situation, Inspector.'

Harris smiled grimly. 'Well,' he said, 'let us try to suspect No. 2, Mervyn Morgan. His story, too, is very straightforward, and, I'm bound to say today, though I didn't think so at first – very plausible. The shop closes at six. The girls who work with him in the shop were gone by six-ten or so. All that has been checked. Mervyn Morgan says he stayed on working at the accounts and order books until about half past six, when he went to the Bell. What he says happened after that, you know well yourself, Sir Richard.'

'Yes. The Bell until nearly seven. Then to the Manor House, where he says he peered through the French windows and stepped back into the rose bushes when Morris and Davies shone a torch on him. Yes. I know.'

'But,' said Harris, 'where was Mervyn Morgan between six-ten and six-thirty? He says he was in the shop during that period. But what is to stop him nipping up to the Manor House, murdering his dad – if I may put it that way, and getting back quickly to the Bell?'

'Then he turns up to see the discomfiture of David Morris and Bryn Davies, whom he had previously summoned by means of anonymous letters. He knocks them both out, and off he goes to the Welcome Home dance. Is that your theory now?' asked Cherrington.

'Well, not a theory. But what I say could have happened, couldn't it?'

'It could. But you have no proof.'

'No proof at all,' Inspector Harris readily agreed. 'The same applies to the third person whose twenty thousand pounds was in danger of being lost if Evan Morgan remarried. I mean Rees Morgan. We have interviewed him in Barry. He says he went to the cinema after the shop closed in Barry on Friday evening. Says he went in at about five-thirty.' Harris consulted his notes. 'And that he didn't get out until seven-thirty, when he went for a drink in the Barry Arms. That part of his story is all right. We have checked on that. He was in the Barry Arms round about seven-thirty. But there's no proof of his visit to the cinema. How could there be? In the dark, these ushers can't be expected to remember everybody they show to their seats, nor the girl in the box office everyone she sold a ticket to. But there is no getting away from the fact that he could have caught the train that gets to Llanddewi at six, and could have left Llanddewi by the train that goes at seven-three. It would have got him into Barry just before seven-thirty.'

'And yet,' Cherrington said, 'if Rees Morgan was seen, as you say, in the Barry at seven-thirty, he couldn't have been in Llanddewi after the train – what did you say it was – the seven-three?'

'Yes. That is unless he went in an extremely fast car, or something like that. He hasn't a car himself, by the way.'

'Let us suppose he had to rely on the train,' said Sir Richard. 'I was wondering if that does not really remove him from our list of suspects. We shall not go far wrong if we assume that the man who made the bogus telephone calls is, directly or indirectly, concerned with the murder. Now how long does it take to get to the railway station from the Manor House?'

'If you ran fast, you could do it in perhaps two or three minutes. An ordinary person walking couldn't have got there in less than five minutes.'

'Good. So that if Rees Morgan was in the Barry Arms at seven-thirty, and had to travel on the seven-three train, he would have had to leave the Manor House before seven o'clock. There is no public phone box at the station, is there?'

'No. But there is one between the Manor House and the station. But the phone calls were made at seven o'clock.'

'Exactly. Which doesn't give Rees Morgan enough time to catch the train at seven-three. So he couldn't have been the murderer, even if we have any reason to suppose he was anywhere on Friday evening other than in the cinema, as he said.'

Inspector Harris was thoughtful. 'Which seems to bring our major suspects down to two, Miss Harper Williams and Mervyn Morgan. Have you any other theory, Professor?'

Cherrington took off his eyeglasses and polished them with care, using a large red silk handkerchief. 'I have a theory,' he said. 'And it has quite a lot to support it. I've been listening to the village gossip – mainly from my aunt – and I've been wondering whether we were right to stress that it was murder for profit. What if it were just a coincidence that the murder was committed just the night before the new will was to be signed? After all, a murder of this kind, with anonymous letters and so on, must have taken some planning. It couldn't have been done on the spur of the moment. We need to know who knew that the will was being changed, and *when* they knew, before we can be certain they are connected – the murder and the new will. I have begun to wonder whether there were not other motives than financial gain. You remember the story of Daphne, Bryn Davies's sister. She was practically engaged to David Morris. He went away to the war. The long separation of overseas service caused Daphne's affections for David to cool

– or that is how I read the story. She was flattered by the attentions of older men like Evan Morgan and, to put it bluntly, seems to have been his mistress for a while. Then tragedy came to set its mark on this wartime flirtation, as it so often came in the war to blow to pieces those temporary liaisons formed in an atmosphere of urgency, uniforms, and devil take the consequences. We have heard of many such stories,' said Cherrington sententiously. 'You know what happened: Daphne was found with child, almost certainly by Evan Morgan. They decided to get rid of the child. It is suspected that Miss Harper Williams acted as an abortionist. You know the rest. It was bungled; blood-poisoning set in. The poor girl concealed her condition until it was too late to do anything. She died. It was towards the end of the war in the west. Many of the facts were in dispute. No one did anything about it. The girl left no statement. Now, it is well over a year since she died, but we now have back on the local scene two vigorous young men, both deeply attached to the girl – her brother and her fiancé, or nearly her fiancé.'

Cherrington paused. 'I believe these two young men decided to take the law into their own hands,' he said, 'and that together they killed Evan Morgan, but in such a way as though it looked that a third person did it. I suggest that they intended to put the blame on Mervyn Morgan. They summoned him to the Manor House for seven o'clock, but themselves got there earlier. Bryn Davies was anxious to tell me that they got to the Manor House at seven o'clock. He told me that he knew it was seven o'clock because he had heard the Town Hall clock strike. But the Town Hall clock has not struck since the end of the war. That was his first mistake. The second was also directed to time. Bryn Davies and David Morris have told us they left the Bell just before seven, but the landlord says it was ten minutes to seven. But the clock in the pub said a few minutes before seven; it was ten minutes fast – most pub clocks are. It is only five minutes to the Manor House. The murder is effected, the lights turned out, the phone calls made and the phone wires cut – all just before Mervyn Morgan arrives. David Morris knocks out Bryn Davies and ties him up with a rope they had previously hidden in the Manor House.'

'Then he skilfully knocks himself out, I suppose?'

Cherrington paused. 'I very much wonder if he was ever knocked out,' he said. 'We have only his word for that.'

'Is ten minutes long enough to do what you say they did?' said Harris. 'It was risky. What if Mervyn Morgan had arrived earlier than he did?'

'As it was,' said Vaughan, 'if we accept Mervyn Morgan's story, he did arrive early and see them both in the Manor House drawing-room.'

'It is the telephones that confuse me still,' said Cherrington. 'I'm damned if I see how they fit in, to my story or any other.'

'I don't think the telephone calls really present any great difficulty,' said Harris. 'Perhaps you did not know that there is an extension upstairs in the Manor House.'

Cherrington pricked up his ears. 'But the lines were cut–' he began.

'The lines at the telephone itself downstairs were cut,' said Harris. 'The upstairs telephone is wired directly to the main telephone point under the stairs.'

'So that–'

'Exactly. So that although the telephone downstairs was cut, and David Morris and Bryn Davies were prevented from using it, the murderer could slip upstairs and make the two bogus telephone calls. Most ingenious.'

'Therefore the murderer must have had a really good knowledge of the way about the Manor House.'

'Well, he must have known there was a telephone in Evan Morgan's bedroom.'

'And that it was independently wired to the incoming phone box under the stairs.'

'Yes. You asked earlier, Professor Cherrington,' said Harris, 'whether there was a public phone box at the railway station, and we said not. There is, however, a call-box just outside the wall of the Manor House. That also could have been used for the bogus phone calls.'

'But is there no way of establishing whence the calls came?'

Harris shook his head. 'No,' he said. 'Llanddewi has a small automatic exchange. The number and duration of local calls are locally recorded, of course, but not the destination of them. It is like any automatic exchange. The only check would be on toll and trunk calls.'

'I see.' Cherrington hesitated. 'But according to my theory there is no need whatsoever to invoke this public call-box outside the Manor House wall. You tell me that when the phone wires were cut downstairs in the drawing-room at the Manor House it would still be possible to phone from upstairs. What more do you want? David Morris, after he has knocked out and tied up Bryn Davies, goes upstairs and telephones the bogus calls to the police and the doctor, then comes down and waits about a while before tottering off to the Police Station and telling his story of attack.'

'All very ingenious,' said the Chief Constable. 'But how could they reckon on Mervyn Morgan not coming into the house?'

'That is not a difficult one to answer,'

replied Cherrington. 'If Mervyn Morgan had come in, he too would have been knocked on the head, and perhaps left in incriminating circumstances.'

Harris roused himself. 'You mean,' he said, 'they intended to knock out Mervyn Morgan and tie him up – that's what the rope was there for – and then leave themselves after telephoning. But Mervyn Morgan ran away, or, as far as they knew, never turned up, and so they had hastily to modify their plans.'

'A fine suspect Mervyn Morgan would have looked – tied up securely,' said Vaughan. 'What sort of murder would we have thought it was if we found the corpse slumped across the desk and the alleged murderer tied up securely alongside?' He sighed, and ran his hand through his hair. 'No,' he went on. 'The truth must out. Here we sit spinning words. We haven't really the faintest idea what happened. We have a few clues admittedly – like the discrepancies to which Sir Richard has drawn our attention. The timings may prove all important. Personally, I find the phone calls very difficult to fit in. But at the moment that's all we have, and from that we weave our theories.'

'What about the cigarette ash?' said Cherrington suddenly. 'The Abdulla 11 cigarette ash and the stub in the scullery. We've forgotten that.'

'No. We haven't forgotten it,' replied Harris.

'But we can make nothing of it. I have myself talked to Mrs Clotbridger, the woman who came in every day and cleaned the Manor House. She is certain that the ash and stub were not there when she left on Friday lunchtime, but apart from that we know nothing.

'On the other hand, we have now had the expert's report on the anonymous letters. They were all done on the same typewriter and on the school typewriter.'

'And that, I suppose, gives us no clue,' said Cherrington.

'I'm afraid not. At the school itself it was of course available to John Davies and to Miss Harper Williams, but then other people visit the school – Ben Anderson, for example, is attending an evening class there – and, anyway, I don't imagine it would be difficult to get in and use the typewriter some evening or during the week-end. It is not kept locked. It is a portable machine, and John Davies sometimes takes it home to do a job of work, so that just occasionally the typewriter is available in Lampeter House to all who live there. He has taken it home once in the last ten days, so that theoretically it would be very easily available to his wife and son. No. I'm afraid the typewriter is not going to give us much of a clue. As the Chief Constable says, we really haven't much to go on except the two odd things you have told us about, Professor Cherrington.'

'You mean the business about the time when Morris and Davies left the Bell and got to the Manor House.'

'Yes, that, and your seeing the Rector walking away from the village when he says he was in the church.'

Sir Richard Cherrington left the dispirited policemen and drove back to Tresaeth House through the rain. He put away his car and went straight into the drawing-room. As he entered the room he stopped abruptly, halted not so much by seeing his aunt talking earnestly to a short, dark young man whose face was vaguely familiar to him as by the fact that the room was filled with the unmistakable smell of expensive Turkish tobacco, and that the young man was quite patently smoking a Turkish cigarette. His sense of the theatrical and a lifetime of jokes about Livingstone and Sherlock Holmes was too much for Cherrington. 'Abdulla No. 11, my dear Watson, I believe,' he said.

CHAPTER 12

THE FEAR OF DEATH

I

The young man stared at Cherrington first with alarm; then his face relaxed into a smile. 'Quite right,' he said. 'Will you have one?'

'Thank you, no,' said Cherrington. 'I was only indulging in a pardonable vanity. Forgive me. It is like being able to fit a name to a face one has seen only once, and that long ago.' He looked keenly at the young man and then across at his aunt.

Miss Cherrington rose with some embarrassment. 'I wasn't expecting you back so soon,' she said. 'Richard, this is Rees Morgan – you know, Evan Morgan's son. My nephew Professor Cherrington.'

'How do you do.' Cherrington bowed. 'I thought your face was familiar, but it must be many years since I last saw you. May I please assure you of my sympathies on the sudden and most tragic death of your father?'

It was rather a challenge than a question

or a statement. Rees Morgan looked away, and Cherrington thought what a contrast he provided to his half-brother Mervyn. Rees was, he supposed, as good a representative of the Mediterranean race as one could expect to find in Wales after centuries of racial mixture. Short, dark, with a sallow complexion, a thin, almost effeminate face, dark eyes, a sharp nose, Rees Morgan could easily have passed for a taxi-driver on the Cannebière or a shepherd on the Meseta or a waiter in Bordeaux. He had a sensitive, nervous face. Cherrington studied it carefully before he spoke again.

'I expect you know,' said Cherrington, 'that I have been helping the police in the investigation of the – er – unusual circumstances of your father's death?'

No one spoke, and Cherrington went on. 'I had intended to call and see you in Barry,' he said. 'But now there is no need. Perhaps I could have a few words with you here?'

'Would you like me to leave, Richard?' Miss Cherrington rose reluctantly from her chair.

'Please don't go, Aunt Mary.' It was the young man who spoke.

'Aunt Mary?' Cherrington looked from one to the other.

'Rees always calls me that,' said Miss Cherrington hastily. 'I'm his godmother. I was a great friend of his poor mother's,' she said. 'And I've always been here when Rees was in any trouble.'

'And he is in trouble now?' said Cherrington.

'Of course,' his aunt said quickly. 'His father's death has inevitably brought trouble. The police, as you know, have been questioning Rees as they have questioned everyone else. Indeed, I begin to wonder why they haven't been here to question me.'

'They will, you know,' said Cherrington easily, 'if you continue to hide relevant facts from them.'

'Me? What do you mean? Richard, you must be jesting. I don't know anything about the murder. You must know that yourself. You were here yourself in this house when the murder was being committed in the Manor House.'

'Yes,' said Cherrington. 'We were all three here, were we not?'

'I don't know what you mean,' she said.

'Just this.' Cherrington spoke crisply. 'When I arrived here last Friday evening, I came into a room in which there had been very recently someone smoking Turkish cigarettes. There were stubs in the ashtray. You do not smoke, my dear Aunt Mary, nor do you allow the refuse of smoking to accumulate in your rooms.'

'Many people smoke Turkish cigarettes,' said Miss Cherrington with an impatient gesture of her hand, but the impatience was with herself.

'That is not so,' said Cherrington. 'Come, Aunt Mary. I won't bother you any more.' He turned to Rees Morgan. 'Why don't you tell the truth to the police?' he said sternly. 'It is a most dangerous mistake to lie to them.'

The young man buried his head in his hands. Cherrington went on: 'Don't you realize,' he said, 'that sooner or later they will find out that you are lying? Someone will have seen you on a bus or train from Barry to Llanddewi and back again. By the way, you did travel both ways by train, I suppose?'

Rees Morgan looked up. 'It's no use,' he said, turning to Miss Cherrington. 'He knows so much he might as well know all. You were quite right. I was in Llanddewi on Friday evening, and I did lie to the police. Very stupidly, I grant you, but I was terrified by Inspector Harris. He seemed to bring out the very worst in me. Yes; and I went both ways by train. I caught the train that gets to Llanddewi at six o'clock – you know, the one that brings the evening papers and the boys back from school.'

'I see. But why did you come to Llanddewi on Friday evening?'

'I had received an anonymous letter summoning me to see my father.'

Cherrington looked sharply at the boy.

'You did? Have you destroyed the letter?'

'No. I kept it. I have it with me.' Rees Morgan took out his wallet and handed to Cherrington a letter similar in every way to that which he had already seen at the Police Station. Sir Richard handed it back. 'Take care of it,' he said. 'Although I suppose it has no fingerprints except your own. Now tell us what you did from six o'clock onwards.'

'I walked up here to see Aunt Mary – to see Miss Cherrington. I showed her the letter and asked for her advice.'

Miss Cherrington interrupted. 'I told him not to go,' she said. 'I thought it was all a stupid hoax, and I told Rees not to have anything to do with it.'

'And you took her advice?' said Cherrington.

'Yes.' Rees Morgan looked steadily at Cherrington. 'Yes; I did,' he said. 'I left here at about six-forty-five or so, and walked back to Llanddewi. I went straight to the railway station and caught the seven-three train to Barry.'

'And as soon as you got to Barry, you went into the Barry Arms, and were having a drink there at seven-thirty.'

'That is so.'

'I see. Now there is just one little detail I want to ask you about again. Your exact time of departure from this house on Friday evening.'

'It takes about twenty minutes to walk from here to Llanddewi Station – perhaps less if you walk quickly. I got to the station just in time to catch the train. So I must have left at quarter to seven or perhaps a minute or two before.'

'And you got here about twenty past six?'

'Yes.'

'Can you confirm these facts, Aunt Mary?' asked Cherrington. 'I don't mean, can you here and now confirm them to me, but will you be able to confirm them to the police and in a court of justice?'

Was there a moment's hesitation in her reply? 'Yes,' she said. 'I naturally didn't time Rees's visit, but my impression was that he was here about a quarter of an hour or twenty minutes.'

'Well,' said Cherrington briskly, 'all this has now to be told to the police.'

'Must it?' It was Miss Cherrington who spoke.

'Of course it must, and without delay. I'm going to drive Rees Morgan in my car straight away down to the Police Station.'

And it was in the car on the way down to the village that Cherrington said, 'Don't be afraid of Inspector Harris, my boy. He is only doing his duty. And it is his duty to discover, if he can, who murdered your father. Help him.' Cherrington paused, and then added: 'And don't hide anything from him.'

231

'Very well. I won't.' The young man seemed more at ease away from Miss Cherrington, and he had answered Sir Richard's appeal readily.

'For example,' said Sir Richard, his gaze fixed on the road ahead, 'you should not, I think, hide from the Inspector the fact that you *did* visit the Manor House on Friday night.'

Cherrington stole a glance at Rees Morgan. The boy's pallor and nervousness had returned at once. 'So you know that, too?' he said in a whisper.

'I do,' said Cherrington. 'And so does Inspector Harris. You hid yourself in the scullery of the Manor House long enough to smoke part of one of your tell-tale cigarettes. Really,' he went on crossly, 'if you were going to get mixed up in crime in this way I do think you should take to smoking a less distinctive type of cigarette. It makes everything almost too easy.'

Rees Morgan said nothing. He sat staring out of the car as the fields gave way to the village and the cottages of Llanddewi closed in on them. They began slowly to thread their way through the narrow streets towards the Police Station. Suddenly he said: 'I didn't do it, you know. I didn't kill my father. I hated him. There was no love lost between us, but I didn't murder him. You do believe that, don't you?' he said earnestly, clutching Cherrington's arm.

Sir Richard shook his head sadly. 'The trouble about you, my boy,' he said, 'is that I don't know what to believe. You tell so many stories.'

II

Cherrington deliberately absented himself from Inspector Harris's examination of Rees Morgan, and the Chief Constable was not there to press him to be present. Instead, he spent the time walking in the fields across the road from the Police Station, and sitting kicking his heels in the charge-room. It was nearly lunch-time when Harris came out and spoke to him.

'I want your help with this young chap, Rees Morgan,' he said.

Cherrington pointed with his finger towards the inner room.

'You have still got him in there?' he asked.

'No. He's off to the cells to cool his heels.'

'You have arrested him for the murder?'

'Oh, no. Perhaps we should have done. Perhaps we will. So far we are just detaining him pending further questioning.'

'Tell me his story.'

They went into the inner room and the Inspector sat on a stool behind a high desk. 'These are only my notes,' he said. 'We shall get him to make a statement later when we get a shorthand writer over. But this is what I have from him to date. The current version, as you might say. He admits the cinema alibi was trumped up. As a matter of fact, we have now a report that he was seen arriving on the six o'clock train at Llanddewi. We would have got round to him even if you hadn't rumbled him first, if you take my meaning. He says he walked to your aunt's house to show her the anonymous letter he had received, and to consult her as to what to do. He says that he stayed there about a quarter of an hour and then walked down to the Manor House, getting there, he says, just about ten minutes to seven.'

'Ten to seven? Has he any proof of that?'

'None at all, as far as I can make out. But I must say that his story hangs together all right. He says that the place was in darkness, but the front door open. He went in, nervously. I can believe that. He says he thought the whole thing was a hoax, just as Miss Cherrington had told him it would be; but he was determined to find out for himself. There was no light at all in the living-room. He struck a match.'

'Yes,' said Cherrington, eagerly.

'And by the light of the match he saw his father's body slumped across the desk – just as we found it later.'

'Ah. Now we are getting somewhere. This

was at ten minutes to seven.'

'That is what he says.'

'Before Morris and Davies had got there? Indeed, just as they were leaving the Bell.'

'Exactly.'

'But we have only his word for this?'

'True. But, as I say, it all hangs together. He says that he had only been in the house a moment. He was standing there in the living-room, shocked, when he heard the gate into the street bang, and voices and footsteps. In a panic, he says, and I can well believe it, he retreated into the scullery.'

'Where, to calm his nerves, he lit a cigarette. The clue of the Turkish cigarette ash. I know. Go on.'

'He says he waited in the scullery, frightened out of his wits. That he then heard voices and footsteps in the drawing-room. Not quite knowing what he was doing, he fled out through the door from the scullery into the hall and out of the house. His only idea was to get away from what he had seen. He made off as fast as he could to the railway station, and just caught the three minutes past seven train.' Harris stopped speaking. 'Well, there it is,' he said. 'That is his story. Now, what do you make of it?'

'I don't know. I must have time to think,' said Cherrington. 'I suppose he did catch the seven-three train.'

'No doubt about it. He was seen in the

235

Barry Arms at seven-thirty and, as I said this morning, nothing else except an aircraft would have got him there in time.'

'We are getting somewhere, although I can't see where at the moment.' Cherrington's tone was excited. 'Evan Morgan was dead at ten minutes to seven, and Morris, Davies, and Mervyn Morgan had not yet arrived at the Manor House. Do you see what I mean?'

'I don't,' said Harris stubbornly. 'I must confess that I don't. I still think that Rees Morgan is lying. All this business about being frightened, waiting in the scullery, and escaping through the front hall–'

'Well?'

'I've been trying to work out the times. Why didn't Rees Morgan bump into Bryn Davies in the hall? Why didn't he leave by the back door?'

'Why, indeed? And we know that he didn't leave by the back door. You remember there were no footprints leading away from or to the back door. No; I think that on this occasion Rees Morgan is telling the truth. But come. We have waited too long for a pint of beer.'

III

When Cherrington returned to Tresaeth

House after lunch he found his aunt standing looking out through the French windows of the drawing-room. She turned as he came in, gave a forced smile, and then went back to the contemplation of her garden. Sir Richard stood with his back to the fireplace.

'Well?' he said.

'Well, what, my dear Richard?' Miss Cherrington temporized.

'Why did you conceal from me the fact that Rees Morgan was here last Friday evening?'

She turned round from the window and faced him. 'You were always hasty, my dear boy. Please remember I asked you down to interest you in the problem of the anonymous letters. That, and because I wanted to see you again and have some company for a while. I do get lonely, you know. But by the time you got here the problem of the anonymous letters was already solved – there was no longer a mystery, a poison-pen mystery for you. I never asked you to solve the problem of Evan Morgan's murder. How could I? I invited you here before it happened. I don't know that I want the problem of Evan Morgan's murder solved,' she went on. 'I don't expect you to agree with me, Richard, but that is just how I feel. He was a bad man, a thoroughly bad man. He had done incalculable harm here in this village and neighbourhood, and was going to do much more by marrying Janet Anderson. Yet all his wickedness was outside the punishment of the law. I'm glad that Evan Morgan didn't get away with it, and I shall not raise a finger to help find the person who killed him.'

'Well, I'm damned. Now at least we know where we stand,' said Sir Richard. 'But, granted all that, perhaps, you very immoral old aunt – and I don't conceal from you the fact that I am shocked, profoundly shocked – you will raise a finger to save a man under suspicion of being a murderer.'

'You mean Rees is really suspected of murder?'

'I do. And that is where you cannot refuse to help. Can you, now he is not here to listen to what we are saying, can you think of anything that fixes the time he arrived and left?'

'I think I can. He did not arrive until after six-fifteen. Of that I am sure. I was listening to the six o'clock news bulletin, and when it got to the sports news at six-fifteen I switched it off. You know that I cannot bear to hear the sports news – the racehorses have such silly names – so I switched off and went straight to the telephone to speak to Mrs John Davies. I spoke to her for three or four minutes, and it was when I heard the front door bell that I put down the receiver.'

'That seems very accurate and satisfactory. Rees would have arrived here then somewhere between six-eighteen and six-twenty?'

'That is so.'

'And his departure?'

'That is a little less easy to fix. I remember that I wanted to listen to a concert of madrigals on the Third Programme – the Lady Somerset Singers, you know; it was due to begin at six-forty, but I wanted to telephone Mrs Anderson at the Post Office. I rang her up, but couldn't get any reply. I thought there was something wrong with the telephone, so I waited a minute or so and rang again. Still no answer, so I went and switched the wireless on. They were in the middle of the first madrigal. I can remember exactly what it was. You know that well-known thing:

How is my pretty fleeting tweeting?
Chuck, chuck, jug, jug,
Jabberwocky, Jollyboo

or something like that. Have I got it right?'

Sir Richard looked at his aunt, puzzled. 'You are making fun of me,' he said.

'My dear boy, far from it. You asked for times and I am telling you how it all is. This programme of madrigals began at six-forty, so that, with my telephone calls – my abortive telephone calls, I should say – Rees must have left here between six-thirty-five and six-forty. Of course,' she added slyly, 'the Third Programme is rather consciously naughty about keeping time, but I hardly think the programme would have got late so early in the evening, if I make myself clear.'

'You do. Yes; you do. You tell me that Rees Morgan was here from six-twenty to six-thirty-five. There was plenty of time for him to murder his father before six-twenty, or after six-thirty-five, if he hurried on the road.'

'There you make a mistake,' said Miss Cherrington quietly. 'I told you before. I know who murdered Evan Morgan.'

'You do? Splendid. Is this to be a confession?'

But his aunt was in no mood for jest. 'You and your police friends make a great mistake,' she said, 'in looking for motive and means and the rest of it. What one must concentrate on is the fear of death or the absence of that fear. You see what deters most people from committing murder is not regret at terminating someone's life nor aesthetic distaste at the shedding of blood. No; it is the fear of being convicted of murder and hanged by the neck until they die. But have you ever thought, Richard, that the fear of death doesn't operate among one group of people – those who know they are going to die soon, anyway?'

'There are such people in Llanddewi?' asked Cherrington.

'Yes; there are. Mrs John Davies is dying of an incurable cancer; not many people know

240

this fact. And Mrs Ben Anderson has such a weak heart that she may drop dead at any moment.'

IV

When lunch was over, Cherrington walked out into the hall. There he found a note waiting for him. It lay on the hall table; he picked it up and turned it over aimlessly. It was in a hand which he did not recognize. Slowly he opened it and read the message. It was from Ellen Harper Williams, and it begged him to call and see her as soon as possible. 'I shall be in all the afternoon,' the note concluded, 'waiting to see you. Please come. It is most important.' Her handwriting was large and florid.

Sir Richard walked straight across to where Miss Williams lived in the now disused flat over the garage which had once been occupied by a chauffeur. He climbed rickety wooden stairs and knocked at the door. A voice bade him enter, and he did so, pausing a moment on the threshold. He had never visited the room in the old days when his aunt's chauffeur lived there. It was a pleasant room, long and narrow, with casement windows the whole length of the end wall looking out to the sea. Miss Harper Williams was sitting on the window seat at the end of the room. She turned as Cherrington opened the door and then quickly turned back again and stared out through the windows. Her movement was not quick enough to prevent Cherrington catching a glimpse of red eyes and a tear-stained face.

'What's the matter?' said Sir Richard, crossing the room. Miss Harper Williams's shoulders shook. She buried her face in her handkerchief and burst into sobs. Cherrington waited a moment and then he said, his voice more gentle than before, 'Shall I go away? I only came, you know, because you sent for me.'

The woman dabbed at her eyes and looked at him. 'No; don't go,' she said. 'And don't pay any attention to me. It's just that I'm – I'm afraid.'

'Afraid?' Cherrington's voice took on a firmer shade. 'Afraid of what? Afraid that the police will find out that you have been the author of all these anonymous letters? Afraid that you are going to be hounded away from Llanddewi, branded as a poison-pen woman for life? Is that it? Bah! You should have thought of that when you started writing them. Afraid, indeed.'

She looked up quickly. 'It's not true,' she said. 'They can't prove it. Anyone can borrow a typewriter.'

'I will prove it to you,' went on Cherrington, his voice now stern. 'The proof is quite simple. My aunt wrote to me in Cambridge asking me down here to help her find out the poison-pen writer who was causing such distress in this village. She wrote and, as was her habit, put her letter in an envelope sealed with one of those emergency sticky label things. She left the letter on the hall table. You posted it. Isn't that so?' He paused, and when she made no reply, went on accusingly: 'Do you deny this?'

'I often posted her letters. I think I do remember posting one addressed to you.'

'Posting it, yes,' Cherrington snorted. 'But what did you do with it before posting? I suggest you steamed it open and read the contents.'

'It is not true.'

'It is true. You know yourself it is true. Because three days later you asked my aunt when I was arriving. How did you know I was coming to Llanddewi?' He paused, and then went on with cruel emphasis: 'Is it that which is making you afraid? The fact that I know these things? Or another reason? Is it because you are afraid the police know you are lying to them about last Friday night?' She made to say something, but he silenced her with an impatient, upraised hand. 'You told my friend Inspector Harris,' he said, 'that you left here at six-forty-five and walked down to the Welcome Home dance. I suppose you went by the road; it was dark;

you were in your party dress and the cliff path to the village is dangerous. But I was driving my car along that road from Llanddewi to Tresaeth House at that time. I didn't see you. Where were you? Is that why you are afraid? Because the police know you are lying.'

His words had an immediate effect. The tears dried quickly, and a trace of sullen obstinacy came into her demeanour.

'It is true that I told the police the wrong times,' she said. 'But you are quite wrong about the other thing. I didn't know about your coming from opening Miss Cherrington's letters – and I didn't open the letter. It is a vile thing to suggest.'

'Then how did you know?'

'Mrs Anderson at the Post Office told me.'

'What?' It was Cherrington's turn to be surprised. 'You really mean that?'

'Certainly. I am telling the truth.'

'Do you then suggest that Mrs Anderson at the Post Office opened my aunt's letter?'

'Yes. It would not be the first she has opened.'

'And that she sent my aunt an anonymous letter about it?'

'Yes. It would not be the first she has sent. I didn't know she had done this to your aunt.'

'But this is preposterous.'

'So are your accusations of me.'

'I have only instanced one example. There are many more. My aunt and I are sure that it is you who started these anonymous letters. I don't blame you for it. You have been through a lot in the war and since. But for God's sake, make these letters stop.'

She looked out through the window at the sea. 'I have stopped writing them long ago,' she said, and when he made to speak, she laid her hand on his arm and said: 'No; please hear me out. You've been beating me down for the last few minutes like some pompous, irate counsel for the prosecution. I'm sorry, but that's what it sounded like. Let me say my say. I admit – to you – that I did start writing anonymous letters. I don't know what came over me – it was just after my little house was bombed, all my few belongings gone. It was a pretty little house; the only real home I ever had. I don't know what made me start. But then I enjoyed it. Frankly I enjoyed it. I enjoyed sending the letters off and then seeing the victims and wondering what they were thinking.' She paused. 'And then the others started,' she added.

'The others?'

'Yes. Other people got the same idea. And I began getting anonymous letters myself. Frightful ones. And I began to be afraid.'

'Have you any idea who was writing these? I mean,' he went on, recollecting the high moral tone he had been taking, 'who was copying your wickedness?'

'Oh, yes. I do know. There were two main people who followed in what you would call my wicked footsteps. Mrs Anderson at the Post Office – and your aunt.'

'My aunt? You can't possibly be serious.'

'Preposterous, isn't it?' she sneered.

'I don't believe you.'

'You don't seem to believe much of what I say.'

'But it doesn't make sense. It was my aunt who summoned me down here for the express purpose of getting to the bottom of the Llanddewi poison-pen mystery.'

'Clever of her, wasn't it? But then your aunt is a very, very clever woman. Take her deafness, for example. It's selective deafness. She only hears what she wants to hear, and when people think she is deaf they say things which she picks up at once.'

'I say again, I just don't believe you. You are lying to me just as you lied to the police about your movements on Friday night.'

'But I have admitted I was lying about them, and I will gladly tell you the truth. I left here about six-thirty; that is why you didn't see me on the road. I walked along the road and then, by the lanes at the back of Llanddewi, to the Manor House.'

'How long did it take you to get there?'

'Between ten minutes and a quarter of an

hour. I walked fairly fast.'

'And you had not been to the Manor House earlier that evening?'

'No. I came home from school at four-thirty, had tea here and was here until about six-thirty, as I've said.'

'Well, go on. What happened when you got to the Manor House, which was presumably about a quarter to seven?'

'I suppose so. I opened the front gate; you know, the one that leads round to the back of the house and directly to the front door – not the little wicket gate opposite the Post Office. I went round that way because I didn't want to be seen.'

'Yes. And then?'

'Just as I had closed the gate behind me I saw a figure come out of the Manor House, which was all in darkness. I was hidden in the shadows of the trees by the gate. This figure came out of the house, crossed the lawn, and went out by the wicket gate opposite the Post Office.'

'You keep saying a figure. What sort of figure?'

'A woman.'

'A woman?' Cherrington stared at her tensely. 'This is most important, and this is no moment for further confusions. You say you saw a woman come out of the Manor House. Can you say who it was?'

'I'm not certain,' she said. 'It was getting

dark, the figure moved quickly, and I was hiding under the trees at the other end of the garden. But I think I know who it was.'

'Well?'

'It was either Mrs Anderson or her daughter Janet.'

Cherrington thought over this surprising piece of information for a moment; then he asked: 'Are you sure of this?'

'Yes; I'm sure it was one of them, from the way they walk. But I wouldn't be sure which one it was.'

'I see. Then what did you do?'

'I was suddenly frightened. I don't know why, nor of what: the house being all in the dark, the woman hurrying away so quickly and furtively. I don't know what I felt, but I didn't go any further.'

'You didn't go into the Manor House?'

'I swear I didn't. I crept out by the gate through which I had come in, and went round the back of the house, along the outside of the garden wall, so as not to meet anyone, and then I went off to the Welcome Home dance. I didn't meet anyone or see anyone on the way.'

'But there is still one thing I don't understand,' said Cherrington. 'I don't understand why you went to the Manor House at all that evening.'

'I thought you knew all that,' she said. 'I wanted to know what was afoot. Mervyn had shown me the anonymous letter he had received, and I was anxious to know what was supposed to be going to happen – if anything – at seven o'clock. I thought it was all a sort of practical joke. Naturally, I didn't tell Mervyn that I should be there. I went to watch.'

'And when you saw the house in darkness and this – er – shadowy figure go across the lawn, you abandoned your plan?'

Something of the doubt in Cherrington's tone conveyed itself to Miss Williams. 'I was afraid,' she said. 'I tell you, I was suddenly afraid. I think it was then I realized what the letters were about – I mean the letter to Mervyn. It's a plot, a plot to murder us – to murder Evan, and Mervyn, and myself – a clever plot which nobody will trace to the murderer or murderers. And you see they have succeeded in their first objective – Evan. They would probably have succeeded in their second objective if Mervyn had only gone into the Manor House on Friday night as was intended. Had he gone in, I am sure now that he too would have been killed. They'll succeed next time.' Her voice was shrill and hysterical. 'And then it will be me. They are out to murder me. Now do you see why I'm afraid, why I sent for you? You must protect me. You will protect me. It is no use going to the police. They won't believe me – won't believe a word I say. But you are different.' She laid her hand on Sir Richard's arm. 'You've got to protect me,' she said. 'You can't sit back and see me murdered, can you?'

Cherrington had been looking out through the windows at the sea during this hysterical outburst. When it was over he turned round and faced her squarely, preparing to comfort her hysteria with reasonable words. But as he stared into her eyes the easy words he had prepared froze on his lips. For in those eyes he saw something naked and horrifying which no hysteria could mask and no easy words assuage – the fear of death.

CHAPTER 13

SIR RICHARD MAKES A MISTAKE

I

When Cherrington left Miss Harper Williams's flat it was with very mixed feelings. At first he had been most genuinely impressed by her story. Then he had begun to explain away her story to himself in terms of hysteria. As he got into his car outside Tresaeth House, he wondered whether it would be wiser to call at the Police Station and tell them all he had learnt since lunch, but he decided that it could all wait until the evening. It was unlikely that, even if Miss Harper Williams's fears were well grounded, she could come to any serious harm between that time and nightfall. She had promised Sir Richard that for the time being she would not go into the village. She had this afternoon off and would either remain in her room or do no more than go for a walk by the sea.

And yet, as he drove up the dark tree-shaded drive that led from Tresaeth House to the main road, Cherrington had misgivings. For one moment he thought he saw a man standing at the head of the drive – a dark shadow against the dappled shade of the trees. But it was only for a moment. As he peered forward he could see nothing, and when he got to the top of the drive there was no one there or, if there had been, he had vanished into the trees. Yet again, as Cherrington drove into Llanddewi, he nearly drove through the village and to the Police Station, but he pulled himself together, saying to himself that he was getting jumpy for no reason at all, and turned his car up the little High Street and drew up alongside the Post Office opposite the still locked gate of the Manor House.

Mrs Anderson was not on duty in the Post Office. He was shown by her daughter Janet through into the house. The older woman was in the kitchen washing up dishes. Sir Richard apologized for the time of his visit and insisted that he be allowed to help. Very reluctantly, Mrs Anderson gave him a cloth and allowed him to wipe the dishes.

'We are very late today,' she explained, 'because we were on duty late this morning.'

'Not at all. I'm very glad you are not upsetting yourself on my account. I shan't stop long.'

'Was it myself you wanted to see?' she asked. 'Or was it really my husband? Because he's gone for a walk. You're unlucky if you wanted him.'

'It was you I wanted to see, Mrs Anderson,' said Sir Richard. 'And I only want to ask you one question. It's about last Friday night.' Was there a sudden tension in the air? Outwardly, at any rate, Mrs Anderson seemed unmoved.

'I expect the police have bothered you already about this,' went on Cherrington, trying to sound as casual as possible. 'All I wondered was if you could bear to tell me again what you were doing between six and seven on Friday evening.'

'Why, of course.' Mrs Anderson went on washing the dishes. 'But I have already told the police all I know. I took over duty on the telephone exchange at a quarter past six, or just after. My daughter Janet had been on until then. It's the time we usually hand over. I listen to the six o'clock news, and then when the sports news comes on I go into the Post Office. I was there on duty until well after seven o'clock.'

'I see. And your daughter, and Mr Anderson?'

'You can ask them yourself, of course,' said Mrs Anderson warily. 'I wouldn't swear to their movements. I was busy all the time on the telephone exchange. I imagine Janet was busy in the house and was upstairs changing until after seven o'clock. She was going across to collect Evan Morgan about half past seven. Of course, as you know, when she did get there she found the place in charge of the police.'

'And your husband?' Cherrington persisted.

'Ben was listening to the news with me. Then he stayed on to hear the sports news. In our telephone exchange room I can just hear the wireless as a faint noise. I heard Ben turn the set off just after the sports news. Some sort of talk was coming on, I believe, and Ben could never listen to talks – neither can I for that matter. Don't know why they bother to have them on the wireless. It's not like music or a play. A talk is just distracting.'

'And then, you say, Mr Anderson went out?'

'That's right. I heard him bang the house

door and cross in front of the telephone exchange window. The exchange, you know, is alongside the house door, and looks across the road to the Manor House.'

'Why do you tell me that so pointedly?' said Cherrington.

'Because,' went on Mrs Anderson quickly, 'it's no good asking me, as the police did, whom I saw going in and out through the gate to the Manor House just before seven o'clock. It was dark, and I couldn't have recognized anybody.'

'There's one other point I would like to clear up,' said Sir Richard. 'You say you were busy in the telephone exchange from six-fifteen to seven. How busy does it really keep you?'

Was there again a wariness, an indefinable watchfulness creeping into Mrs Anderson's manner?

'It is an automatic exchange, of course,' she said, 'as you know. So that we have to deal mainly with trunk calls, inquiries, and telegrams.'

'And was there much business on Friday evening?'

Mrs Anderson stumbled and hesitated. 'I can't remember,' she said. 'Is it important?'

'It may be,' said Cherrington. 'It may be. You see, I must tell you, in confidence, of course, that one person who is suspected by the police says that he or she rang you up at

254

a certain time between six-fifteen and seven – rang you up twice – and couldn't get an answer.'

There was a crash as Mrs Anderson dropped to the floor the dish she had been holding. 'Oh dear,' she said. 'How clumsy I am! Don't trouble yourself,' as Cherrington began to pick up the pieces. 'Really, you shouldn't bother.'

'Not at all,' said Sir Richard. 'It is no trouble at all. And now I must be going.' He turned at the door. 'By the way, you didn't answer my question.'

'Did you ask one? I thought you just made a statement,' said Mrs Anderson, whose composure seemed to have returned. 'You said that somebody had telephoned the exchange and been unable to get hold of me. They must have been mistaken. Perhaps they dialled incorrectly, or maybe they are inventing this telephone call to try and prove an alibi,' she added.

II

Joseph Stanley Thomas looked up from the seed catalogues he was studying. 'Professor Cherrington, isn't it?' he said, getting up and shaking hands. 'I was wondering when you would get round to me.'

'And I'm not going to be here long,' said

Cherrington. 'Inspector Harris has shown me your statement, and I have corroborated it with your brother.'

'You have been busy.' The voice was scornful.

Cherrington ignored it. 'You got to the Bell soon after opening time,' he said.

'Correct,' said Thomas briefly.

'But not so soon after opening time that you couldn't have murdered Evan Morgan at six-six,' said Cherrington swiftly, but in a casual tone of voice.

'That is a strange allegation,' said Thomas. 'Evan Morgan was murdered at seven o'clock.'

'How do you know that, my friend?'

'How do I know? But really, this is absurd. It was in the papers. Everyone knows.' Joseph Thomas spluttered.

'And if I tell you that he was not murdered at seven o'clock, but much earlier,' Cherrington chanced, 'what now? There is no need any longer to bother about your alibi for seven o'clock precisely, is there?'

'My alibi for seven o'clock?'

Cherrington sighed. 'Come, come, Mr Thomas,' he said. 'I can think a little, you know, if not up to the high standards of cerebration set by fictional detectives. You were at the Bell from shortly after opening time. You could have killed Evan Morgan between six o'clock and when you went in to the pub. You did not kill him at seven o'clock because he was dead already. Why all this mystery about where you were at seven o'clock? Your brother says you left the bar for a few minutes, probably to go to the lavatory. You know that will not do; you know it yourself. It just will not do. You must think up something better. It is no defence to a charge of murder to say that you were in the lavatory.'

'I never said I was in the lavatory. That was my brother's kind alibi on my behalf. Unsolicited, too. Bless him.'

'So you did leave the pub?'

'I did. I walked up to the Post Office and called on Janet Anderson.'

'Ah. And at what time did this happen?'

'Somewhere about twenty to seven. I can't be certain of the time. I called on Janet because I knew that she and Evan Morgan were planning to announce their engagement at the Welcome Home dance. I made a last effort to try and persuade her to abandon the scheme. You see,' he went on shyly, 'I wanted to marry her myself.'

'I do see,' said Sir Richard. 'And she wouldn't listen to you?'

'She listened to me. In fact, we talked for quite a bit. I rather think she was beginning to have doubts about her engagement to Evan Morgan. I think she was having doubts ever since I told her I was divorcing my wife

257

and citing Evan Morgan as co-respondent.'

'She knew all that?'

'Yes. Yes; she did.' He went on: 'I suppose we were talking together for a quarter of an hour or so.'

'And then?'

'Then? Oh. Then I came back to the Bell, rather dispirited, and had some more to drink.'

'You met nobody on your way from the inn to the Post Office and back again?'

'Nobody.'

'And you did not go near the Manor House?'

'No nearer than the front door of the Post Office – or, rather, the side door of the Post Office, the main door of the Post Office house, across the road from the Manor House gate.'

'And if I told you you were seen going in through the gate of the Manor House?' It was a long chance, but Cherrington took it.

'It would be a lie. Who says so?'

'Think now,' Cherrington persisted. 'Who could have seen you without being seen himself or herself?'

'What do you mean?' He hesitated. 'Oh I see. You mean Mrs Anderson at the Post Office. But that's nonsense. It was dark when I called, and the exchange telephone room was lit up. I could see in, but she wouldn't have been able to see out. And, anyway, she wasn't there when I went to the Post Office.'

'Say that again,' said Sir Richard. 'And say it slowly.'

'Why? Is it very important? All I said was that if Mrs Anderson is now saying that she saw me go into the Manor House she is lying. She wasn't in the telephone exchange when I got to the Post Office. I tell you, if she says she saw me go in through the gate of the Manor House, she's mistaken or deliberately lying, and I can't imagine why she is doing that.'

'I never said,' replied Cherrington, 'that she did say so.'

III

It was a thoughtful man who drove his car from Sealands Farm to the only garage in Llanddewi. Sir Richard found the garage to be in the charge of Roger Thomas and explained what he wanted done – greasing and oiling, the brakes tested, and the road springs sprayed. The car was promised ready in two hours' time, and Cherrington walked off.

He did a great deal of walking in the next thirty minutes or so, and anyone who had followed him would have been very surprised at his manoeuvres. He walked first to the Manor House via the Bell and Evan

Morgan's grocery shop and noted the times: five minutes from the Bell to the Manor House, and just over a minute from the shop to the inn. Then he walked from the Manor House to the railway station at a reasonable pace, and made it four and quarter minutes, and then retraced his steps to the Manor House and walked quickly from the Manor House under the railway bridge and up to the Davieses' house. He arrived, out of breath, in just under nine minutes. He paused at the gate to recover, and then walked up the garden path. He had noted as he passed the garage that the car was out, and no one there.

John Davies was in his greenhouse, and Cherrington went straight there. The schoolmaster looked up from the plants he was repotting. 'Still sleuthing, Professor?' he asked, taking his pipe out of his mouth and pointing with it to an old, upturned box.

'That's it,' said Cherrington with forced amiability. He took the proffered seat; John Davies himself sat on top of a small, folding stepladder, and began cleaning his pipe with an old piece of wire.

'And I think I'm getting somewhere at last,' went on Cherrington. 'I may be wrong, but I believe and hope that I shall be able to give the police something definite quite soon.'

John Davies spoke very slowly. 'You can't expect me to be very excited,' he said. 'Evan Morgan was a bad man.'

'And murder is a bad thing.'

Davies looked away – out through the windows of his greenhouse and across the garden. But he said nothing. Then he turned back to Cherrington and asked: 'Why have you come here if you are in the last stages of your investigation? Do you suspect me or my son? Come on. You might as well tell me the truth.'

Cherrington laughed. 'A fine detective I should make,' he said, 'if I came and warned my suspects that they were in danger. I should put them on their guard and put my own life in danger. Of course I suspect you and your son; suspect everyone remotely connected with the case until I have proved that it is impossible they could have been murderers. But seriously,' he went on, 'my purpose in calling this afternoon is a simple one. I just want to check on some information regarding other suspects. I want to talk with your wife, if I may.'

'My wife? But what on earth has she got to do with it? You know that she is practically bedridden?'

'I do indeed. That is exactly why I want to see her. If people wanted to talk to Mrs Davies, they had to come here or use the telephone.'

John Davies frowned. 'But I still don't see–' he began.

'I'm not expecting you to see,' said Cherrington. 'And if you don't mind, I shan't give away the importance of this bit of information I want confirmed or denied by your wife. It is just that I am checking up on a phone call your wife made between six and six-thirty on Friday evening last.'

'I see. A call my wife made?'

'Yes. It is no use my asking you about it, because you were out of the house yourself, working in the garden.'

'Quite right. I was working in the garden and in here from teatime onwards. I didn't go into the house until after half past six. But my son Bryn will be able to tell you about the phone call as well. He was in the house at that time. He went in just in time to turn on the six o'clock news and came out changed half an hour later. You can ask him. He's down in the garage tinkering with the car.'

'Not at the moment,' said Cherrington. 'The garage is empty.'

'Very well. Let's go into the house, then.' John Davies led the way in through the back door and the kitchen into the hall of the house. He changed from his gardening boots into slippers and shouted up from the well of the hall: 'Mother, I'm bringing a visitor to see you. Sir Richard Cherrington. Is that all right?'

A voice came back saying it was all right, and they went upstairs. Mrs Davies was reclining on a divan along the window of a small bedroom, so that where she lay she could look out across the garden and the road, and across the road and the fields opposite to the Bristol Channel in the distance. John Davies introduced Cherrington and left them together. Sir Richard sat in a chair drawn up beside the divan. Mrs Davies's face was a deathly white, her features drawn, and her eyes had the glazed look of someone who was being drugged.

'I hope you are not in great pain,' said Cherrington softly.

She smiled wanly. 'Only now and then,' she said. 'Dr Wynne Roberts is very good to me.' She waved her hand at the bottles of pills at her bedside. 'I always have a remedy ready, you know,' she said.

Cherrington nodded. 'It is very kind of you to see me,' he said. 'And I won't distress you, I hope. My business will not take more than a few minutes. You know, I expect, that I am giving some unofficial help to the police in their investigation into Evan Morgan's murder.' Mrs Davies said nothing, and he went on: 'One of the minor clues I have got on to is a matter of timing, and this is where you can help me. It is bound up with a telephone call which you made to my aunt. It would help if you went through the events of Friday evening, so that we can fix this phone call.'

'By all means. When shall I begin?'

'At six o'clock, please.'

'Very well, then. At six or just before I was sitting here. My son came in from the garage and switched on the wireless.'

'That is up here?' Cherrington looked round the room.

'No. The set is downstairs in the drawing-room. We have only one wireless, and this up here by my bedside is an extension of it. I can turn this speaker off if I want to, but I can't turn the set off and on. It's a little awkward, but there it is.

'I had the wireless on continuously until late in the evening. It kills time – a little,' she added pathetically.

'So that you can, perhaps, as I had hoped, fix your telephone call?'

'I can. Let me see, it was just after the news had finished – the national news and they were just beginning the regional news from Cardiff. So it was just on six-fifteen as near as I can make out.'

'Good. That is really just what I wanted to know.'

'We didn't talk together for long – three or four minutes at most. Then I put the receiver down and went on listening to the regional news. Then the sports news. It was just when the sports news was over that Bryn came in and kissed me goodnight and went out. He had been changing in his room.'

'Yes.' Cherrington hesitated. 'I really think

that is all I wanted to know. Oh, no. One other small point. Your telephone. It is up here by your bedside, as I see.'

'That, like the wireless, is an extension. The main phone is in the drawing-room downstairs, on my husband's desk. This extension was put up here when I became ill.' Her face twitched with a spasm of pain. Sir Richard got up quickly. 'I'm sorry,' he said. 'I'm tiring you. Stupid of me. Thank you for your help.' He bowed and walked quickly across the room. As he turned at the door he looked back. Mrs Davies was fumbling with her bottles. He shut the door quickly behind him and went out of the house. As he passed through the garden, he waved a hand at John Davies, who was back in the greenhouse. As he was outside the garage a car drew up and made to turn in. It was Bryn Davies. He waved to Cherrington.

'Walking, Professor?' he said gaily. 'And it's just beginning to rain. Let me drive you down to Tresaeth House.'

'That is really most kind of you,' said Cherrington with alacrity. 'But not to Tresaeth House. I'm only going down to the garage at Llanddewi, where they are fixing my car.'

'Nothing serious, I hope?'

'Oh, no. Just a routine check.' Cherrington got into the car, and Davies turned it and drove down the hill.

'Wait a minute,' said Cherrington as they

passed under the railway bridge and came up on the other side near the Manor House. 'Will you put me down here, please? By the telephone box. I want to telephone my aunt.'

'It's out of order, I'm afraid,' said the young man. 'Been out of order since last week. You can telephone from the garage.' They drove on to the garage. As Cherrington got out, he turned to Bryn Davies and said, 'Wait a minute. That phone box. You said it was out of order – had been out of order for some while. Since when?'

'I don't know since when. All I know is that it was out of order on Friday when I tried it.' He became conscious that Cherrington was staring at him very intently. 'What's the matter?' he asked.

'You may well ask,' said Cherrington cryptically.

IV

Cherrington's car was ready, and he was driving across the Market Place when a policeman on a motor-cycle drew across his bows and signalled him to stop. It was Police Constable Roderick. He touched his cap and said, 'I'm very glad I've found you, sir. You are to go to the Police Station at once. Chief Constable's orders.'

Cherrington turned his car in the Market Place and drove off to the Police Station. He found Colonel Vaughan alone in Sergeant Williams's office. Vaughan was sitting at the desk. He turned as Sir Richard came in.

'It's Miss Harper Williams,' he said. 'Her dead body has been found at the base of the high cliff between Tresaeth House and Llanddewi Beach.'

'She threw herself over?' Cherrington spoke quickly, his question coming almost automatically.

'Might have done. Or it might have been an accident. You know that cliff path is treacherous.' He paused. 'Or she might have been pushed over. The Inspector and Sergeant Williams are out there now with the photographers and the rest of them. And I'm waiting for a line to Scotland Yard. This settles it. We must have expert assistance. It's far too much for us.'

Cherrington buried his forehead in his hands. 'I'm a fool,' he said. 'A bloody, cocksure fool.'

'What's the matter?'

'The matter?' Sir Richard looked up. 'It is just that I am in part responsible for this woman's death.'

'You?'

'Yes. I think I could have prevented this second tragedy.'

The Chief Constable made as if to say

something. Then he stopped. The telephone bell began ringing.

'You knew it was going to happen?'

'No. No. Not exactly,' said Cherrington. 'But I made a mistake. I think I know now who murdered Evan Morgan. But it is too late.'

The telephone went on ringing insistently. 'You know?' The Chief Constable turned to the telephone and picked the receiver. 'Hullo,' he said, and a voice replied telling him he was through to Scotland Yard. Colonel Vaughan drew a pad of notes towards him, stuffed a finger into left ear, and began speaking.

CHAPTER 14

INSPECTOR COLWALL INVESTIGATES

Richard Cherrington was sitting in a deck-chair on the lawn in front of Tresaeth House when his aunt came out and announced that Detective Inspector Colwall of Scotland Yard had called to see him. Cherrington rose to greet a tall, well-built man of, he supposed, forty-five, whose chubby face belied the age he must be, to judge from his rank and manner.

'Please don't move,' said Colwall after they had shaken hands. He spoke easily, agreeably. 'I'll sit here if I may.' He indicated a rustic-work chair.

'I want,' he went on, 'to talk to you about the death of Miss Williams. I've gone over the evidence fairly carefully, such as it is, and I've been over the ground. There's nothing to say that she slipped, or, for that matter, that she didn't slip. All we know is that her body was found on the beach by this man Anderson from the Post Office at five-thirty, and that, according to the doctors, she had been dead about three quarters of an hour to an hour and half, and that her death was due to a fall from the cliff. Her head was battered in by the rocks on which she fell. I repeat: she may have fallen over, she may have thrown herself over the cliff or, as the Chief Constable seems to think, she may have been pushed over.'

'It would be easy to do.'

'It would. The cliff path is very narrow and there is a thick thorn hedge along one part of it. It would have been easy to lie in wait.'

Cherrington snorted crossly. 'I told her not to go into Llanddewi until I had spoken to the police. I told her not to set foot outside Tresaeth House or its immediate vicinity. I thought the cliff paths close to the House would be safe.'

'Perhaps you would tell me what exactly passed at your talk yesterday with Miss Harper Williams – in your own words. I have read the statement you made yesterday at the Police Station. Begin at the beginning. Tell me why you went to see her.'

The Detective Inspector listened carefully as Cherrington went over his interview with Ellen Williams. Cherrington concealed nothing, not even his half-formed suspicions that he had seen a man lurking in the drive of Tresaeth House as he drove away.

When he had finished, Colwall said: 'So you formed the opinion that she genuinely believed somebody – one or more people – was planning to kill Evan Morgan; herself, and Mervyn Morgan?'

'I did,' said Cherrington. 'And I must confess that I gathered she thought it was the people at the Post Office.' It was the first time he had put her suspicions into his own words.

'Mr and Mrs Anderson?'

'Yes.'

Colwall leaned forward and said, with a trace of boyish eagerness: 'Would you mind, Sir Richard, if I ran through the suspects with you? It will help me to get the case clear in my head, and I shall have the benefit of your comments and counsel.'

Cherrington nodded, welcoming the academic politeness of his approach. Colwall took out a file from his despatch-case and snapped it open. 'I'm confining myself to the known murder, of course,' he said. 'The murder of Evan Morgan. After all, we don't know what was the real cause of Ellen Williams's death.' He tapped his file. 'I've made a list here,' he said. 'Just before lunch this morning. Shall I read it to you with my notes?' The question was a rhetorical one, and he went on: '*First*, Mervyn Morgan. Stands to gain a great deal by his father's death; to lose a lot if his father lived another day. That's enough motive for you. Opportunity: Could have done it between six-ten, when the girls left his shop, and six-thirty, when he was seen in the Bell. Could have dealt with David Morris and Bryn Davies and then telephoned upstairs from the Manor House to distract the police and doctor.

'*Second*, Miss Harper Williams. I must modify my notes, by the way, following what you have told me. I have down the same motive as Mervyn Morgan, but under "Opportunity" I merely have: "No alibi". Says she was alone in her flat from four-thirty to six-forty-five. Now I have to put down that she was in the grounds of the Manor House at six-forty or thereabouts.

'*Three*, Rees Morgan. Motive same as for one and two. Opportunity: By his own admission was at the Manor House – and hid in the scullery. Could have murdered his

271

father and dealt with Bryn Davies and David Morris. Could have telephoned from the phone box just outside the Manor House and caught the seven-three train. He would have had to be pretty smart. The timing is almost too close to be credible, but I'm leaving him for the moment.

'*Four,* David Morris. Motive rather thin. An attempt to revenge himself on the man who, so it appears, virtually killed his fiancée, Daphne Davies. Opportunity: Could have done it between six-fifteen, when he left the Rectory, and six-forty when he appeared in the Bell. Goes back to the Manor House with Bryn Davies – knocks him out and ties him up. Fakes the telephone calls and then, after a suitable delay, totters into the Police Station saying he had himself been knocked out.

'*Five,* the Reverend Hugh Morris, his father. Motive: Even thinner than his son, and, of course, his cloth is all against him being seriously considered. But he could have done it. Says he left the Rectory at six-fifteen, and was praying and working in his church until he went to the Welcome Home party. It remains true that he had no alibi from six-fifteen to seven, and that he was seen by you walking towards the church at a quarter to seven from the village. Is that right?'

'Quite correct,' said Cherrington. 'And

you are bearing in mind the possibility of a conspiracy between your suspects four and five.'

'Between father and son? H'm. Hadn't thought of that one, but, of course, it is possible. Improbable, but possible.' Colwall made a note on his file. 'Of course, you realize,' he said, 'I am doing all this entirely as a theoretical exercise from the notes and reports I've been given. I haven't yet seen any of the people.'

'Never mind,' said Cherrington with amiable patronage. 'You are doing very well. Very well indeed. Go on.'

'Let me see, how far had we got. Oh, yes. *Six*, Mr Benjamin Anderson, the Postmaster. Motive: To prevent Evan Morgan marrying his daughter. Opportunity: Left the Post Office soon after six-twenty and went to the Welcome Home party. His time of arrival there cannot be fixed – quite naturally. But it remains possible that he could have murdered Evan Morgan soon after six-twenty, gone to the party, and escaped later for long enough to deal with Bryn Davies and David Morris and make the phone calls – and get back to the dance. His absence might just not have been noticed.'

Colwall hesitated. 'I've got down as *Seven*,' he said, 'Mrs Anderson. But she is not a very strong candidate. Motive as for husband. Opportunity: I suppose she had opportunity.

273

She says she was on duty at the telephone exchange from six-fifteen onwards. But she could, I suppose, have left the exchange.'

'She did leave the exchange.'

'Oh?'

Sir Richard told Colwall what he had learnt from his aunt and from Joseph Stanley Thomas.

'That's interesting. That's very interesting,' said Colwall. 'She definitely moves up in the list of suspects. And yet, you know, it doesn't sound a woman's job to me: I mean, particularly all that went on at seven o clock – dealing with the young men and the phone calls.'

'Number *Eight*,' he went on, 'Joseph Stanley Thomas of Sealands Farm. Don't think much of him as a suspect. Motive: Wanted to prevent Evan Morgan marrying Janet Anderson, so that he could marry her himself. Opportunity: He was in the Bell from six-fifteen onwards, but was missing for a short while, according to his brother, the landlord; and now, according to your information, he was, on his own admission, missing for a long enough time to pay a visit to the Post Office and speak to Janet Anderson and therefore perhaps long enough to cross the road and murder Evan Morgan. Just the man to deal with the two young chaps, I imagine, and he was away from the pub until seven o'clock or thereabouts.'

He paused. 'Well, there's eight for us, anyway. And now we come to the Davieses, father and son.'

'Not mother?' interjected Cherrington.

Colwall looked up from his notes. 'I have it down here that she is bedridden,' he said. 'Isn't that so?'

'It is apparently so.'

'I'll add her to my list if you think I should.'

'Not really. I think she can really be left out.' Cherrington hesitated. 'Or do I?'

'Well, then, back to husband and son. *Nine*, Bryn Davies. Motive: To avenge the death of his sister. Opportunity: that is the snag. I don't see how he had the opportunity. He left the house at six-thirty or thereabouts and went to the Bell. Went with David Morris to the Manor House, and there they found Evan Morgan murdered. I'm not sure I shouldn't rule him out of the list of suspects – or at least put him in the second team.'

'You have a second team?'

'Certainly. But I'll leave him in the first team for the moment. After all, there might be a conspiracy between himself and David Morris or himself and his father. His father is a more definite suspect, so I have down as *Ten*, Mr John Davies, schoolmaster. Motive: Same as the son. Opportunity: Quite considerable. For example, he is supposed to be working in the garden and greenhouse from six to six-thirty. That just gives him time to get down to the Manor House, murder Evan Morgan, and get back. Then, he has no alibi for seven o'clock. Yes: I think John Davies is rather high up on the list of suspects, don't you?'

Cherrington shook his head. 'I'm only a listener at this session,' he said, 'I'm waiting to hear your second team.'

Inspector Colwall frowned. 'It is very much a reserve list,' he said.

'I have put Mrs Davies down at your suggestion. Then there is Janet Anderson herself. It's just possible, isn't it, though not probable?'

'Unless the evidence of Joseph Stanley Thomas clears her?'

'Yes. There is that.'

Cherrington looked keenly across at Colwall. 'And you have two more names on your list – myself and my aunt; isn't that so?' he said.

Colwall looked uneasily away, then turned back to Cherrington and smiled. 'I must consider all the possibilities, mustn't I?' he said.

'Quite right,' said Sir Richard, and laughed unamusedly. 'So these are our two teams of suspects. Team One: Mervyn Morgan, Miss Williams, Rees Morgan – the three beneficiaries – the Morrises (father and son), the Davieses (father and son); the Andersons

276

(husband and wife) and Joseph Stanley Thomas. Team Two: Mrs Davies, Janet Anderson, my aunt, and myself. A pretty wide choice, isn't it?'

'Too wide.'

'And yet,' said Cherrington, 'it is not as wide as you make out. I think I know where the choice really lies.'

'You do? I wish that I thought the same thing,' said Colwall ruefully. 'Of course,' he went on, 'if one assumes – and it is a rather big assumption – that Miss Williams was also murdered, then that narrows the field very considerably.'

'Exactly. That is what I was hoping you were going to tell me.'

'Inspector Harris and Sergeant Williams and their men have been pretty quick off the mark on this matter,' said Colwall. 'Miss Williams's body was, as I say, found at five-thirty. According to the doctors, this means she was killed somewhere around four-thirty – let us say somewhere between four and four-forty-five. Now, of course, our main suspects come down to nine at once. Miss Williams herself goes out.' He looked at his notes. 'And of the remaining nine, three have alibis: Rees Morgan was in his shop in Barry the whole time, the Reverend Hugh Morris was at a Diocesan meeting at Llandaff, and Mrs Anderson was serving in the Post Office. I think, therefore, we can now narrow our field of suspects to six; but all six are possibles. Mervyn Morgan was out on his country rounds – he could have killed Miss Harper Williams – John Davies was working in the garden the whole time, Joseph Thomas was working on his farm the whole time, Bryn Davies was tinkering with the car and admits taking it for a trial run along the road towards Tresaeth House – what more natural thing to do? – and Ben Anderson says he spent the afternoon wandering about the cliffs. Apparently he collects fossils in his spare time.'

'Yes. But this process does get us down to six people at last. And now?'

'And now the rigid, soul-destroying business of police questioning. Checking up on everybody's movements. Trying hard to find any little extra clue. Hoping someone will make a mistake or mention a new fact he had hitherto thought unimportant. Anything that pulls the six down to one or two at least.'

Cherrington said slowly: 'Always assuming that Miss Harper Williams was murdered.'

'Yes. Yes. I'm aware of that.' Inspector Colwall got up. 'And what puzzles me is this: How could her assailant – if she had one – be sure that she would be killed? The cliff is a high one, but she might only have broken an arm or a leg or suffered concussion. She might just not have been killed.'

'Exactly,' said Cherrington, getting himself with difficulty out of his deck-chair. 'That is just what makes me sure that Miss Williams was murdered – the fact that the assailant didn't care whether she was murdered or not. I know that sounds pretty odd – but I think all her attacker wanted to do was to push her off the cliff. To hurt her.'

Colwall stared at him. 'What a horrible thought,' he said.

Cherrington turned to the house. His aunt was at the French windows, obviously trying to attract his attention. 'Don't bother about me,' said Colwall. 'I shall just glide unobtrusively away.'

'No. Wait a minute,' said Sir Richard. 'My aunt may have something to say which concerns you.' He went into the house and was gone five minutes. Colwall had nearly decided that it was nothing to do with him, and that he should go away as he had suggested when Cherrington came out on to the lawn. His face was serious.

'It is something concerning you,' he said. 'Something very important indeed. It is Mr and Mrs Anderson from the Post Office. They have come up especially to see me and to seek my advice. They have more to tell than they have hitherto told the police.' He paused. 'I think I have persuaded them to allow you to be present when they tell me whatever it is they have to say. Would you remember one thing, Inspector, please? Don't ask them anything. Leave it all to me. Their official examination can take place later down in the Police Station.'

Colwall grinned his acquiescence, put his papers in his dispatch-case, and followed Sir Richard into the house. He found Miss Cherrington standing with her back to the fireplace and Mr and Mrs Anderson sitting unhappily on the sofa. Cherrington introduced him as Mr Colwall to the Andersons, and they smiled weakly and Miss Cherrington made to go.

'You won't want me here, I imagine,' she said.

'Please don't go,' said Mrs Anderson. 'Please don't go. You see, Miss Mary, you are the real reason why we are here.'

'Me?'

'Yes. I've been trying to persuade Ben to see the police again today, but he wouldn't. We're both frightened of them, to tell the truth. They twist round what you say and make it all sound worse. And we hadn't told them all we should have done, I'm afraid,' went on Mrs Anderson.

'Well anyhow, Mrs Anderson,' said Sir Richard, 'suppose you tell us in your own words now what you have on your mind. We won't interrupt you, I promise you.' And he looked sternly at Colwall and his aunt.

Mrs Anderson twisted her handkerchief in

her hands. 'Your friend was quite right,' she said to Cherrington. 'I was away from the telephone exchange on Friday night, but only for a few moments. I went over to the Manor House. Oh, no; not for what you think. I didn't stab Evan Morgan. I couldn't have done that. I went over because I was afraid – afraid for Ben, for my husband here.' She paused. Nobody moved in the room. Ben Anderson was looking at his boots.

'I told you yesterday,' said Mrs Anderson to Cherrington, 'how I went into the telephone exchange when the news came to an end, and the sports news began. That's true. And I said that I heard my husband switch off the wireless when the sports news was over, and bang the front door as he went out. That was true. What I didn't say was that I watched him go away from the house. I looked out through the window of the telephone exchange. It wasn't dark then. I saw him cross the road and go into the Manor House, and I was afraid. We'd been having talks about Evan Morgan; and we neither of us wanted Janet to marry him. Janet is a good girl,' she went on simply, 'a very good girl, and he's a bad man. I should say he *was* a bad man – a wicked man that never did anybody any good.'

Then Ben Anderson spoke, and it was the first time that Cherrington had heard his voice. It was a soft voice – soft and hesitant.

'Aye,' he said quietly. 'We had had discussions; that's quite right, and I'd spoken out of my turn a bit, I think. It is true that I had said I would do anything to stop Evan Morgan marrying my daughter. But what I meant was anything short of murder. I wouldn't have killed him – and what's more, I didn't kill him.'

His wife took up the story. 'So that when I saw Ben go into the Manor House, I was frightened,' she said. 'I knew that the engagement of Evan and Janet was going to be announced at the Welcome Home dance on Friday evening, and I thought perhaps Ben was going to argue with Evan. They are both hot-tempered men, though Ben doesn't look it, and I was afraid they might come to blows. I just didn't know what to do. I dithered about for a while, but there was no sign of Ben coming out from the Manor House, so I left the exchange and slipped across the road and through the wicket gate. I went up the path to the front door of the Manor House. I don't really know what I intended to do. Reason with them, perhaps. Then I noticed that the house was in darkness. It was all quiet and dark, and I turned and ran away quickly and came straight back to the Post Office. I was shaking all over.'

'Aye, lass,' said her husband. 'She was afraid, d'you see, because she thought maybe that I'd done something to Evan Morgan.

But I hadn't, you know. I changed my mind as soon as I went through the gate. I found the house in darkness, and so I walked out by the far gate and went away.'

'And that is all you both have to tell us?' Cherrington spoke deliberately.

'Er – yes.' There was the slightest hesitation in Ben Anderson's reply which Cherrington noticed.

'You can, I imagine, fix the times of your visits to the Manor House within some limits,' he said. 'You say, Mr Anderson that you went across after the news – say about six-twenty?'

'I'd say it were a little later. A few minutes after. Say six-twenty-five.'

'Do you agree, Mrs Anderson?'

'Yes, I do. That would be right. And I went over myself in about ten minutes from then.'

'Now, of course,' said Cherrington briskly, 'I have only one piece of advice to give you, and you won't like it. You must go straight down to the Police Station and tell Inspector Harris all you have told me. You have nothing to fear.'

'But we have,' said Mrs Anderson. 'Don't you see we have? It is only my husband's word against theirs. He could have killed Evan Morgan, do you see? I know they suspect him. He could have pushed Evan Williams over the cliff. If we go to the police there will only be one sure result. They'll arrest Ben. That's why we came to see you: to protect us from the police, to save Ben from being falsely arrested. He didn't do it. I know he didn't do it. You do believe that, don't you?'

'I should be more ready to believe it,' said Cherrington slowly and deliberately, 'if I didn't feel that your husband was still concealing something from us.'

Ben Anderson looked up at Cherrington and stared him straight in the face for the first time. 'You don't miss much, do you?' he said.

'Why did you change your mind about calling on Evan Morgan so abruptly?'

'The house was in darkness.'

'Yes?' There was a long pause. Cherrington could hear the ticking of the grandfather clock in the corner. 'Yes?' he said again, and his voice was gentle, almost wheedling. 'There was something else you wanted to tell us, Mr Anderson, wasn't there?' he said.

'Yes; there was,' said Anderson, and his voice was little more than a whisper. 'I saw a man come out of the Manor House and half-walk, half-run down the path and out by the other gate.'

'You recognized him?'

Ben Anderson looked at his boots again. 'Yes; I did,' he said reluctantly. 'Mind you, I might have been mistaken. And, anyway, it doesn't prove that he murdered Evan Morgan. He couldn't have done. He's the last person in Llanddewi – in the world – who could have done such a thing.'

'The last person in Llanddewi.' Cherrington caught at he words. 'You mean to tell us,' he said, 'that the man you saw come out of the Manor House at six-thirty or thereabouts was the Reverend Hugh Morris?'

Anderson stared at the Professor. 'Yes,' he said. 'That's right. But I'm damned if I know how you guessed.'

CHAPTER 15

REVELATIONS IN THE RECTORY

I

Cherrington had been sitting waiting in his car outside the Police Station for over an hour and a half when the Reverend Hugh Morris came out, 'Cheer up, Rector,' he said. 'It could be worse. At least they haven't detained you for further questioning.'

Morris didn't smile. 'No,' he said. 'Nor have they arrested me for murder – yet.'

'Jump in my car. I'm going to drive you straight back to your house.'

'You are very kind,' said the Rector as he

got in, and did not speak again till they reached his home.

'You must come in,' he said then. 'Come in and warm yourself by the fire.' He led the way into his study and stirred the logs in the fireplace. He straightened his back and looked round the room. 'Everything seems exactly the same,' he said. 'Exactly as I left them this morning.'

'But, my dear Rector,' said Cherrington, 'for Heaven's sake, you must pull yourself together. Why shouldn't everything be the same? The heavens have not fallen down because you have been interviewed again by the police.'

'They were quite kind,' said Morris. 'I will say that for them. They have their job to perform, but they were very kind, and all I had to do afterwards was wait while my answers were typed out. I signed their papers. They had got everything right.' He looked at Cherrington depressedly. 'I'll tell you exactly what happened, although frankly I do not properly understand your position in all these inquiries. My story is simple. I had an idea last Friday that I would go and talk to Evan Morgan. There had been a lot of talk recently about Daphne Davies' death. It had been said that she died through blood-poisoning brought on by an illegal operation to get rid of the child she was carrying. Evan Morgan's child, it was said.'

286

'I know,' said Cherrington. 'I have heard all the gossip. And Ellen Williams was supposed to have performed the operation.'

'That's it. Shocking, of course. Well, you know, my son David was very much in love with Daphne Davies. I didn't want him to be told the facts – or the rumours – about her death. But somehow he did learn of them. I was horrified. I was afraid that he might do something violent, so I went to see Evan Morgan and to warn him of the possible danger. I wanted to suggest to him that he saw my son and made a full explanation and apology.'

'And when did you get to the Manor House?'

'I suppose it was about twenty-five minutes past six,' he said. 'I was so busy with my thoughts. I was wondering how to broach this difficult subject with Evan Morgan. He wasn't an easy man, you know. I was wrapped up in myself, so that I didn't notice there were no lights on in the house until I was on the doorstep. I noticed the drawing-room door was ajar, and I knocked at it. It swung open under my knock and I saw–' He buried his face in his hands. 'Well, you know what I saw.'

'But I don't. Was Evan Morgan dead?'

The Rector nodded.

'I see,' said Cherrington. 'So Evan Morgan was dead at six-twenty-five, according to your story,' he added ungraciously.

The Rector looked up. 'I am telling the truth this time, anyway,' he said. 'I have nothing to lose. Evan Morgan was lying across his desk. In the firelight I could see the knife sticking out of his back.'

'Why didn't you telephone the police?'

'I was frightened,' said Morris. 'I was suddenly frightened. I turned tail like a coward, and fled as fast as I could. I don't know what I wanted to do, all I knew was that I wanted to get away from the Manor House, from the ghastly thing I had seen. I didn't know where I went or whom I saw. All I know is that in due course I found myself in my own churchyard; I went into the church and prayed.'

'And this is what you told the police?' asked Cherrington. 'All that you have just told me?'

'Yes. It's the truth – the whole truth. I kept nothing from them.'

'And when you saw the dead body of one of your parishioners lying there, murdered in his own house, you fled at once, believing that the police would suspect you. Why didn't you go to the police straight away? Why should you have been so afraid? What need was there to go to the church and pray?'

'I went to pray that God would grant me forgiveness.'

'Forgiveness for what? You hadn't done anything wrong? Or had you?'

Morris stood up and defied Sir Richard. 'I won't have you browbeating me in my own house,' he said. 'I knew that you were part of the tactics of the police. It's abominable. They examine you peacefully in the Police Station and then send a plain-clothes man to question you in your own house, to abuse your hospitality. I order you to leave my house at once.'

'Certainly,' said Cherrington. 'I am leaving. But do not imagine that I am deceived by your show of temper. There is only one good reason ever to lose one's temper, and that is when every other device is useless.'

'Get out of my house.'

'A final word, Mr Morris. Let me tell you why you were praying for forgiveness. Let me tell you why you fled from the Manor House when you saw Evan Morgan's dead body. I will use the words you have used yourself. You were afraid – afraid that your son David would do something violent. That is what you said. When you saw Evan Morgan's body, I think you knew at once that the violent thing you were fearing had happened. Is that not so?'

Hugh Morris's temper disappeared as quickly as it had been aroused. He collapsed into an armchair and buried his face in his hands. Cherrington turned away from him

289

and faced the door, and as he did so he heard a voice, cool and collected, say: 'My poor father was as mistaken as you are, Professor Cherrington.'

David Morris stood in the doorway, a different David Morris from the man who had confronted Cherrington on his previous visit to the Rectory. 'If you step this way,' he said with a trace of insolence in his voice, 'I will tell you why. What my father needs is some bromide and a sleep. I'll deal with you first.'

II

David Morris led the way out of his father's study across the hall and into a disused drawing-room. 'We won't be disturbed in here,' said the young man, and for a moment the thought flashed across Cherrington's mind: 'Am I closeted here with a murderer?'

'So you think I murdered Evan Morgan,' said David Morris. His tone was quiet and conversational.

Cherrington rallied to this frontal attack. 'I think your father thought you might have done so,' he said. 'And that is why he concealed from the police the fact that he visited the Manor House last Friday evening.'

'It's true then, what I heard you saying in the study? My father did actually visit the

Manor House on Friday evening.'

'He admits it, and he was seen there.'

'When?'

'Your father was seen in the grounds of the Manor House at six-twenty-five. Evan Morgan was alive at six-five. According to your father, he was dead at six-twenty-five.'

'Then there's no more mystery about the whole thing as far as I'm concerned.' The young man's face broke into a smile.

'I'm very glad to hear it,' said Cherrington. 'And so will the police be.'

'You are making fun of me. What I meant is that if Evan Morgan was murdered between six-five and six-twenty-five, it lets us all out.'

'Unless he was murdered at six-twenty-five by your father.'

'But that's preposterous. You can't be serious. My father wouldn't hurt a fly. He wouldn't hurt anyone in a moment of temper or excitement, leave alone plan an act of violence. You really must put that idea out of your head. You can suspect me – you obviously do – and the others. But my father – why you might as well suspect your aunt or – or Bryn Davies's mother.'

'But I do. I do. They are all on my list of possibles until they are proved to be innocent.'

'You do, eh?' said David Morris. 'Then I'll tell you a fact you haven't yet considered.

Last Friday night an attack was planned on Evan Morgan; it was a silly practical joke, really. Planned by three people who bore him a grudge – Joseph Stanley Thomas, Bryn Davies, and myself. It was Joseph Stanley Thomas's idea. He broached it at the party given by Mrs Davies ten days ago, and we all had a game of golf to discuss the details. It was not a plan to murder Evan Morgan. All we planned to do was gag him and bind him up, so that the announcement of the engagement should not be made during the Welcome Home party. We planned our scheme for seven o'clock last Friday night. We were all three to meet at the Manor House. We had sent Evan Morgan an anonymous letter saying that if he were in at that time he would hear something to his advantage. And to safeguard ourselves in case anything went wrong we sent anonymous letters to ourselves.'

'The ones I have seen?'

'Yes.'

'Who typed them?'

'I did. I went into the school one evening and typed out the notes to Evan Morgan, Bryn Davies, Joseph Thomas, and myself. An unnecessary dramatic touch, I suppose, but then the whole thing was rather an undergraduate prank. We had planned to tie handkerchiefs around our faces so that Evan Morgan wouldn't recognize us.'

'I see. And you are sure you only typed

four notes.'

'Yes.'

'You sent none to Rees Morgan or Mervyn Morgan?'

'Certainly not.' The answer seemed genuine and spontaneous. 'Why should I? They weren't in the scheme.'

'You did the letters. Whose idea was that?'

'I don't remember. We split the responsibility. Bryn Davies was to provide the rope – beforehand. We were to meet on the lawn of the Manor House at seven o'clock.'

'And that is what happened?'

'No. Bryn and I were there. Not Joseph Thomas. Bryn and I met, as you know, in the Bell and walked up together to the Manor House. We saw no sign of our third man.'

'And you hadn't seen him in the pub? He was there.'

'Well, if he was, he wasn't in the lounge bar with us. We waited for him at the Manor House and then, puzzled by there being no lights, we went in. You know the rest.'

'I know your account of the rest,' said Cherrington severely.

'What Bryn Davies and I have told you is the truth. The only thing we have kept from you until now is the story of our planned escapade.'

'Why? That's what I don't understand. Why? I can imagine you didn't want to be discredited by admitting the plan you had formed. But why not tell the police at the beginning? That is what puzzles me. And what also puzzles me is your change of attitude. When I first spoke to you, you were frightened. Now you have all the composure in the world. Why? Has it taken you all these days to think up this story?'

'Wait a minute. Hear me out. I knew the moment I recovered from the blow on my head what had happened. Someone who knew of our original plan for a practical joke had improved on it. And I was afraid – afraid that it had been so improved that the murder could be laid at our door.'

'I begin to understand, my boy. You were afraid that your friend Bryn Davies had improved on it? Isn't that so? It could only be him or Joseph Thomas. You were afraid not only lest you should be suspected, but that Bryn would be suspected, and, what's more, you suspected him yourself. You were half-afraid you would be used to prove his innocence – an innocence you didn't believe in. Isn't that so?'

David Morris nodded his head.

'Why didn't you untie Bryn Davies when you came to yourself?' went on Cherrington. 'You left him there so that the police should untie him. Isn't that so? Your story is a good one, but it doesn't remove the possibility that Evan Morgan's murder was the concerted plan of Davies and yourself.'

'You have forgotten the evidence of my father. Evan Morgan was dead by six-twenty-five. Between six-five and six-twenty-five is the crucial time for this murder. At that time I was walking about on the cliffs. Ask the newspaper boy; he saw me at about a quarter past six near Tresaeth House, when he was delivering the evening paper to your aunt. So I couldn't have been at the Manor House at the same time. And Bryn Davies was in his bedroom changing. His father and mother can prove that. There was only one person who could have murdered Evan Morgan during that time – Joseph Thomas. And he did. He used us in laying this plot, and then he double-crossed us.'

III

As Sir Richard Cherrington was to say later – indeed, to say often in his later years with boring regularity as he recounted his few exploits as an amateur in detection – it was as he drove away from the Rectory that morning after talking to David Morris and hearing of the plan to play a practical joke on Evan Morgan that he was really sure of the identity of Evan Morgan's murderer. What was the next stage? To tell the police of his suspicions, put the case to them as he saw it, and then leave it to them – going away for a holiday at once as far as possible from the closely inbred domestic affairs of Llanddewi? Cherrington paused at the top of the hill where the road plunges down to the church. All the village lay in front of him, straggling up the opposite hill like a small Mediter-ranean township. He thought how wise it would be to leave – to leave at once; to drive quickly down to Southampton and try to ship his car across to Cherbourg or St Malo. Tomorrow he could be crossing the Loire, and the next day sitting in his beloved Perigord, the poplars along the banks of the Dordogne casting their long shadows across the water-meadows. He could sit with a glass of Monbazillac in his hand, eating wild strawberries and listening to the rasping wail of the sawmills. To escape from it all, from the intricate emotions of other people's lives into which he had stepped. If I stay, he said to himself, if I stay, there must come another death to Llanddewi. And yet, he thought, even without me, the police are bound to find out the truth; perhaps already they have made an arrest. Then his professional vanity began to reassert itself. It would be interest-ing, he thought, if I did solve this before Inspector Colwall and Inspector Harris. And he felt he was at last very close to the solution. He sighed. The foie gras and truffles must wait. He would pursue to its unpleasant end this investigation.

He drove down to Llanddewi across the Market Square and out along the road to Sealands Farm. Mr Thomas was again in his little office behind the old stables. He got up and scratched his head. 'Hello,' he said. 'I wasn't expecting another visit from you. I was expecting the police. Shouldn't be surprised to see them here any moment – come to arrest me.'

'Why?'

'I gathered that after our last conversation you were satisfied I had murdered Evan Morgan between six and six-thirty under cover of visiting Janet Anderson. I imagined you would tell the police your suspicions and that they would come round and arrest me. Am I wrong?'

'You misunderstood me. I never said that I believed you had done these things. I only said you could have done them. And so you could. Especially since you knew that the two young men were going to be there at seven o'clock anyway.'

A puzzled look came over Thomas's face. 'But that is just what I don't understand,' he said. 'Why were they there?'

'You need not hedge any more, Mr Thomas. David Morris has told me about the plan to tie up Evan Morgan.'

Joseph Thomas turned his face away. 'It was a rather silly, schoolboy thing to do,

297

wasn't it?' he said. 'I suppose it never pays to take the law into your own hands,' he went on ruefully. 'And this time it seems to have paid worse than ever.'

'You realize the position you are in at the moment, do you?' said Cherrington. 'You three planned an attack on Evan Morgan. Presumably you three were the only people who knew about the scheme. Two of the three were knocked out; two of the three say they saw Evan Morgan dead. Isn't a jury likely to assume that you – the third member of this gang – that you knocked them out, and that it was your hand that stuck the dagger into Evan Morgan's back?'

Joseph Thomas's face was white. He passed his tongue nervously over his lips. 'Do you suppose,' he said quietly, 'that a jury will be asked to make that deduction?'

'I think it is very likely,' said Sir Richard, his voice surprisingly cheerful. 'Yes; I think it more than likely. And yet there is one thing – or, rather, at least one thing – that I don't understand about all this business.'

'And one main thing that I don't understand. Why the whole thing was called off.'

Cherrington made no attempt to conceal his eagerness.

'The arrangements were called off?' he said. 'When and by whom?'

'I was rung up about half past five on Friday evening and told that we would have

298

to postpone our little joke.'

'Who rang you up?'

'David Morris.'

Cherrington spoke abruptly, almost rudely. 'Look here, man,' he said. 'The answers you are giving me at this moment may one day lead someone to the scaffold. Can you for a moment give over this appalling business of telling half-truths. Are you sure it was David Morris?'

Joseph Thomas hesitated. 'I'd never thought of that,' he said. 'It never occurred to me it might be someone else. It was, after all, only a voice. A voice which said it was David Morris, and that our whole scheme had to be postponed.'

'And it was postponed?'

'As far as I am concerned, yes. You may not believe me. I swear that I did not go to the Manor House on Friday evening at any time. I am not sorry that Evan Morgan is dead, but I didn't kill him.'

CHAPTER 16

CHERRINGTON INVESTIGATES

On Thursday morning, Sir Richard asked his aunt if she would arrange a dinner party for him. 'A small dinner party; just the police and ourselves. Colonel Vaughan, of course, and the two inspectors who are engaged on the case, Colwall and Harris. You and me. Just five of us. Can you organize it for tonight? Or am I giving you too short notice?'

Miss Cherrington said it could be arranged, and Sir Richard drove down to the Police Station. Harris and Colwall were going over some papers together, and they accepted Cherrington's invitation. 'Unless, of course,' said Colwall, 'something very urgent or pressing turns up that keeps us away. You'll understand, of course?'

Cherrington rang up the Chief Constable, who said he would be delighted to dine with them that night. He put down the receiver and turned to Harris. 'I don't want to discuss the case now,' he said 'because I have several little inquiries to make beforehand. And, first, I have two things I would like the police to find out for me.'

'We are at your service,' said Colwall with a mock bow.

'The first thing relates to the Manor House,' said Cherrington. 'Is there a wireless set there? Or, rather, was there a wireless set there on Friday evening, and, moreover, one in working order? That is the first thing I would like to know. And the second is the phone box near the wall of the Manor House. Bryn Davies told me it is out of order and has been out of order since last week. Can you find out when it was first reported out of order? I want to know – we all want to know – whether it was available for use on Friday evening.'

Cherrington left the Police Station and drove up the hill to the Davieses' house. He drew up at the garage. Bryn Davies was lying under the car, and emerged wearing a filthy, oil-stained pair of brown dungarees.

'Still on the same job?'

Cherrington nodded. 'Yes,' he said. 'But the enquiry is nearly at an end.'

'Is it?' The young man seemed only mildly interested. 'That will be a great relief to my mother and father. They have taken it all very hard. They think we are all suspected – particularly my father and myself; and I expect we are. I've tried to reassure them, but it's no good.'

'But now they know about the plan to beat

up Evan Morgan, they must be a little re-assured.'

'My father knew before.'

'He did?' Cherrington tried not to show his sudden quickening of interest.

'Yes. I don't want you to think he was a party to the scheme, of course,' said Davies. 'He wasn't. Far from it. It was just that he noticed the coil of rope missing from the garage and wanted to know what had happened to it. It was all rather silly – rather like a schoolboy prank,' he added reflectively.

Cherrington spoke slowly. 'But it is Evan Morgan's blood which is cold as a result of what you call a schoolboy prank,' he said.

Bryn Davies looked Cherrington straight in the eyes. 'I say,' he blurted out, 'you don't seriously think that he was murdered as a result of our prank, do you?'

'What other conclusion is to be drawn?' said Sir Richard, a trace of exasperation in his voice. 'What simpler way exists of committing a murder than of improving slightly on a scheme which was in existence for another purpose? All the murderer has to do is to add one small feature to the plan – in this case, just a seven-inch dagger of steel stuck through Evan Morgan's back at a suitable moment.'

'But if you think that,' said Davies, 'you are practically accusing Mr Thomas or David Morris – or myself.'

'Or your father.'

'My father? That is quite preposterous.'

'Is it? You told me yourself he knew of your plan. He could have murdered Evan Morgan between six-five and six-twenty-five. All we know is that he was in his garden during that time – or says he was there. No one saw him between the time you went into the house at six and came out again at six-thirty to talk to him about the sports news. This gives your father a whole thirty minutes; plenty of time to get to the Manor House and back again, having murdered Evan Morgan, cut the telephone wires, and plunged the house into darkness.'

The young man looked at him contemptuously. 'It appears you can trump up a case against my father if you are so inclined. But all you've done is say that he could have been at the Manor House between six and six-thirty. You haven't proved, for example, that he could have been there at seven o'clock to deal with David Morris and myself.'

'Do I have to prove that?'

'Of course.' Bryn Davies spoke hotly. 'You don't think do you that David Morris and I knocked each other out?'

'Why not?'

'What?'

'I said, "Why not?" Yes, why not? What proof have we of what went on after seven o'clock in the Manor House?'

'Proof?' began Bryn Davies. 'You have my statement and–'

'I know,' interrupted Sir Richard. 'Your statement. We all know what you said happened. We know what David Morris said happened. But we still don't know what really happened.'

Davies got up. 'You think we are both liars?' he asked.

Cherrington brushed the unpleasant appellation aside as though it were of no consequence. 'Sit down,' he said. 'And let me tell you what I think happened. David Morris knocked you out and then tied you up securely with your own rope. He then went upstairs and telephoned the police and Dr Wynne Roberts.'

'Upstairs in the Manor House?' The young man's tone was one of genuine surprise. 'Is there a telephone up there?'

'There certainly is. It is wired independently to the phone box under the stairs. As I was saying,' he went on. 'David Morris then comes downstairs, waits a while, and goes off to the police and gives a fine imitation of a man who has been knocked out.'

'Do you also suggest,' Davies's tone was scornful, 'that our plan included the use of a telephone upstairs of whose existence we didn't know?' He shook his head. 'It won't do, you know, Professor Cherrington,' he said. 'As I've said before, it is all very well to think up these ideas, but they won't work. You must know as well as I do that there was someone in the Manor House when we got there last Friday evening – someone who was desperate and who would do anything to avoid being captured by us. And you know as well as I do who he was.'

'Do I?' Cherrington didn't conceal his surprise.

'Of course you do. You know as well as I do that Joseph Stanley Thomas murdered Evan Morgan. He was free from five to six-thirty, and he knew we were going to be there at seven. It was he who knocked us both out – in the dark.'

'Pshaw!' said Cherrington, his confidence returning. 'Pshaw and bah! Use your intelligence. Why should Joseph Stanley Thomas, if he had murdered Evan Morgan between six and six-thirty, return to the scene of the crime at seven?'

'To try and fix the crime on us.'

'But I ask you again, is that likely? Two men are knocked out on the scene of the crime, one of them is tied up by rope. Are we likely to think of them as murderers? A murderer gets away from the scene of his crime as quickly as possible. Isn't that obvious?'

'I suppose so. Then perhaps he wanted to delay the discovery of the body.'

'You suggest that he disposed of David Morris and yourself and telephoned the police and the doctor so as to delay the discovery. But why? Joseph Thomas hasn't produced an alibi for seven o'clock, nor one for between six and six-thirty. And then, if his object was delay, why did he take no action regarding the others who turned up at seven o'clock?'

'The others? What others?'

Cherrington paused. 'The anonymous letters which you and David Morris and Joseph Thomas Stanley received summoning you to a rendezvous you already knew about were copied and sent to other people,' he said. 'You didn't know of this?'

The young man shook his head. 'First I've heard of it,' he said.

'And you didn't telephone Mr Thomas on Friday evening telling him the whole escapade – your schoolboy prank – was off?'

'Me? Certainly not. Why did you ask? You mean – somebody did? Or, rather, he says that somebody did?'

'He says,' went on Cherrington deliberately, 'he says that he was telephoned by David Morris saying that the plan had to be put off for a while.' Sir Richard made a gesture of impatience. When he spoke again his voice was testy. 'Why do you go on shielding your friend all the time, my boy?' he said. 'It is a fine display of loyalty, I grant you, but have you thought where it is going to land you? No? Into the South Glamorgan Assizes charged as an accessory after the fact – the fact of murder.'

Bryn Davies said nothing, and Cherrington went on: 'Don't you see how obvious it is becoming to all that only one man could have murdered Evan Morgan, and that that man was David Morris? He could have sent the additional anonymous letters, at the same time warning Joseph Thomas off the scene of the crime. The crime is apparently fixed for seven o'clock, but you and he arrive earlier. You set off from the Bell by the clock there, which is always ten minutes fast. You arrived at the Manor House well before seven. You know this perfectly well. Why do you go on shielding him, pretending that you heard the town clock strike seven when you know it hasn't struck since the war?'

Davies bit his lip and turned quickly away from Cherrington's glance. Then he said: 'It's easy, as I said before, to twist the happenings of Friday night into any shape you want them. But you still haven't proved a thing. You might just as easily build up a comparable case against me? All you say, I could have done – sent these additional anonymous letters you speak of, used the pub clock to get to the Manor House before seven, and all the rest of it. Why not me? Why not set out the case against me, or is that what you are trying to do in a roundabout way?'

'No,' said Cherrington. 'You have an alibi from six to six-thirty. You were in the house changing your clothes. That is one reason. And the second you have just given me now. You didn't know there was a telephone upstairs in the Manor House. It was installed during the war, when you were abroad.'

'And David Morris knew of its existence?' Cherrington smiled non-committally.

'But in any case,' went on Davies, 'there was always the telephone box up the road – the one on the way to the station.'

'Was there?' asked Cherrington. 'Think again. Didn't you tell me yourself that it was out of action last week?'

'So it was.'

'When did you find it was out of action?'

'On Friday evening.'

'Not, I imagine, at seven o'clock,' Cherrington smiled grimly.

'No,' Davies said. 'I did not use it at seven o'clock to telephone the police and doctor. I tried it at five-thirty. I wanted to telephone David Morris, and I was down the road in the car. It was out of order then, at five-thirty. I telephoned him later from the house at six-fifteen but he had gone out. Only his father was there.' He laughed, and his laughter broke the tension. 'You're quite right, Professor Cherrington,' he said. 'It's no use trying to turn me into a murderer. I'm afraid I just won't fit your bill.'

'But David Morris does.'

'You are making a great mistake,' he said. 'A very great mistake.'

Cherrington looked at him steadily. 'I wonder if I am' was all he said, and with that they parted.

When he reached Llanddewi Police Station, Cherrington was met by Constable Roderick, who said: 'I was asked to tell you, sir, that there isn't a radio set in the Manor House. Mr Evan Morgan did not think much of the wireless, although he did have a set. It had been out of order for some while and has been down at the garage for repairs for over a week.'

'The garage does wireless repairs as well?'

'Oh, yes,' said Roderick. 'Mr Humphreys' garage is a sort of jack-of-all-trades place for the village, you might say. And now that he has young Roger Thomas working there it will be more so. Roger is very clever with his hands at most things.'

CHAPTER 17

DINNER FOR FIVE

It had been a very delightful dinner. Miss Cherrington had taken very special trouble over it. The promised Michaelmas goose with which she had tried to entice her nephew down to South Wales had been preceded by an excellent *timbale maison* with *quenelles*, mushrooms, and crawfish, and followed by an equally good cheese soufflé. They had drunk Chablis with the *timbale* and the goose and cheese had been perfectly matched with some fine bottles of the Richebourg 1929 which Sir Richard had been delighted to discover in his aunt's cellar. The table had been cleared and they sat eating Cox's orange pippins and drinking Château Filhot 1929.

'I sincerely hope that you do not mind drinking Sauterne,' said Sir Richard. 'You do not, I hope, consider it, as some do, a woman's drink.' He turned to Inspector Harris, who had never drunk any before in his life, was a little fuddled by all the wine he had already consumed, had a raging thirst, and would have loved a glass of water, but thought it would be rude to ask for it.

'Oh no, certainly not,' he lied easily. 'Very nice, I'm sure.'

'And you, Inspector Colwall? Is it to your taste? Or would you have preferred a glass of port?'

'Suits me very well,' the Detective Inspector said with no conviction and little truth. He had been longing for a pint or two of beer all through the evening.

Cherrington solemnly took some sheets of paper out of his pocket and straightened them out on the table. 'Here,' he said, 'are some jottings I have made. An after-dinner paper, you might call it. Inspector Colwall asked me for my views the other day, when he gave me his. I wasn't then ready to say anything. Now I am. If you can all bear to listen.'

'By the way, Sir Richard,' said Colwall, rousing himself. 'There is one thing I should say before we hear your analysis of the case. You asked us about the phone box between the Manor House and the station. You wanted to know when it was reported out of order.'

'That is so.' Cherrington nodded.

'I am afraid we cannot tell you. All we know from the Post Office authorities is that it was reported out of order on Saturday morning when someone went to use it.'

'Bryn Davies says it was out of order when

he tried to use it on Friday evening at five-thirty.'

'Does he? I didn't know that. Well, that gives us the earliest time when it was out of order, I suppose. We have no earlier information, anyhow. But there is another thing,' went on Colwall. 'One thing which we should have missed if you hadn't put us on to investigating the business of the call-box. It was no technical defect that put the box out of order. Someone had cut through the wires.'

Sir Richard cleared his throat and looked at his notes. 'When I went over what we know of this affair of last Friday night,' he said, 'and the affair of Monday afternoon – because I believe Ellen Harper Williams's death is closely linked with Evan Morgan's murder – I started with two headings. First, the Psychology of the Crime, and then the Psychology of the Potential Criminals. Let us take the crime itself first.' He warmed to his theme as he spoke, and his left hand occasionally twitched at the hem of a non-existent black gown. 'We have been told,' he went on, 'of three motives for the murder of Evan Morgan. First, financial gain, second, revenge for the death of Daphne Davies, and third, to prevent him marrying Janet Anderson. The first motive fits Mervyn Morgan, Rees Morgan, and Miss Williams – you might say that Miss Williams was equally engaged in preventing the marriage to Janet Anderson. All these motives are bound up. What I am still not clear about is how many people knew that the new will was to be signed on the Saturday morning.'

'It was not necessarily so,' said Colwall. 'Mr Rendle wasn't certain that the will would have been signed on the Saturday morning. Mr Morgan had already changed his instructions once or twice, and he might still have wanted a few things altered.'

'Then,' said Cherrington, 'we cannot assume either that it was only a coincidence that the murder took place before the will was to have been signed, or that it wasn't?'

'That's it,' said Colonel Vaughan. 'I think that your first motive must be thought of as a general one of financial gain, not a specific one of gain by a certain time on the Saturday morning.'

'The second motive,' continued Cherrington, 'is revenge for the death of Daphne Davies. This takes in Bryn Davies, John Davies, and David Morris – according to my appreciation of the case. The third motive was to prevent Evan Morgan marrying Janet Anderson, and that takes in Bryn Davies again, Joseph Stanley Thomas, and Ben Anderson. So much for motives. The other aspect of the Psychology of the Crime which I think important is the actual mode of the crime. I don't merely mean here the dagger stuck in Evan Morgan's back. I mean the surrounding circumstances – the anonymous letters, the plan for attacking and tying up Evan Morgan. I believe we can draw some kind of valid conclusion from that. First of all as to the mind of the criminal. He (and when I say "he" I mean, of course, "he" or "she") is using existing situations. The anonymous letters have been going on in the village for a long time. Then the scheme for attacking Evan Morgan and tying him up was a scheme certainly known to three people, and possibly more than three – at least four, and perhaps five or six people. This scheme, like the existence of the anonymous letters, is used by our criminal. To do this successfully, you must have a very carefully thought out plan, and that is the second thing that strikes me so forcibly about this murder; it is so carefully planned. Behind the murder must be someone with a clear mind and organizational ability.'

He paused and turned over his papers. 'So far, perhaps,' he said, 'I am merely repeating the obvious. But let us now turn to the Psychology of the Criminals. We have all between us made rather a long list. I think this evening we can conveniently exclude all those present, and also I suggest, on the grounds of her health, Mrs John Davies – she is a dying woman, virtually bedridden. Also, on the grounds of psychology and probability, Miss Janet Anderson. She was working at the telephone exchange from six o'clock onwards, and if we believe, as I think we should, the testimony of the Rector, Evan Morgan was dead by six-twenty-five p.m. We should also exclude, I hope, the mysterious Mr X – the unknown person who has hitherto been unmentioned by us, and who arrived from nowhere and departed, leaving no certain trace. Inspector Colwall told me he was concentrating on six names; Mervyn Morgan, John Davies, Bryn Davies, Ben Anderson, David Morris, and Joseph Stanley Thomas. I think they are all possible and I would have added a seventh, Miss Harper Williams. As it is, all that can be usefully said is that she did not kill herself. I don't think she was acting when she interviewed me and said she was afraid of being killed. And what is more, if one were contemplating suicide by jumping over the cliffs between Tresaeth and Llanddewi, surely one would arrange it when the tide was in. After all, if one's object is death, it would be quite horrible to be carried back to Llanddewi with no more than severe concussion, a broken arm, and a broken leg. That is the first key-point I want to make: the criminal who pushed Ellen Harper Williams off the cliff was not, I think, concerned with killing her. All he wanted to do was to hurt her. That is why, in my analysis, on purely psychological grounds which you may disallow, I rule out Mervyn Morgan, her son.'

He paused. 'I know this runs counter to a theory that has been, I believe, entertained officially by the police; I mean the theory that the murder was a conspiracy between Mervyn Morgan and his mother. But, for all that, I rule out Mervyn Morgan. I will give you further reasons later. Let us now turn to our five possibilities. Ben Anderson is a quiet, retiring man who, when roused, I suspect, could be most violent; one of those shy, unobtrusive men who is stubborn and determined. John Davies is a more normal, open person. His real feelings are nearer the surface, but I suspect, however, that he is a man of deep convictions, of enduring hates and affections. I believe he felt the death of his daughter most deeply, and it may be that the return of his son, the knowledge that his wife is dying of an incurable cancer – these things may have driven him over that short frontier zone that separates theoretical deeds of violence from actual ones. Joseph Stanley Thomas is a different proposition. He is a much younger man, but he, like John Davies, has suffered a great loss – his son in whom he was enormously bound up. He has also for years virtually lost his wife; they have been living separate lives for years, and recently he has, as you allow, started proceedings for divorce. I think that his anger at the death of his son may have been turned against the world and crystallized against Evan Morgan, whose final act of calumny, in Thomas's eyes, was to propose marriage to the young girl, Janet Anderson, in whom his dead son Nigel had been interested and in whom he himself had taken a similar interest.

'As to the young men, I can say very little, nor, I think, can anyone else. They come to this post-war scene of Llanddewi right from six years of war. I shall say no more than that I think in the immediately post-war period of any man's life anything is possible. I remember only too clearly in my own life the years 1918–19.' He shuffled his notes again and went on: 'Now let us leave these five main actors and turn to the crime itself. The time problem is easy. We must, as I have said, accept the Rector's reluctant evidence as well as take him out of our list of suspects. Evan Morgan was, then, murdered between six-five and six-twenty-five. The real issue to solve is who could have done it during that time – which of my five potential criminals could have done it. Then we can ask who actually did it. But before we ask and try to answer these questions, there are two other matters to discuss. First the plan for beating up Evan Morgan and, secondly, what happened in the Manor House between six-fifty and seven-ten on Friday evening, and why it happened.

The plan for attacking Evan Morgan and tying him up was a real one; a stupid, school-boy prank, perhaps, crossed with memories of happenings reported during the war. It is an unpleasant little history; and it arises out of intense and perhaps justified hate for the man. I think we can assume that the plan arose among the three men who said they had planned it and make no denial of this fact – namely, David Morris, Bryn Davies, and Joseph Stanley Thomas. They all had very good reason to hate Evan Morgan.

'And now what happened in the Manor House between six-fifty and seven-ten on Friday evening? I believe it was like this. Rees Morgan arrived first, found his father dead, heard voices in the garden, and retired into the inner part of the house. The voices were those of Bryn Davies and David Morris; they then discovered Evan Morgan's corpse. At this stage Mervyn Morgan arrives and sees them through the window. So far, so good; the torchlight is shone accidentally on the French windows and Mervyn Morgan flees. Rees Morgan decides to clear off. I believe that neither of the Morgans knocked out David Morris and Bryn Davies. I believe they were either knocked out by John Davies, Joseph Stanley Thomas, or Ben Anderson – or that they knocked each other out.'

318

'A conspiracy between the two young men. Is that what you mean?'

'I do not. I have expressed myself stupidly. I mean this. Either Bryn Davies knocked out David Morris then, after telephoning the police and doctor, tied himself up in the rope; or David Morris knocked him out and tied him up and, after telephoning and a suitable interval, tottered off to the Police Station pretending he had been assaulted himself.'

'But why? What was the point of this elaborate move?' said the Chief Constable.

'I find no difficulty in understanding why Morris and Davies could have done this. If they were – either of them – the murderers, what better way of proving an alibi than to find the corpse when you arrived on the scene of the crime, and show that you were knocked out yourself by someone who must be assumed to be the murderer. If they were the murderers, or one of them, they were not to know that the Rector was going to prove that Evan Morgan was dead at six-twenty-five. If one of them was the criminal, then what he has been trying to do is to show that the crime took place just before they arrived, and that the murderer, disturbed by them, was driven into the back of the house and knocked them out when they followed him.

'Our real concern now is with the relation

319

of the plan to attack Evan Morgan to the murder. If we solve that, we solve the whole thing. To my way of thinking, there are only two possible relationships to consider. First, that someone knew of the plan to attack Evan Morgan and used it – improved on it; and, secondly, that the murderer didn't know of it and that it was a coincidence. The second solution is hardly worth considering. I once toyed with the idea that David Morris and Bryn Davies had arrived at seven o'clock to carry out their plan and found by a strange coincidence that their victim had already been murdered: that they then concocted the business of themselves being knocked out to make it look as though they had nothing to do with the real crime. But that sort of thing wouldn't do. It is the sort of coincidence that would not be allowed to pass the publisher's reader even of our most desperate detective stories. Besides, if that idea were right, what had happened to Joseph Thomas? He was part of the original plan to attack Evan Morgan; he should have been there. I know that he says he had a message allegedly from David Morris calling the whole thing off.'

'Which David Morris denies sending,' said Colwall.

'He does? That is also very interesting,' said Cherrington. 'My point here is that it is unacceptable to suppose other than that the murder is an improvement on the plan to attack Evan Morgan. Then who knew the plan, and who could have murdered him between six-five and six-twenty-five? Here is the crux of the matter. I haven't very much more to say. We have to look for our murderer among five men only. If what I have argued is right – namely, that the murderer must have had knowledge of the plan to attack Evan Morgan – we ought to be able to reduce the number from five to three. That is what I thought yesterday, but by today I realize that this argument does not, unfortunately, help us. The plan was admittedly well known to Bryn Davies, David Morris, and Joseph Stanley Thomas, but alas! we cannot reduce our suspects to those three. John Davies knew of the plan: his son told him of it. And there is the possibility – or, perhaps, one should say more than the possibility – that Ben Anderson knew of it.'

'How do you make that out?' asked Colwall.

'Miss Harper Williams told me that after she had started sending anonymous letters, others had taken up the same unpleasant habit. She told me that one of the others she suspected was Mrs Anderson.'

'But surely not!' Miss Cherrington was scandalized.

'That is what she said,' went on Cherrington. 'She denied opening and reading your letter to me asking me to come down here. She told me her information on the subject came from Mrs Anderson. It is therefore possible that Mrs Anderson did open letters and herself send anonymous letters. She might therefore have intercepted one of the letters sent by David Morris on his own admission and improved on the occasion.'

'You are suggesting a conspiracy between Mr and Mrs Anderson?' asked the Chief Constable.

'Not necessarily,' interrupted Colwall. 'We have been speaking as though Mrs Anderson was the only person who could have opened these letters, but Mr Anderson could have done it himself equally well.'

'Quite so,' said Cherrington. 'However we look at it, we must at this stage admit that there were five men who fit the bill for the murderer of Evan Morgan. Our last question is, then, which of the five could have murdered him between six-five and six-twenty-five? Which of them did? David Morris first. He went out for a walk soon after six o'clock, and was, I understand, seen by the boy delivering the papers round about six-fifteen somewhere near Tresaeth House. Leastways, that is his story.'

Inspector Harris bestirred himself. 'It is substantially correct,' he said. 'I've checked all that up with Miss Rodgers, the house-keeper at the Rectory, and with the paperboy. David Morris was near Tresaeth House at six-fifteen. He says he spent between then and his appearance at the Bell walking about on the cliff path.'

'H'm. So it is just possible he could have been the murderer,' commented Cherrington. 'He could have got to the Manor House in ten minutes. That makes it six-twenty-five. At which time, however, his father had seen Evan Morgan dead.'

'Possible, but a little difficult,' said Colwall. 'We should have to assume that the six-fifteen was a few minutes earlier and the six-twenty-five a few minutes later. That would make it possible.'

Sir Richard nodded. 'Next, Ben Anderson,' he said. 'That is also a little difficult. His wife says he left the house after the sports news – that is to say, he couldn't have left before six-twenty. Now, if Evan Morgan was dead at six-twenty-five, he just had time to commit the murder, but only just. And this doesn't strike me as one of those split-second murders. After all, there were telephone wires to cut and the lights to put out. The Rector says he found the house in darkness when he arrived.'

'Yes,' said the Chief Constable. 'Anderson is a difficult proposition, but he too must remain a possibility – just.'

'Yes,' agreed Cherrington. 'And so must Bryn Davies, though he seems more difficult still to fit into our required mould. He enters his own house at about six o'clock, puts the wireless on, goes upstairs to change, telephones the Rectory at six-fifteen, listens to the sports news, and is leaving the house at six-thirty, having changed his clothes.'

Miss Cherrington coughed and said quietly: 'Isn't there something odd there in what you say, Richard? You say that Bryn Davies telephoned the Rectory at six-fifteen. It was just at that time that his mother and I were talking together on the phone. There is only one telephone at Lampeter House. Have I said something silly?'

'Not at all,' said her nephew. 'I had thought of this difficulty earlier on. There is only one telephone at the Davieses' house, but it has an extension upstairs to Mrs Davies's bedroom. It is possible that Bryn Davies telephoned a minute or two before six-fifteen – say, from the downstairs telephone – and your call to Mrs Anderson was a minute or two afterwards. We can't be quite certain of these times, can we? And so we come to the two last suspects. John Davies and Joseph Stanley Thomas. There is no confusion about them. John Davies was in his garden and greenhouse from six to six-thirty. It gives him time to slip away, murder Evan Morgan, and return. And as for Thomas, there is no alibi at all. He isn't sure when he set out from Sealands Farm, and it isn't possible to say exactly when he arrived at the Bell. So there it is.'

He looked across at his aunt. 'If you agree,' he said, 'I think this would be a good moment to go next-door and drink our coffee?'

In the drawing-room he sat down and concluded his lecture. 'So there we are,' he said. 'That's how I see the problem. Now which is it to be? One of the two men with no alibi, or one of the three with some kind of alibi?'

'Or someone quite different,' said Miss Cherrington. 'There is one serious discrepancy that I find very interesting. Mervyn Morgan said he told no one about the anonymous letters, but Miss Harper Williams knew he had received one. How did she know? He might have told her, it is true, but it might be that she herself sent them. Somewhere in all these statements there must be one or two things that give the lie to the whole business.'

'That particular discrepancy is easily explained,' said Cherrington. 'Mervyn Morgan could so easily have told his mother, but denied it to us, as he didn't want to drag her into the whole business.'

'That is possible,' admitted Colonel Vaughan. 'But I am interested – most interested – in Miss Cherrington's remarks. It still makes it possible for the murderer to be

Mervyn Morgan or Miss Williams, or both working together. I had meant to show you this before, but our discussions were so interesting and so rapid.' He took out a sheet of paper from an envelope and straightened it out. 'Of course, this may not be authentic,' he said. 'It is typed in capitals just like the anonymous letters and is unsigned. It purports to come from Ellen Williams. It arrived at my house yesterday, Wednesday, and its postmark is Tuesday morning. She could have posted it before she threw herself over the cliff on Monday. There is no afternoon collection out here at Tresaeth Bay, is there?'

'No,' said Miss Cherrington. 'Anything posted in the box up on the main road is collected by the postman in the morning when he delivers the letters. That is why I used to get Miss Williams to take my letters to Llanddewi and post them for me.'

'May we hear what this letter says?' asked Cherrington.

The Chief Constable read from the paper he was holding.

MISS HARPER WILLIAMS PRESENTS HER COMPLIMENTS TO COLONEL VAUGHAN AND INFORMS HIM THAT WHEN HE RECEIVES THIS LETTER SHE WILL BE DEAD. HE NEED LOOK NO FURTHER FOR THE MURDERER OF MR EVAN MORGAN. IT WAS IN

THE GENERAL INTEREST THAT HE
SHOULD DIE, AND IT SHOULD BE
MADE QUITE CLEAR THAT MR
MERVYN MORGAN WAS AT NO TIME
A PARTY TO HIS MURDER, EITHER
BEFORE, DURING, OR AFTER.

Colonel Vaughan stopped reading and took
off his spectacles. 'That's all,' he said. 'No
fingerprints, of course. Typed on the village
school machine.'

'And as you say,' said Cherrington, 'might
have been written by anybody – Miss Harper
Williams, Mr Mervyn Morgan, or any one of
my five suspects.'

'Exactly. It doesn't help us much,' said the
Chief Constable. 'I propose we should dis-
regard it.'

'And yet,' said Cherrington, 'if it was not
written by Miss Harper Williams, then I
think it does help us.'

'In what way?' asked Colwall.

'It means, I think, that someone is beginning to panic; that someone has taken a step
to divert attention from himself, don't you
think?' He turned to Colwall. 'What do you
think about the case by now? You have heard
my maunderings, but you haven't said much
yourself.'

Colwall smiled. 'I was following your con-
clusions until Miss Cherrington here made
us all think about the case again. There is

one aspect of the evidence at our disposal which you didn't stress, Professor, and from which I hope for a great deal.'

'What was that?'

'You said that everything turned on what five people were doing during the period six-fifteen to six-twenty-five. And what they were doing in that period seems to depend very much on the wireless; and particularly on news bulletins. Do you remember? Mrs Davies rang up Miss Cherrington when the sports news was on, Mervyn Morgan came into the Bell just after the sports news, the Reverend Hugh Morris left the Rectory after the sports news, Mr Ben Anderson left the Post Office after the sports news, Bryn Davies left his house after the sports news and gave the results to his father. Now, all this confused me for a while until I realized what I expect has been obvious to others for a while. There are, of course, two sports bulletins broadcast every night; or, rather, shall I say that the same sports news is read twice every night – first on the London Home Service at six-fifteen after the main news, and, secondly, at six-twenty-five on the regional programmes. If you live in the London area and your set is normally tuned to the main London Home Service, you hear the sports news at six-fifteen. But if you live down here in Wales, as I have found out only yesterday, your set is tuned into the

Welsh Home Service, with the result that at six-fifteen you automatically get ten minutes of regional Welsh news, and then the sports bulletins at six-twenty-five.'

'I congratulate you,' said Cherrington. 'That point had completely escaped me. Completely escaped me; and yet I should have noticed it. Of course I should. It stands out a mile, and it escaped me. Mrs Anderson in her evidence said that her husband left after the sports news, when a talk of some kind came on, while Henry Thomas at the Bell said that Mervyn Morgan came into the pub just after the sports news, when dance music was beginning. What a fool I am! How stupid I have been!'

'Exactly,' said Colwall. 'I mean, that is exactly the difference. Last Friday night the Home Service sports news was followed by a talk; the Welsh Home Service news was followed by dance music.'

'But I still don't see,' said the Chief Constable crossly, 'what this business of the two programmes will prove for us. We have established the simple fact that people were listening to different programmes. The Davies–Cherrington phone call took place during the six-fifteen London sports news, and the Post Office people listened to the same news. Bryn Davies, however, was listening to the six-twenty-five Welsh Home Service sports news, and so was Henry

Thomas at the pub. So what? – if I may be permitted that rude phrase. Is that all it adds up to?'

'Does it not add up to something more,' said Colwall. 'Surely someone has gained ten minutes if they lied about the sports news.'

Cherrington looked at him sharply. 'Do you mean the Andersons?' he asked. 'But that wouldn't help us. If Ben Anderson really left after the six-twenty-five news, why, that would completely clear him. Why should he lie about it, or his wife lie about it?'

'Perhaps lie was too strong a word,' said Inspector Colwall. 'I was wondering if someone might be mistaken about the time.'

'And you can't mean the Davies household,' went on Cherrington. 'Or can you?' He turned to his aunt. 'Let us go over again this business of your phone call,' he said. 'Mrs Davies rang you up?'

Miss Cherrington nodded. 'That is so. Just at the moment when the sports news – the six-fifteen news – I always have my set tuned to London – was beginning. I said before that I switched off my set as the phone was ringing.'

'Yes,' said Cherrington quickly. 'And when you were talking to Mrs Davies, could you hear the wireless at her house booming away in the background?'

'I certainly could. In fact, Mrs Davies

mentioned it to me.'

'She did?'

'Yes. She did. She said something about hoping the wireless didn't disturb me, and could I hear her all right. She can't turn it off, as you know; the wireless set there is downstairs, and she was telephoning from her bedroom.'

'You actually heard the wireless,' persisted Cherrington.

'Yes. Yes.'

'But you couldn't say what was on, I suppose?'

'Oh come, Cherrington,' said Colonel Vaughan. 'You don't expect your aunt, who is slightly deaf, as we all know (begging your pardon, Miss Mary), to be able to give us evidence whether the wireless at Lampeter House was on which programme. Is that what you're after?'

'I think it is,' said Colwall with excitement in his voice. 'If Miss Cherrington heard at the other end of the phone the very same sports news that she had just turned off in her own house – then, of course, we have been misled about the sports news being heard by Bryn Davies at six-twenty-five.'

'He could have left his house at six-twenty, not six-thirty. He would have had ten minutes in hand,' said Cherrington.

'But I still don't see,' persisted the Chief Constable. 'What is the use of this ten minutes? It would get him to the Manor House at six-twenty-five. The same time as Hugh Morris, who saw Morgan dead at that time.'

'Unless,' said Cherrington quietly, 'the Rector was mistaken in his times, and arrived a few minutes late.'

'He's pretty absent-minded,' said Vaughan. 'I know Hugh well. Dammit, he's my brother-in-law. Ring him up. Find out what really happened on Friday night.'

'May I?' asked Colwall.

'By all means. The phone is in the hall.' Miss Cherrington waved her hand towards the far door.

When Colwall came back into the room, no one spoke for a moment. Then Vaughan said, 'Well? Did you get any satisfaction?'

'Hardly satisfaction,' said Colwall. 'But information.'

'You mean he doesn't confirm the theory?'

Colwall flushed a little. 'The Rector is quite clear about the sequence of events,' he said. 'His set is always tuned to the London Home Service, just as is Miss Cherrington's. The sports news had just begun when he was rung up by Bryn Davies, who wanted to speak to his son. David Morris had already gone out. The Rector told him this and then rang off. It was only after that he turned the wireless off. As he did so, it was still the sports news from London. He went out immediately, and he says he is certain that the time he got to the Manor House was around six-twenty-five.'

'H'm. So we are back at the very beginning again,' said the Chief Constable.

'It looks like it,' said Colwall gloomily.

'I don't agree with you,' said Cherrington suddenly, and there was a note of triumph in his voice. 'We are at last at the end of the case.' He stood up with his back to the fire, a brandy glass in his hand. The faces of the Chief Constable and Inspector Colwall registered their surprise.

'God, what a slow-witted fool I have been!' said Sir Richard. 'I see at last how the murder was done. The Rector's statement clinches it – if only this time he is telling us the truth.'

CHAPTER 18

UP THE GARDEN PATH

I

Miss Mary Cherrington eyed her nephew across the breakfast table with a whimsical disfavour. 'I am furious because I haven't been able to solve your riddle,' she said.

'My riddle?' Cherrington's eyes twinkled.

'You know perfectly well what I mean. Last night, when I thought we had all argued ourselves round in a full circle, you suddenly announced that a perfectly harmless piece of corroborative evidence from the Rector had solved the whole mystery.'

'And so it had.'

'Richard, dear,' his aunt said. 'You are being serious, are you not? And you are sure? The Cherringtons are always so vain, and an intellectual academic life is so bad for the vanity. You are not leading Colonel Vaughan and Inspector Colwall and myself up the garden path, are you?'

'I am not.'

Miss Cherrington was silent for a moment, and then she said quietly: 'Well?' She hesitated. 'Well? What are you going to do?'

His face became very serious. 'I told you all last night,' he said, 'that I would go to the police on Saturday morning – tomorrow morning – and if they had not got all the evidence they wanted themselves by then, I would put before them the proof they need.'

'But why the delay? Why not go and see them now? Why couldn't you have told them last night?'

'Because there are one or two loose ends that I must deal with,' he said, pausing, 'And I have a feeling that more evidence will be forthcoming. That letter, for example – the letter which Vaughan read out to us last night and which was supposed to have been written by Ellen Williams.'

'Could have been written by her,' said Miss Cherrington.

He shook his head. 'No. No,' he insisted. 'That letter wasn't written by her. I saw her a few hours before she was killed. The fear of death was in her eyes. She was afraid of being murdered herself.'

He walked across the room and opened the door into the hall. He paused at the threshold and looked back over his shoulder. 'I wish you had not asked me to come down here,' he said. 'When one sympathizes with a murderer, when one likes him as a person, detection ceases to be an amusing intellectual game.' He went out and closed the door quietly behind him.

II

As Sir Richard drove down the High Street of Llanddewi, he met Bryn Davies walking up the street carrying one of those canvas bags which air transport companies call nightstop bags. He drew up alongside, greeted the young man, who smiled and then glanced hurriedly at his watch. 'I'm afraid I can't stop and talk,' he said, 'if you don't mind. I must catch a train.'

'Then let me give you a lift to the station?'

'That is very kind.' Davies got in and Cherrington drove on. 'I've just put our car in the garage,' said Bryn Davies. 'The brakes need adjusting, and that's a thing Roger Thomas can do better than I can.'

'You are going away for long?' asked Sir Richard.

'I'm going up to Oxford to look for a college that will take me in as an undergraduate in October.'

'Any particular college in mind?'

'No.'

'It's just going to be a dreary tramp from one admissions tutor to another? That's your plan, is it?'

'Afraid so.'

'What do you intend to read?'

'Medicine. I started before the war. I was going up to Cardiff just as war broke out.'

They drew up at the station gates, and Bryn Davies got out. 'Thank you very much. I'll just say goodbye.'

Sir Richard also got out of the car. 'I'll come with you on to the platform,' he said. 'I've nothing to do this morning. You get your ticket. I'll look after your bag.'

They walked across the footbridge and on to the up platform. The train was a few minutes late, and they paced up and down.

'You won't be here, then,' said Cherrington, 'when the arrest is made?' He spoke abruptly.

Bryn Davies stopped in his tracks. 'The arrest?' he said blankly.

'Yes. I expect the police to arrest the murderer of Evan Morgan late tonight or early tomorrow morning.'

There was a moment's silence and in that silence the approaching train could be heard whistling as it came round the curves of the line from Bridgend.

'Would it be improper,' said Bryn Davies hesitantly, 'to ask who is going to be arrested?'

'Don't you know as well as I do who murdered Evan Morgan?'

The young man laughed. 'You must be joking, because if you believe what I believe about his death the case is virtually closed.'

'Closed?'

'I have never had any doubt that it was Ellen Williams who murdered Evan Morgan, with Mervyn Morgan as accessory. And, by the way, there is a fact you ought to know – a fact I should have told you before. You know the knife with which he was stabbed – the one I brought home from the Far East. It was missing after my mother's party.'

Cherrington nodded his head.

'Well,' Bryn went on, 'I've remembered who was the last person I saw handling it at the party.' He paused. 'It was Mervyn Morgan.'

'I see. How convenient to remember this

at this late date,' said Cherrington rudely.

'What?'

'I said how convenient to remember this now. How is it that it didn't occur to you earlier when you were giving evidence to the police.' His voice was harsh.

'I don't know. I don't think it's odd. You know how things slip your memory.'

The train came in and Bryn Davies got into a compartment. He pulled down the window and leaned out.

'So the whole thing is to be laid at Ellen Williams's door, is it?' asked Cherrington.

'That's my view.'

'Did she also knock out David Morris and tie you up?'

'Mervyn Morgan probably did that part of it.'

'If it ever happened.'

Bryn Davies stared at Cherrington. 'What do you mean?' he asked.

'Why do you go on shielding the murderer?' said Cherrington. 'Why not tell the police all you know? Why are you running away?'

'I'm not running away. I'm deliberately going away preparing to build myself a new life – at Oxford and after Oxford, somewhere I can forget – forget about the war, and Llanddewi.'

The guard waved his green flag. 'Then I must wish you goodbye,' said Cherrington.

Bryn Davies shook him by the hand. 'You sound as if it is to be a long goodbye,' he said.

'It is,' said Cherrington. 'I am going to France tomorrow – also to forget Llanddewi.'

The train moved off. 'Goodbye,' said Bryn Davies, waving his hand.

'Goodbye,' said Cherrington. 'Good luck.' But his words were swallowed up in the noise of the train. Sir Richard stood until the train had cleared the platform and curved out of sight. The station was as quickly deserted as it had suddenly for a moment leapt into activity. A cold wind blew across the empty platform. Leaves and bits of paper eddied across on to the line. Cherrington turned up his coat collar and walked slowly back across the footbridge to his car. His face was very grave.

III

Cherrington drove from the station into the village and drew up in front of the garage. Roger Thomas was serving petrol and when he had finished he came over to Sir Richard's car. He was as cheerful and ebullient as ever. He touched his dirty beret respectfully and said, 'Now what can I do for you, Professor? Petrol? Any coupons left?'

Cherrington smiled. 'What I want from

you is information,' he said. 'You have the Davies car here at the moment, haven't you?'

'Yes.'

'And it is fitted with a radio?'

'It is. One of those ordinary portable radios.'

'Does it work?'

'I don't know. But why not? I'll go and look.' Roger Thomas turned as he was going into the garage, a puzzled look on his face. 'This is on the level, isn't it?' he asked.

Cherrington nodded. The young man was away for about five minutes. When he came back he said, 'There's nothing the matter with the set. It goes perfectly well. It's one of the small portable radios: they hardly ever go wrong.'

'And if they did,' persisted Cherrington, 'would it be difficult to put them right again?'

'Oh, no,' said Thomas. 'No difficulty at all – at least for people like us old soldiers who had to work and understand wireless sets in the war.' He grinned.

'That goes for Bryn Davies?'

'Yes. We all had to have a reasonably good knowledge of radio before we were sent out on jungle patrols in Burma.'

'Thank you,' said Cherrington. 'You've been most helpful.'

IV

Cherrington's next call was on Dr Wynne Roberts.

'I haven't called to see you about my own health,' Cherrington said at once, introducing himself: 'In fact, my visit is of a most unprofessional kind. I have come to ask you to give away some of your professional secrets.'

Wynne Roberts looked up sharply from his desk and glanced hurriedly at his watch. 'I can only give you a few minutes, I am afraid, this morning,' he said. 'I have a long list of visits.'

'I shall not keep you more than five minutes, if you can see your way to answering my questions,' said Sir Richard. 'They are private questions, by the way. I am in no way officially connected with the police. I am acting entirely on my own.'

'Quite.' Doctor Roberts tapped his desk impatiently with Cherrington's card. 'Quite so.'

'I have a theory,' went on Cherrington, 'that the murder of Evan Morgan was done by someone who didn't fear the death penalty, because he or she knew they didn't have long to live. I have in mind people like Mrs Anderson or Mrs Davies – people in their state of health, or sickness.'

'Impossible. Fantastic idea.'

'I beg your pardon.'

'I said it was quite impossible that Mrs Anderson or Mrs Davies could have murdered Evan Morgan.'

'You mean physically impossible?'

'No. No. I don't mean that at all. It is physically possible,' said Roberts. 'It wouldn't have been outside the bounds of possibility for either of them to have stabbed Evan Morgan. A woman, even an old woman, could have done it.'

'If they could have got to the Manor House?'

The doctor frowned. 'I mean,' went on Cherrington, 'Mrs Davies is virtually bedridden, isn't she?'

'Oh, no. Where did you get that idea from? She keeps to her room most of the time, of course, and I suppose in the village they think she is bedridden. But she's not. Certainly not.'

'Then, as I said, either Mrs Anderson or Mrs Davies could be murderers.'

'Really!' said Wynne Roberts impatiently. 'I said it was physically possible and it is. But psychologically, no. It is quite impossible. You must remember, Professor Cherrington, that in a small place like Llanddewi, a doctor is much more than a medical man; he has to be. Perhaps every doctor is much more than a medical man; he ought to be if he does his job properly. I know the people of Llanddewi. Believe me, I know them all well.'

Cherrington spoke slowly and quietly. 'I have been thinking,' he said, 'that if you knew death was coming to you, one might commit a crime because one no longer feared the consequences. At first I thought of death as physical death, and that is why my mind turned to Mrs Anderson and Mrs Davies. But there is the death of the spirit,' he went on. 'You know what I mean? How often you as a doctor must have met it. A man who dies because he has not the will to live. For example, a man whose wife dies, an old man, may immediately go into a decline and is soon in the grave himself. There is nothing for him in life, and so he leaves it. I am right am I not, in assuming that both Ben Anderson and John Davies knew that their devoted and beloved wives had not long to live?'

Dr Roberts got up quickly from his desk and hastily put some papers and instruments into an attaché case. He smiled at Cherrington – a forced, formal smile. 'If you don't mind,' he said, 'I can't stay here gossiping with you any more. I must think of my patients.' But as he bustled Cherrington out into the street, his manner was nervous and uneasy.

V

Cherrington left his car in the market place and walked through the narrow streets down to the church. The mid-September sun gave the whitewashed, thatched cottages a late warmth whose deceptive nature was felt the moment one stepped into the shade. He stood at the lych gate and looked down the flight of stone stairs into the churchyard. Around there was a sea of grey tombstones pitching and tossing with years of neglect and decay. As he walked down the flagged path he thought that no one would ever know how many of those interred around him had been hurried to their ends by the helping hands of friends, enemies, or the dear ones they had left behind. He paused in front of a crumbling, lichen-covered tombstone; it was a nineteenth-century slab set up to some local spinster. 'A diligent and honest teacher,' read the inscription. 'This memorial is erected to her memory by her friends and relatives, who are witnesses to her modest worth.'

'A charming sentiment, is it not?' said a voice behind him, and Cherrington turned to see the Rector, who had just come out of the church.

'Good morning,' he said. 'Yes; you are right. A charming sentiment. And how few people these days would dare use such a phrase as a compliment. Modest worth – that

344

really goes for all of us, doesn't it, if we but thought clearly and honestly about ourselves.'

'I don't know,' said the Rector. 'I just don't know. I have been thinking up what to say this afternoon. Modest worth would not do, I fear me.'

'This afternoon?'

'Yes. Evan Morgan's funeral.'

'It is this afternoon? I did not know. Is it private?'

'No. A public funeral. As a matter of fact, I have had to decide most of the details about it. Rees Morgan is the person really responsible, but I haven't been able to get much sense out of him. If one were uncharitable, one would say that he didn't care a thing about the disposal of his father's mortal remains.'

'And Mervyn Morgan?'

'Legally, you see, he has no status in this matter.'

'But his mother? Is Miss Williams also being buried today?'

'No. The inquest on her has still to be held. In Evan Morgan's case, as you know, there was no problem about the manner of death, and the inquest decision was a simple one. Miss Williams's inquest has been adjourned. If it was suicide, there will be another problem – the problem of the disposal of her remains.'

'Ah, yes,' said Cherrington agreeably. 'Now, that is where your profession and mine overlap. The disposal of the dead. That is my special subject, you know.'

'Your thoughts run too much on murder,' said the Rector, rather severely. 'Are you still busying yourself with the case here?'

'No,' said Sir Richard. 'The Llanddewi murder mystery is over.'

'Over?' The Rector lifted his eyebrows in surprise. 'I don't think that the police consider it is over. They were telephoning me only last night about some trifling detail.'

Cherrington swung round on him. 'I was the cause of that telephone call,' he said. 'And believe me, it was not a trifling detail. It was very important. You told them you were listening to the news on the London Home Service, that it was six-fifteen – that is to say, the sports news had just begun – when you were rung up by Bryn Davies. You spoke to him for a few minutes: he only wanted to know if your son was in. Then you turned off the wireless. The sports news was still on. Is that right?'

'Quite right,' said Morris. 'But I still don't see what is so important about it.'

'I don't expect you do. I wish that your statement were fuller, but that would be hoping for too much. I suppose that as your own wireless set was on you won't be able to say whether there was a wireless at the other

346

end of the phone call?'

'You mean at the Davieses' house?'

'From where Bryn Davies was speaking.'

'He told me he was speaking from his house. But no, I am afraid I couldn't say. Wait a minute though. Wait a minute. Bryn Davies said something about that himself.'

'Are you sure?'

'Yes. Of course I'm sure. I can't remember the precise words. Something like "I must ring off now and listen to the wireless!"'

'H'm.' Cherrington was silent.

'I wish someone would tell me what all this mystery is about,' said Hugh Morris, a trace of petulance in his voice.

'The mystery is the mystery of the death of Evan Morgan,' said Sir Richard, 'which to me at least is no longer a mystery. I can't tell you more now; you will learn all in due course. Meanwhile, I must leave you to your duties. My concern is to get Evan Morgan's murderer. Yours to lay his body to rest.'

The Rector seemed uncertain how to take this curious phrasing. 'Shall you be at the funeral this afternoon?' he asked.

Cherrington shook his head. 'I think not,' he said. 'No; I think not.'

'Everyone will be there.'

'Not everyone. I do not expect the murderer to be there.'

VI

It was early in the evening when Cherrington walked up the garden path of the Davieses' house. He had on leaving the Rector telephoned his aunt to say that he would be out to all meals that day, and then he had driven the few miles inland to Cowbridge, where he sat for two hours in the Duke of Wellington drinking stout and beer and eating sandwiches, sausage rolls, and pickled onions. It had been a very thoughtful man who set out in the sun of a September afternoon to walk on Stalling Down. When he walked back into Cowbridge about five o'clock, Cherrington's mind was made up. He went back to the Duke of Wellington, ordered some tea, and sat writing for over an hour until it was time for more beer. Then he finished his letter and added this postscript: 'I am only writing all this out and posting it to you in case – just in case – anything happens to me before tomorrow morning. It is unlikely, but one never knows. I think I must reckon tonight with a murderer who may very well know that I know his identity.'

He stuck up the envelope, sealed it, addressed it to Colonel Vaughan at the Llanddewi Police Station, took it across the road, and dropped it into the letter-box. That done he got into his car and drove slowly over to Llanddewi.

He found John Davies sowing seeds in shallow boxes in his greenhouse: 'Well, Mr Davies. Here I am again,' said Cherrington with a great show of affability.

'So I see,' said John Davies. 'And here I am, Professor Cherrington. You always find me in the same place, but not doing the same thing. The last time you called I was transplanting my gloxinias and my caladiums. Today I'm sowing schizanthus and antirrhinum and, in a few minutes, salvia. There is such a lot to do.' He sighed.

'I didn't come to talk to you about gardening, you know,' said Cherrington, his voice little more than a whisper.

John Davies busied himself with his seed-boxes. 'No,' he said. 'I didn't suppose that you had. What a pity.' He spoke deliberately. 'I suppose you have come to talk again about the murder.'

'Yes. But I have come to talk on this subject for the last time. There is no more mystery. I know who murdered Evan Morgan.' He paused. 'Don't you, Mr Davies?' he added quietly.

'That is not a question which you really expect me to answer, is it?' Mr Davies put down his packets of seeds and spoke quickly and earnestly. 'Why don't you give up all this sort of thing?' he said. 'It's doing nobody any good. It's only stirring up things that were better left alone. Evan Morgan's dead. Dead and, by now, buried. Leave him alone. Nothing you can do will unbury him. Or does your question mean I murdered Evan Morgan?' It was as though he were asking Sir Richard's advice on some simple gardening problem.

'I suppose you could take it that way,' Cherrington spoke abruptly.

'Well, I didn't, you know,' said John Davies. 'Evan was a bad, bad man, a wicked man. I hated him all my life. I'm glad he is dead, but I didn't kill him.'

'Are you sure?' said Cherrington. 'Let me ask you one question to help you clear your memory of last Friday evening. I think you told the police and myself that you were working in your greenhouse from six to six-thirty. You saw your son go into the house at six o'clock; he spoke to you at six-thirty after the news, and told you some of the sports results. That's so, isn't it?'

'Yes.'

'You were in the greenhouse at six-thirty. Tell me this. Which way did your son come when he came to talk to you? From the house or from the opposite direction?'

'Why, what a strange question. And I don't know. I wasn't looking.'

'I think you don't know, Mr Davies, because you weren't there.'

There was no doubt about the amazement which John Davies registered: 'I wasn't here?'

'I suggest that you left this greenhouse as soon as Bryn had gone into the house, that you went down to the Manor House and murdered Evan Morgan, and that you were just getting back at six-thirty when your son was in the garden looking for you. That's why he's gone away, isn't it – because he knows who murdered Evan Morgan? You knew about the scheme for tying up Evan Morgan. It was you, Mr Davies, who wrote those anonymous letters on the school typewriter, wasn't it? Isn't all I say true?' Cherrington's voice was coaxing.

'There seems no use in my saying anything, does there?' said John Davies. 'You seem to know all.'

'No,' said Cherrington quickly. 'I don't. I'm only guessing. Will you not help me?'

'Help you? You seem to be doing pretty well on your own,' said John Davies. 'What's the next step, anyway. Have you told all this to the police?'

'I shall speak to them tomorrow morning.'

John Davies smiled – a wry, tired smile. 'So I have until tomorrow morning, have I?' he said. 'Is that what you mean?'

'I think you understand my meaning.'

John Davies turned back to his seed-boxes. 'I think I shall go back to my gardening if you don't mind,' he said. 'It is more soothing than your conversation. I still have to sow my salvias.'

'And if I may, I will pay a farewell call on Mrs Davies.'

'You are not to upset her in any way.' John Davies's tone was fierce. 'Don't disturb her.'

'I only want to wish her goodbye,' said Cherrington.

'Very well,' said the schoolmaster reluctantly. 'You know your way in, don't you?'

Cherrington crossed the lawn and entered the house. John Davies turned back to his seed-boxes. Then, after a moment, he crossed the lawn himself and went into the house. He tiptoed into the hall and stood listening. Then he took off his shoes and walked upstairs in his stockinged feet, making as little noise as possible. His pipe was still unlit. His face was anxious and weary. It was the face of a tired man who can go no farther.

VII

Sir Richard tapped at Mrs Davies's bedroom door, and a quiet voice bade him enter. He went in quietly. Mrs Davies was lying on her divan bed in the same position as on his previous visit. She looked up from the illustrated journal she was reading.

'Come in,' she said. 'This is a surprise.'

'Good evening,' said Cherrington. 'You must pardon my intrusion. Your husband said I could come up and see you on condition I didn't upset you.'

Mrs Davies smiled, a thin smile of resigned politeness.

'I shan't do that,' went on Cherrington quietly. 'I've only called to wish you good-bye.' He hesitated. 'Goodbye and good luck,' he added.

'You are leaving Llanddewi?'

'Yes. Tomorrow.'

'Are you leaving Llanddewi with the mystery left unsolved?'

'No; not unsolved, Mrs Davies,' said Cherrington. He crossed over to the window and looked out into the garden. As he spoke he did not look at her. His voice was barely audible. It was as though he was talking to himself.

'Who murdered Evan Morgan?' said Cherrington. 'What member of this household? Was it your husband, who was entirely un-attended in his garden for half an hour from six to six-thirty? Was it your son, who was allegedly in this house from six to six-thirty? Or was it neither of them?' he went on. 'You hold the key to the mystery, don't you?' He turned and faced her. 'You are not really bedridden, Mrs Davies, are you?' he said, and lifted his hand as she made to speak. 'Please, the time for pretences has gone. You simu-lated an agreeable surprise when I came into the room, but you knew I was here all the time. As I walked across the lawn from the greenhouse I saw for a moment your face at the window as you were putting the curtains back. Tell me this: did you walk across your room last Friday evening between six and six-thirty and look out through the window? And if so, what did you see? Your husband or your son stealing up the road back to the house? Someone must ask these questions; and the police will not do so until tomorrow, at least.'

Mrs Davies said nothing. 'I am sorry,' said Cherrington. 'Believe me, I am sorry.'

When Mrs Davies spoke her voice was hard, but hard with a jerky, rasping character. It was as though she was controlling it with the greatest difficulty. 'And I am sorry for you,' she said. 'You are deluding yourself.'

'Am I?' said Cherrington. 'Am I really? How I wish I could believe that I were.'

'Perhaps you are not deluding yourself on every point,' she replied. 'It is quite true that I am not bedridden. I did look out of the window and see you. It was silly of me to pretend that I hadn't seen you. And I did look out of the window last Friday evening as you suggested. I saw my husband working in the greenhouse.'

'Was this before or after you had telephoned my aunt?'

She hesitated. 'Before and after,' she said.

'And Bryn? Was his telephone call to the

Rector before or after your call to my aunt?'

She bit her lip. 'I couldn't be sure,' she said. 'I am afraid I couldn't be sure on that point. You see, he would have telephoned from downstairs. I used this phone here.'

'Both phones are connected to the same outside line?' Mrs Davies nodded her head. 'And if I tell you, Mrs Davies,' said Cherrington, 'that your son's call to the Rectory and yours to my aunt were at exactly the same time, what then?'

'Then,' she said, 'your information is at fault.'

'I see,' Cherrington smiled. 'I'll go now,' he said. 'Of course, I have disturbed you. That had to be. Goodbye.' He turned at the door. 'May I say how much I admire your bravery?'

'It is very easy to be brave,' she said, 'when you are as certain of the future as I am. It is fear and uncertainty of the future that makes cowards of us.' Cherrington paused with his hand on the door handle. 'It won't be long now,' she said, her voice no more than a whisper, 'before I go and join my daughter.' Then she went on in a firmer voice: 'Please go. Please go.'

Sir Richard went out of the room without looking back. He walked quickly down the stairs and out of the house the way he had come. As he walked down the gravel path to the front gate he had a wild urge to turn round and look at the upstairs windows of the house. He resisted the urge and walked on to the gate.

VIII

John Davies stood by the open casement of the front bedroom window. The room, which was next door to his wife's, was in darkness. He had listened with his ear to the thin wall as Cherrington and his wife had talked together. Then, as he heard Cherrington leave, he stood in the dark shadows by the window. As Sir Richard came into view and began walking down the garden path, John Davies lifted a shot-gun to his shoulder and aimed it at Cherrington's back. His finger was on the trigger when a voice spoke beside him. In his concentration, he had not heard his wife open the door and cross the room.

'No, John,' she said. 'No. That is not the answer.'

They stood together in the dark watching Cherrington walk out of the gate and get into his car. He switched on his lights and for a moment everything was brilliantly lit up. Then he drove off, and it was dark again.

CHAPTER 19

THE BEGINNING OF THE END

The telephone rang as Sir Richard Cherrington was coming down to breakfast on Saturday morning. He answered it himself, and was greeted by the Chief Constable. 'I wonder if you would be so good as to come down to Llanddewi Police Station as soon as you can,' he said.

Cherrington readily agreed and, after a hurried cup of coffee, he drove down to the village. The Chief Constable was sitting in the inner room of the station with Inspector Colwall and Inspector Harris. They did not smile as Sir Richard came in.

'Well,' said Vaughan briskly. 'The Llanddewi murder mystery is over.'

'How?' Cherrington looked round from face to face.

'The murderer has confessed,' replied Vaughan. 'We have charged him with the crime to which he readily confesses. He is at the moment locked up in the cells.'

'Splendid,' said Cherrington. 'Splendid. What more could you want? Of course, he will plead not guilty at his trial, but that will be only a matter of form. Having a confession is marvellous. I didn't think it likely for a moment.'

'Neither did we,' said Colwall. 'The most unlikely of the five suspects to which you narrowed it down.'

'You mean unlikely because at first we couldn't see how it could be done. But I can explain all that,' began Cherrington.

'No,' interrupted Colwall. 'There was no difficulty in seeing how it could have been done. It was psychologically that I thought it unlikely, relying as I did – as I had to do – on the portraits of the man which the Chief Constable and others gave me.'

The Chief Constable nodded. 'Same here,' he said. 'And I've known him since I was a boy.'

Cherrington turned sharply to Colonel Vaughan. 'What did you say?' he asked. 'Since you were a boy, or since he was a boy? Whom have you got locked up in there?'

'Who?' It was Colwall who spoke. 'I thought you knew. John Davies, the school-master.'

'John Davies. Oh, I see.' Cherrington took off his spectacles and tapped his hand with them. 'Oh, I see,' he repeated. 'Then we have been talking at cross-purposes. You say that John Davies has come here and con-fessed to the murder of Evan Morgan?'

'Tell the Professor what happened,' said Vaughan.

'It all took place last night,' said Colwall wearily. 'I was here talking to Harris and Sergeant Williams when Mr John Davies came into the Police Station. He looked all in. Tired, but also sad. He had a sort of resigned appearance that made me think that the end of the world had come – or his wife had died, which to him might be the same thing. He was silent for a moment or two, and then he said he had come to confess to the murder of Evan Morgan and Ellen Williams. After we had recovered from our shock, we cautioned him but he said he wanted to make a statement there and then. He did. It was all very simple. He said that he had heard from his son the plan to attack Evan Morgan, and that he had decided to improve on it. He sent out the anonymous letters and when his wife was listening to the wireless and his son was changing he slipped down to the Manor House, murdered Evan Morgan, and got back just as his son was coming out of the house at six-thirty. Then, he says, when his son had left he crept back to the Manor House, hid himself, and dealt with David Morris and his son.'

'He said all this?'

'Yes,' replied Colwall. 'He said he knocked out David Morris first, then dealt with his

359

own son, tying him up securely. He also admits to the murder of Ellen Williams. Says he just pushed her over the cliff.'

He stopped talking, and Cherrington said nothing. Then he sighed. There was something of a weary impatience or annoyance in that sigh. The Chief Constable looked up. 'That's what we feel,' he said. 'That's why we sit here loath to go on any further with the next part of the proceedings. John Davies should have been brought to a magistrate's court this morning and formally charged with murder, but we are still detaining him for further questioning. You see, there are so many things in his confession that are puzzling.'

'Such as?'

'Well,' said Colwall, 'he says for example that he went into the Manor House through the back door. Yet there were no footsteps outside the door on the gravel, as we know. Then he says he was there in the back room of the Manor House at just the time when we know Rees Morgan was there; yet he mentions nothing of this.'

'His confession is bogus,' said Cherrington.

'Oh, come,' said the Chief Constable. 'There are curious things in his statement, but I'm not prepared to discount it like that.'

'I don't believe any part of John Davies's

alleged confession,' said Cherrington roundly.

'No part of it?'

'None at all. And I'll tell you why.' He hesitated. 'There are many reasons, but there is one fairly simple and straightforward one. Had John Davies murdered Evan Morgan, he would have had to be at the Manor House somewhere between six-five and six-twenty-five. Yet he was seen at his own house twice during that period of twenty minutes.'

'By whom?' asked Colwall.

'By his wife,' said Cherrington. 'By Mrs Davies. She told me yesterday. You ask her yourselves.'

'That will not now be possible,' said the Chief Constable.

Sir Richard missed the purport of Colonel Vaughan's remark and the tone in which it was made. 'I know that a wife's evidence for or against her husband is necessarily suspect,' he said, 'but you should question her on this point. And by the way, you should disabuse yourselves of the idea that she is entirely bedridden.' He stopped speaking and looked from one face to another.

'Mrs Davies is dead,' said Colonel Vaughan quietly.

'Dead?'

'Yes.' It was Colwall who replied. 'She died last night in her sleep. Overdose of sleeping tablets.'

361

'She took her own life?' asked Cherrington.

'No doubt of that,' said Colwall. 'Her husband was here in the Police Station at ten-thirty last night. She left two notes behind: one to the police telling us what she was going to do. It was midnight when she wrote that note. If we had gone round last night, we might have saved her life,' he went on. 'As it was, we didn't go round to the house until this morning.'

Cherrington spoke slowly. 'She wouldn't have wanted to be saved,' he said. 'Poor soul. Now I know what she meant when she said that she hadn't long to live. I thought she was only referring to her own ill-health. So she couldn't stay and face it. And I don't blame her. She was a brave woman,' he added with apparent inconsequence.

'The second letter,' said the Chief Constable coldly, 'is addressed to you, Sir Richard.'

'To me?'

'Yes. That is why we asked you to come and see us this morning. That and the fact that I have received a letter from you mysteriously marked "Only to be opened if Professor Cherrington is missing on Saturday morning".' Cherrington smiled, a wintry smile. 'I am not missing,' he said, 'you can read it at your leisure.'

'There is also the fact,' said Colwall, 'that,

362

apart from her husband, it seems you were the last person to see her alive yesterday.'

'You have been keeping a track of my movements?'

'Not yours,' said Colwall. 'But we have been watching all main suspects for some time. And here is the letter to you.'

Cherrington opened the envelope, meticulously splitting open the fold with a penknife.

'Dear Professor Cherrington,' he read. 'I don't know why it should be easier to write to you on this occasion than to my husband or to the police, but it is. Perhaps the outsider will understand more easily what I am doing and why. And then, in any case, you have, I think, already guessed my secret. My husband has not, and that is why I hope it may be possible for him and for my son to live on their lives without knowing.

'I don't know when you first guessed that I had murdered Evan Morgan. It was clever of you. I thought that the phone call would have fixed all, but you saw through that. It was a bad piece of luck that Bryn should have telephoned at the same moment from the house; but there, murder is difficult to arrange.

'I have wanted to kill Evan Morgan ever since I heard what he did to my daughter. Daphne was a lovely girl: she would have grown into a beautiful woman. Mothers are

363

not supposed to be more fond of their daughters than of their sons, are they? Of course, I love Bryn, but somehow Daphne was most dear to me. I think that part of me died when she died, just as part of me only came to life when she was born and developed as she grew. When Dr Roberts told me I hadn't long to live, I decided to kill Evan Morgan. I do not think it was wrong of me. The world is the better without him, and getting rid of him has been one useful thing I have been able to do before I die.

'You know how I carried out my plan almost as well as I do. You will be able to tell the police the details that are not worth bothering to put down here. I slipped out of the house when Bryn was changing, and was back by six-twenty-five. As you guessed, I telephoned your aunt from the Manor House: it was my one attempt at fixing an alibi. You see, I suppose, that though I was quite prepared to kill Evan Morgan, I didn't want to suffer the consequences of my crime – not that they would hang me, an old woman, already under sentence of death.

'I knew that Bryn and David Morris had planned to go to the Manor House at seven, and I was prepared to use their visit in the hope that it would confuse the whole issue, which it did, though I did not know that they would do it so successfully. Of course, as you guessed, Ellen Williams was not murdered by anyone. Whether she threw herself over the cliff or slipped, I do not know or care. These are, as you may say, academic issues.

'Tomorrow I shall be where the natural course of disease would have taken me in a few weeks, or two months at least. When you read this, all of me will be past, including my crime. Here is my confession. You will handle it with the police very well, I know.

'I am sorry for my husband and for Bryn but I was leaving them, anyhow. I hope they may be spared knowing I committed a murder. It should be so simple to explain that Ellen Williams killed Evan Morgan and then committed suicide herself. Colonel Vaughan is a kind man. I desire no post-humous notoriety for my crime. Daphne is dead, Evan Morgan is dead, Ellen Williams is dead, and when you read this I shall be dead. Let us all rest in peace, and trouble no more the living with our crimes, if crimes is the right word. Are you sure in your conscience that mine was a crime?'

Cherrington set down the letter. He took out his handkerchief and, under pretence of an elaborate cleaning of the lenses of his spectacles, he wiped the tears from his eyes. He blew his nose vigorously and in silence handed the letter to the policemen. They gathered round the table and read Mrs

Davies's moving letter. Cherrington got up and stood looking out through the window for several minutes. When he turned round he had regained the composure which had temporarily deserted him while reading the letter with its dramatic disclosures.

'Well?' he said.

'I'm damned,' said the Chief Constable. 'That's all I can say. I'm glad in one way. I never thought of John Davies as a murderer. I suppose he guessed and gave himself up to save his wife. And to think of it: she wasn't even on our short list of suspects.'

'It's a masterpiece of a letter,' admitted Colwall. 'Pulls at the heart strings and all that, but–' he hesitated.

'This letter,' said Sir Richard, 'was meant to be the last enclosure on the file of the Llanddewi murders. That was its purpose, but it fails. I think it fails because it puts the burden on us – particularly on me – of explaining away the crime. I can explain the crime, and have done in the letter I sent to the Chief Constable, but not in the way Mrs Davies hoped I might be able to do. What she says in effect is: "Evan Morgan and Ellen Williams killed my daughter. I've killed them. Now I'm dead. Leave it at that." Something like that is what she, in effect, says. But it isn't all right. You said with surprise, Chief Constable, that she wasn't on our list of suspects, our short list. That was true, and for a very good reason. We had no real reason to suspect her. Nor does this letter alter my view. This letter is intended to shield the murderer from the consequences of his crime.'

'To shield her husband?'

'No,' said Cherrington. 'And yet in a way yes: to shield her husband from the consequences of the crime. But he was not the murderer. His confession, like hers, is a fake.'

'We are getting cluttered up with false confessions in this case,' said Vaughan. 'There was the document from Ellen Williams? Was that genuine or bogus, do you think?'

'It was when Bryn Davies typed that document,' said Cherrington, 'that he took the first active step to destroy his own defence. He took the second step yesterday when he told me that he had seen Mervyn Morgan or practically seen Mervyn Morgan take his dagger from the party at the Davieses' house.'

The police looked at him with renewed attention.

'You mean?' asked Vaughan.

'I mean that Bryn Davies killed Evan Morgan and Ellen Williams. I have known for some time it must be him, yet the proof has been difficult to obtain. I had all the proof by yesterday. I felt that both his father and mother suspected him. They knew or feared that he had done this thing. That is why I went to them yesterday. I made it clear to them that I also suspected him – so clear that if they knew of any evidence which might prove me wrong they would bring it out. But they could say nothing except to manufacture evidence.' He paused. 'You were, of course, quite right about John Davies. The events at his house at seven o'clock or thereabouts prove he was not there. The important thing is that David Morris and Bryn Davies arrived at the Manor House well before seven, although the anonymous letters said seven. John Davies didn't leave his house until ten to seven. He couldn't have remained unseen by Rees Morgan; his footsteps would have been on the gravel outside the back door; he arrived in the Bell soon after seven.

'Nor could Mrs Davies have done what she said. It involves her getting to the Manor House and back, between six and six-thirty, without being seen by her son or husband. And she gave herself away by saying that she telephoned from the Manor House. She telephoned my aunt, and during that call my aunt heard the wireless at the other end of the line. There was no wireless set in the Manor House. Mrs Davies telephoned from her own house.

'It was her son who telephoned from the Manor House. It was a coincidence that he could not have anticipated. He telephoned the Rector at the same moment as his mother telephoned my aunt. Ergo, he was not at his own house at the time he said he was.

'I think Bryn Davies may have planned the murder of Evan Morgan,' he said, 'before he heard of Joseph Stanley Thomas's scheme for attacking him. Whether that be so or not, he realized, I suspect, that this plan was a Heaven-sent opportunity to murder Evan Morgan. He sent round the anonymous letters to Mervyn Morgan and Rees Morgan hoping they would be there at seven o'clock. The whole keynote of the affairs of seven o'clock was that they were part plan, part improvisation. It couldn't all have been planned in the way it turned out.

'But first the actual murder. Having arranged a rendezvous at the Manor House at seven o'clock, Bryn Davies then proceeded to murder Evan Morgan before that. I suggest he did this. He went into his own home just at six o'clock and switched on the wireless. He established his presence in the house by talking to his father on the way in and his mother on getting upstairs. Then, when they thought he was in his bedroom changing, he left the house quickly, and cut across the fields to the Manor House. I think he could have been there by six-ten or six-twelve. It would be the work of a few minutes to murder Evan Morgan. Then – he was a man of courage – he stood at the desk in the Manor House and with Evan Morgan's dead body by his side, he telephoned the Rector with the purpose of establishing he was at his own house at that moment.

'The call over, he cuts the phone lines, switches the house in darkness, and escapes through the back door and the fields back home. He could have been back in the house by twenty-five minutes past six, but I think he went to the garage, where he switched on the portable radio in the car and listened to the sports news while he hurriedly changed. Then, an overcoat covering him, he probably crossed over to the house, shouted goodbye up the stairs to his mother, and emerged from the house again to talk to his father in the greenhouse and tell him about the sports news.

'That's how I see the whole thing happened. A cleverly built-up alibi – his father saw him enter the house at six or a few minutes to six and saw him leave it a few minutes after half-past; his mother heard him upstairs and heard him wish her goodbye at half-past. And apparently he telephoned the rector at six-fifteen from his home. In any case, he couldn't have been at the Manor House; that is what we were being asked to believe, because he was changing and listening to the news. Changing would have taken ten minutes, the sports news he was supposed to have listened to was six-twenty-five. There couldn't have been time for him to go to the Manor House. That is what we were supposed to conclude, and indeed did.

'And now let's go back to the subsequent events,' went on Cherrington. 'Here was a daring attempt to throw suspicion on others. He set out to implicate as many people as he could – Mervyn Morgan, Rees Morgan, David Morris, Joseph Stanley Thomas. He couldn't be sure that the first two would turn up. The last he telephoned, saying he was David Morris, and told not to turn up. He hoped by this that Thomas would have little alibi or none for the times concerned. All he was doing was providing the ingredients that might be used to confuse the police when the time came.

'The fixed element in his plan was to be at the Manor House first with David Morris, to deal with anything that required fixing. They set out from the Bell by the pub clock and got to the Manor House early. They find Evan Morgan dead, the house in darkness, and the telephone wires cut. I think Bryn Davies invented the noise in the inner room, and then knocked David Morris out. Then he left the house and telephoned from the phone-box between the Manor House and the station.'

'Why not from the phone upstairs in the Manor House?'

'I don't think he knew that existed. He was genuinely surprised when I told him about it. It had been put in during the war. The other things he would know about from being in and out of the house as a youth – I mean the phone in the living-room, the electric light switches, and so forth. So he went to the phone-box.'

'But wasn't it risky?'

'If he had been seen it would have been easy to explain. He had gone to telephone the police and the doctor. As it was, it was dark and raining and he wasn't seen. So he made his bogus calls and got back to the Manor House. From then on it was still, I believe, improvisation. He could not be sure whether he would not find Mervyn Morgan and Rees Morgan there. What he would have then done I don't know. Actually, he found no one there when he returned. The rope was there; he was an experienced Commando and had specialized in escape methods. He tied himself, relying that the first thing the police would do was to untie him.'

'Which, of course, they did,' said Inspector Harris crisply.

'Which, of course, they did,' agreed Cherrington. 'Well, there it is. That is how I see the case. A clever piece of work.'

'And the motive is simple, of course,' said Vaughan. 'Revenge for the death of his sister, and to prevent Janet Anderson from marrying Evan Morgan.'

'And there may even have been a third motive,' said Sir Richard. 'Financial gain. It seemed to be generally known that Evan Morgan was changing his will in favour of Janet Anderson. It might have been assumed that the settlement was to have been signed before the engagement was announced at the Welcome Home dance. We thought it a coincidence that the murder took place before the will was signed. Not at all. It was odd that it hadn't been signed earlier.'

'But even if it had been signed–' said Inspector Colwall. And then he stopped. 'Oh, I see,' he said. 'The devil. He was hoping that with Evan Morgan out of the way, he might marry Janet Anderson, by then a rich heiress.'

'That's what I think. All that remained was to get rid of Ellen Williams. We know Bryn Davies was driving his car along past Tresaeth House on the afternoon she was killed, on his own admission. It would have been child's play for him to push her over the cliff.'

Cherrington paused and looked at the three men. 'Are there any snags in the story as I have reconstructed it?' he asked.

'It won't be easy to prove in a court of law,' said Vaughan. 'But, anyway, now we have a scheme to work on we shall be able to check every detail of it. The machinery of the law can now roll on. That will be the headache of the Director of Public Prosecutions. My job is merely to arrest him.'

'For that,' said Cherrington, 'you may have to go to Oxford.'

'No,' replied Harris. 'Like the rest of the suspects, we have had our tabs on him. He didn't leave Cardiff last night. He clocked in at the Bute Arms Hotel under an assumed name, took a room, and spent the night with a girl he picked up on the streets.'

'Oh, what the hell,' said Sir Richard suddenly and rudely, his nerves snapping. 'What the hell does it matter how he spent the night? Isn't it likely to be his last out of gaol?'

Two hours later when police officers, led by Inspector Harris, entered the Bute Arms Hotel they found Bryn Davies alone in a corner of the bar. He had not shaved, and although it was only half-past-eleven he had been drinking heavily. He did not say anything when arrested and walked quickly and quietly out to the police car drawn up alongside the kerb. It was when the car was halted by traffic lights on the outskirts of Cardiff that he turned to Inspector Harris and said in a whisper: 'Keep this from my parents as long as you can, will you?' Harris said nothing; he looked fixedly ahead. The traffic lights changed and the car moved on. Bryn Davies spoke again. 'Especially my mother,' he said.

CHAPTER 20

FAREWELL, DEATH

'Someone once said that a successful murder must look like an accident,' said Cherrington, turning from the window and facing his aunt. His bags were packed and the car waiting at the door of Tresaeth House to drive away. His aunt looked up from her embroidery. 'The one thing that this case didn't look like was an accident. It had all the appearance of being carefully planned – the anonymous letters, the telephone calls, the timing, and all the rest of it. And that is what set us all so wrong for so long. It is only when I realized there was not an overall plan that I began to be on the road to solving the mystery. There was only a plan which was improvised – altered and modified – to meet the occasion. It was when I appreciated the significance of the events at seven o'clock that I got near to the mind of the murderer. It seemed to me impossible that anyone could have knocked out both David Morris and Bryn Davies, but equally impossible that the events that occurred could have been allowed to occur as a plan by either of them.

I realized it was no master mind that had developed a plan staged for seven o'clock; merely a resourceful man using a series of circumstances presented to him.

'And once I realized this,' he went on, 'I realized that it was not seven o'clock that mattered. All that was to confuse us. The time that mattered was earlier. It was a pity for Bryn Davies that the police were able to narrow down the time of the actual murder so well, but even then he had what seemed to be an unshakeable alibi. For a long time it seemed to me quite foolproof. The first thing that made me suspicious was his insistence on mending the radio in his car. I suppose he was anxious to show that the only place he could have heard the sports news on Friday night was in Lampeter House. The second thing was his insistence that the phone-box between the Manor House and the Post Office was out of order from before the murder; it is now clear that he telephoned Joseph Stanley Thomas from it at five-thirty pretending to be David Morris, and then cut the wires after he had made the call at seven o'clock. I was, admittedly, subconsciously made on the alert by all this. That is to say, my attention was drawn to radio and telephones. Then there was no reason why he should have been so surprised at the existence of a telephone upstairs in the Manor House. His surprise showed he was vitally concerned with radio and telephones in building his alibi, and I drove myself to think of these things in the hope I could break what seemed an unshakeable alibi.

'Then there were two things that put the pattern into shape. First, the realization that there were each night two sports news bulletins. That was Inspector Colwall's contribution to the solution. And then yours. The accident that you were speaking to his mother at the very time he was speaking to the Rector. This seemed to me of the most vital importance, especially when you were able to say the wireless was playing at Lampeter House when Mrs Davies was telephoning.'

'So I really solved the murder,' said Miss Cherrington.

'You might say that!'

'And equally well can make or mar the future legal proceedings.'

'What do you mean?'

'Only that it may be my recollection of these phone calls may not be so precise when I am called to be a witness for the prosecution in Bryn Davies's murder trial.'

Cherrington waved a hand crossly. 'There will be so much corroborative evidence by then,' he said. 'Your evidence may not be so vitally important as it was when we did not know for certain how the murder had been achieved.'

'But if it is?'

'That is for your conscience to answer.'

'And yours? Are you leaving Llanddewi a happy man? Will not Bryn Davies's face haunt you for the rest of your days?'

Sir Richard affected to laugh at his aunt's question, but as he drove down to Southampton and across western France to the Dordogne he kept being painfully aware in sleeping and waking hours of the Davies family of Llanddewi. On the fourth day in France he returned to his hotel at Les Eyzies to be told that a police officer from Paris had called to see him. He walked out on to the terrasse and was delighted to find his old friend, Monsieur Coquilhatville of the Sûreté, sitting at a table with a large Dubonnet in front of him. They greeted each other warmly, and then the French policeman said: 'I was delighted to hear that you were on holiday in these parts. I am down to assist in a most curious investigation.' He hesitated. 'And I wondered, if you are free, whether you would like to be associated with me – in a purely informal capacity, of course.'

Sir Richard shook his head. 'I'm afraid not,' he said. 'I have a strong distaste for crime at the moment. I am purely on holiday.'

'Ah, but this is a most interesting and unusual case,' persisted Coquilhatville. 'Most extraordinary. It is like a novel. It all happened in a little château a few miles from here. A French professor took it for the vacation, and when he opened a cupboard in his bedroom, a dead body fell out.'

'There's nothing odd about that,' said Cherrington.

'Perhaps not,' said the other. 'But this man thought it odd, and went and told the police. They came back to his house.'

'I know what you are going to say,' said Cherrington. 'The body had gone. The Professor had been drinking too heavily. A bad thing.'

'Next day,' said Coquilhatville, 'the Professor's wife opened another cupboard; this time in the attic.'

'H'm. And another body fell out, I suppose?' Cherrington laughed.

'Not at all. There she found her husband, hanging from the roof. He was quite dead.'

Cherrington made as if to get up from the table. Then he made an impatient gesture, sat down again, and smiled. 'Tell me more,' he said.

And that night for the first time his dreams were not disturbed by memories of Llanddewi.

This Large Print Book, for people
who cannot read normal print,
is published under the auspices of

THE ULVERSCROFT FOUNDATION